The Eagle Murders

The Eagle Murders

by
Jean McCord

The Eagle Murders
By Jean McCord

SECOND EDITION
Copyright © 2023, 2024 by Jean McCord
Originally published by Zero Latitude Books,
Cuenca, Ecuador.

This is a work of fiction. Names, characters places, and incidents are either the product of the author's imagination or are used fictitiously.

All rights reserved, No part of this book may be reproduced in any manner whatsoever without written permission, except in the case of brief quotations in critical articles and reviews.

ISBN: 978-1-3041-5687-7
Printed in the United States of Americas

Dedication

To the many police officers and firefighters with whom I did ride-alongs, and especially the regular deputies and reserve deputies with whom I worked for three years as a Pierce County reserve deputy.

Chapter 1

I reached the motel cabin in the north Cascade Mountains just after 8:00 p.m., earlier than I'd expected. The clearing in the woods was pitch black, except for the glow from cabin porches and the tall light over the phone booth across from the Meeting House. The blocky wooden structure was an old-fashioned campground church dating from when the motel was a summer Bible camp and revival ground. It was a bona-fide historic attraction open 24 hours a day, according to the folder I'd picked up when I registered.

I wasn't ready for bed, and since my best friend Sharon had changed her mind at the last minute about coming, she and I weren't going to talk half the night. Playing tourist was my usual time filler when I traveled by myself, and as good as any. Visiting the church would shorten a long evening of reading before going to bed alone.

Inside the church was dark, the only light coming from the utility pole over the phone booth. I felt around on the wall to the right of the door and flicked the switch. Two rows of dim lights came on, brightening the room's center while leaving the walls in shadow. I walked around, then sat on a pew near the front to take in the peace and quiet of the place.

Church hadn't been part of my life for a long time, other than an occasional wedding or funeral. But I've always liked visiting places that give a sense of how people used to live and what they thought was important. Such visits are trips into the past, into a world I never knew and never can know firsthand. Some of us are tourists wherever we go, and like any dedicated tourist I try to see the local sites. After all, I'm not likely to pass this way again.

The Meeting House, smack in the center of the motel grounds, was as plain as the Southern church of my childhood. Clear glass windows broke the white plaster walls. At the front, three steps led up to a platform on which an unadorned lectern stood facing the empty pews. A small nativity scene was arranged at the front of the stage, and three chairs backed the pulpit. A simple cross hung on the wall. The rows of photographs I'd noticed hanging in the vestibule were the only things distinguishing this church from that of my childhood.

Most days I think I've made the move emotionally as well as physically from Turtle Creek, Georgia, to Washington State. Probably, though, I'll never get completely away—at least not as long as a place or smell or song can hurl me back to the past.

This small trip would be my last adventure in 1989—and I hadn't had many adventures this year or even in the decade that was almost over. I'd meant my pre-Christmas trip to see eagles along the Skagit River to be relaxing, a break from thinking and writing about street people for grant proposals and a break from all the false holiday cheer. Even being in this building was part of that break, something different. I liked sitting on the curved pew, hearing the rain pound on the corrugated tin roof. The tension accumulated during the long wet drive from Tacoma to this site not far from the Canadian border drained away and a wary peacefulness began to take its place. No hymns came to mind, just Ray Charles' voice filling my head with *A Rainy Night in Georgia*. "Seems like it's rainin' all over the world."

I was about as relaxed as I ever get when the door at the back of the church opened. I turned around and saw someone enter. In the dim light, at first all I could see was a fuzzy coat in a vile shade of pinky-orange, looking like a mutant caterpillar. I realized it was a girl, and knew I had not gotten away from street people.

"Hi," I said, more so I wouldn't scare her than in welcome.

She didn't respond as she explored the space with a wobbly walk and a loud clacking sound. When she passed my pew I saw that her pink plastic high heels explained her gait and her noisiness.

When she reached the front she finally answered me, "Hi."

Her cheap powerful perfume assaulted me. I sneezed. She sniffled, as though she snorted drugs or had a cold.

As she moved closer to the light I saw her face. She looked like my little sister playing dress-up in our mother's makeup. My first impulse was to hug her, my second to demand that she wash off her garish makeup. Of course I did neither; I had no right. Marilu had died twenty-six years ago. I had last seen her in a coffin, in a room that looked like this one.

The girl sat down in a pew on the other side of the aisle. "Sure doesn't look like a church ought to," she said. "No stained glass or statues like at Holy Rosary."

I grunted, "Doesn't matter; it's peaceful," relieved that she didn't sound anything like my sister.

"What good is a church that doesn't look like a church?" She coughed, clutching the coat around her throat.

"I don't know. Maybe it just gives people a place to think about whatever it is they believe in." Sometimes I get contrary and say the opposite of whatever the other person says, and this was one of those times. If she'd said something good about the place I wouldn't have defended it. Funny what I hear myself saying sometimes.

"Believing doesn't do any good, anyway."

I answered, "Maybe not, but believing in something makes some people happier. And it can give them a kind of pattern to live by."

"What if you don't like your pattern?" She coughed again.

"Then believing can help you change." That, at least, fit in with what I believed about my higher power.

"Change!" She spat out the word with disgust.

Before I could answer, a horn sounded and she jumped up.

"Gotta go. He said to stay in the car."

She slipped out the door. As I got up to close it, I heard a man's voice demanding, "What were you doing in there? Get in. And to whom were you speaking?" Something about his voice and diction bothered me, but I couldn't pinpoint it.

"Just some woman," the girl replied. A car door slammed and a vehicle roared away. I wondered what the girl was doing far from any city, in a church at a motel in the northern Cascade Mountains.

***

After a good night's sleep, I caught a big breakfast of bacon and eggs at a nearby inn and drove to the staging area where we would leave our cars and take a bus to start our raft trip. A young woman in what looked like REI's top-level outdoor gear directed me to the back of the bus with others assigned to the third raft. "Your first float trip?" I asked the little girl next to me.

"Yes," she said. She looked down at her hands clasped on her lap. As she spoke, the smell of bubble gum mixed with the scent of baby shampoo and the musty smell of the bus.

"I'm Sarah Tierney," I said, "and this is my first trip too. What's your name?"

"Angie."

"Didn't I see your family at the Meeting Ground Motel this morning?"

Angie glanced up at me and nodded, then looked back at her hands. I figured she was only seven or eight. Her mother, sitting behind us, spoke up. "We're Pete and Rose Rimbaud from Gig Harbor. Angie's really been looking forward to this trip. She thinks eagles are 'real cool.'"

The door closed, the last passenger settled in, and the bus started moving.

The tall young woman in the REI gear stood and picked up a microphone. "I'd like your attention, please," she announced, adjusting the mike until its squeal cut out. "My name is Abby and I'm your guide today on raft three. We're going into some sensitive areas, and you need to know about the Skagit River Bald Eagle Natural Area regulations."

My mind wandered as she talked. She sat down and a young man rose and told about the eagles, followed by another young man—with astounding freckles—who cautioned us about raft safety and said to follow the guides' directions no matter what. Like the young woman, they were dressed in high-quality outdoor gear, but theirs looked much more worn.

When we reached the launching site, the people on the first

two rafts followed the two young men's directions while our third-raft group watched from the bus and exchanged names. I didn't catch who the two older women said they were, just that they were from Panorama City retirement home in Lacey. A fortyish man said he was Walt from Tacoma and introduced his teenage son as Frank. With the Rimbauds and Abby and me, we had a full load of eight rafters and one guide.

At Abby's direction, we layered on our unprofessional rain gear, then clambered into the greenish rubber raft. Walt and Pete volunteered to paddle as needed and Abby positioned them on either side of the middle seat. She sat at the back and steered, while the river's current did most of the work. A few minutes later, before we even reached midstream, a heavy drizzle started. This changed to a steady downpour that leaked through the seams of our rain jackets and ponchos and distorted the images in our camera and binocular lenses.

Abby cautioned us to keep our voices low. Conversation would probably have died out anyway, as the rocking of the raft, the sound of the paddles, and the steady beat of the cold rain drove us inside ourselves. Cloud drifts obscured all but an occasional outline of the mountains, and the water-soaked air muffled everything except the sound of the river. Snow fell just a few hundred feet higher and clung to the trees.

"The lead raft's spotted something," Rose whispered behind me. "Over to the left!"

"Ooh, it's an eagle up high on that dead tree," blurted one of the two older women. "Look, there's another one below it."

Those were our first bald eagles: shapes that hunched in the trees, then flapped away. Soon we floated close enough to see the fine fierce white heads, curved beaks, and bright yellow eyes of a pair of eagles. I scanned the trees, then gasped with exhilaration when another spread its wings and lifted right in front of us while I was wiping my binoculars. Its wings must have stretched at least six feet.

Frank, the teenager who sat next to me, grinned and murmured a quiet, appreciative, "Awesome."

An hour or so into the float, we drifted close to three eagles on a gravel bar, feasting on the mottled carcasses of spawned-out salmon. The birds seemed like vultures, standing on the huge fish and ripping pieces out of the bodies. Occasionally the stench of rotten fish floated toward us, but smells, like sounds and colors, were softened by the rain. Muted conversation flowed around me, mostly about what we were seeing.

I kept quiet, lost in wonder at seeing the birds up close. From time to time we glimpsed the lead and second rafts bobbing to the right on the broad river, while we drifted toward the left, away from the road. Trees and shrubs lined both banks. Silhouettes of hills and mountains rose around us, their tops lost in layers of cloud and snow.

Angie's mother, Rose Rimbaud, had kept up a running commentary on every major piece of litter we passed, so I almost didn't look up when she said, "What a mess up ahead! You'd think people wouldn't dump such an eyesore!" Then she added, "But look at that eagle; it's one of the biggest we've seen."

I raised my binoculars to examine the eagle, but the pink heap caught my eye first. *It's her*, I knew right away, *the girl I saw last night*. "Abby," I said, "we've got to land. That's a person!"

Abby looked at me. "Are you sure?"

"Almost sure," I said. "I recognize the coat."

Abby took one quick look through her field glasses. "Pull hard toward the gravel bar," she directed the two men with the paddles.

The sodden heap of pinky-orange fuzz didn't disturb the eagle's dinner any more than the drenching rain did. I guess only living human beings bother eagles. The birds probably see a body that still smells and looks human as just another piece of garbage washed up by the river, not nearly as appealing as a well-rotted salmon.

The eagle chittered to warn us away, then ripped hunks out of the enormous fish he stood on. When the raft was only a few yards distant he gave a final "kak-kak-kak," lifted off with strong slow strokes, and flattened into a long glide down the river. Only the salmon carcass and the body of the girl remained.

By that time I could clearly see the ugly fake fur coat, unmistakably the one I had seen the night before. Matchstick legs protruded, and a small white hand stuck out of one sleeve and moved in the river's current.

We hit the gravel bar hard. I leaped from the raft and splashed toward the dirty pink pile. My boot caught on a rock and pitched me forward; I righted myself just in time to keep from falling into the water.

When I was about three feet away I saw the girl's face, swollen and as mottled as the huge fish corpse beside her. I stopped. I could hardly bear to look at her, and not just because her face was so distorted. Even in death she reminded me of Marilu.

She wasn't much bigger than the fish the eagle had been eating. The current had grounded her upper body on the gravel bar, then jerked her legs around, pulling her coat and short black skirt nearly crotch-high before letting go. Her dark stockings were ripped, leaving her inner thigh exposed, white and vulnerable. Ankle straps held the pink shoes to her small feet. The heel was broken off one shoe.

I had thought the girl pitiful when we talked the night before. Now she was infinitely more so.

My seatmate's father, Walt, was right behind me. He bent to pull her skirt down.

"We'd better not touch her," I said, putting my hand out to restrain him. "This might be a crime scene, and we don't want to mess up any clues."

He bent toward her again. "What do you mean? There won't be any 'clues' after she's been in the river."

"Come on, Walt." I kept my hand on his arm. "Something might still be there. Let's give the experts every chance."

"Okay, lady," he said with a sneer. "I guess somebody died and made you God. Whatever you say." He backed off and joined the others standing about six feet from the body. One of the older women raised her camera, but evidently thought better of taking such photos. She spoke quietly to the other woman, while Pete and Rose Rimbaud pulled Angie close.

I stayed where I'd stopped. Apparently I was in charge, as the expectant semicircle of faces waited for direction. Then Rose asked, "What should we do?"

Abby secured our raft and came toward us. She looked at the others, then moved closer to me and asked, "Yeah, what do we do?" She'd been our leader until now, but she turned to me for direction, just like the others. *Guess they don't have much about bodies in the guide curriculum*, I thought.

"Leave everything as it is and call the sheriff or the police or whatever they have around here," I answered.

"We ought to take her with us," Walt objected. "She might wash away, or the law might not find her."

"No, Dad, Sarah's right," Frank put in. "When the cops talked to my Scout troop they said people shouldn't do anything to mess up an investigation."

"What investigation?" Walt blustered. "You think she was killed? It doesn't have to be murder. Maybe it was an accident or she killed herself."

"Look at her face—and the mark around her neck. Did she strangle herself and jump in the river?" I sounded colder, harder, than I intended.

The group looked at the girl, then back at me. Rose was weeping silently as her husband held her and Angie.

"Do you have some way to contact the other rafts?" I asked Abby.

The rafters looked relieved when she reached into her inner layers and pulled out a two-way radio. She opened it and punched a button, then looked up. "Guess I forgot to charge it," she said.

I looked at the others, but no one else said anything. "I'll stay here, then, while you find a phone," I said, not knowing what I was going to say until the words came out.

"You can't," Abby objected, taking back her authority. "It'll take time for the deputies to get here."

"I'm staying," I insisted. I looked at the frail figure in its ridiculous coat and felt a wave of dizziness as again I saw my sister's face. "I feel obligated. I mean, I may be the last one who saw her alive."

Abby shook her head. "No. I'm in charge on this raft and I'm not leaving you here. We stick together and call the sheriff. There's a launching site and a phone a mile or so down river. We'll make sure they find her. If you insist on staying, we all have to stay, and we're the last raft. They won't come looking for us until long after we don't show up."

"We've got to get Angie inside and away from this," Pete Rimbaud said.

"We don't want to stay either," one of the older women said. "Let's do what Abby says and go for help."

I looked at the others; everyone but Frank was nodding in agreement.

I didn't have much choice. I looked at the girl one last time as the raft started, then sent her a mental goodbye. *I'm so sorry.* ≠

Chapter 2

Our raftload split up once we landed. Abby, our guide, headed straight for the phone, Walt following close on her heels. Picnic tables were scattered around the area but there was no shelter.

The Rimbauds took Angie to one table, while the two older women stood under a tree for whatever little shelter it offered. I moved to a more distant table and stared at the river.

Frank, the teenager who had sat next to me on the raft, moved to the opposite bench. "Mind if I join you?" he asked.

"No; have a seat," I said. He couldn't have been more than sixteen or seventeen, but he seemed bright. I liked the way he had kept quiet on the raft and how he had shown his appreciation of the eagles.

"I'm glad you kind of took charge," he said. "Nobody else knew what to do, especially not my dad."

"Thanks. I guess I just felt responsible. Crazy, huh?"

"Not so crazy if you met her last night. What happened?"

I faced downwind to keep the rain from pelting my face while talking with him. I've sometimes been accused of providing too many details for my written accounts, but when speaking I try to be brief. I told Frank only an edited version of the church encounter, glad to talk about it but not wanting to relive it. "I think she was someone without a whole lot of options," I ended.

Frank grimaced. "Any ideas about who did it?"

"Yeah. The man she was with. And I wonder if he killed all

those others, too."

"You mean the Skagit River Killer?"

I gestured at the silver-brown water behind Frank's back. "Seems possible, doesn't it?"

The rain continued beating on us as we looked at the river rushing by. Neither of us spoke, but the wind gusted from time to time, and an occasional car or truck whooshed down the wet pavement.

Frank broke our silence. "I don't think I understand about the church," he said. "This was at the motel?"

"Yeah, the Meeting Ground Motel. It used to be a church campground and they built the church for the crowds of people who came each summer. After a while people built cabins instead of using tents, and later the owners turned the cabins into guest quarters."

"And they kept the church?"

"Something about respecting history, according to the information in the brochure. The campground was one of the earliest developed sites in this area besides the logging camps, and the church was its first permanent building. I saw some neat photos in the back, of the logging camps as well as the campground. The church is unlocked all the time so people can meditate and rest. It was restful until the girl came," I added.

I shivered and hunched forward, wrapping my arms more tightly around myself and pressing my hands into my armpits for warmth.

Frank glanced at his father, who stood with Abby near the phone. "You're cold," he said. "Maybe we should huddle together and wrap our ponchos around both of us."

I looked up in surprise.

"Body heat," he said, his face flaming. "They taught us in Boy Scouts how to keep from getting hypothermia. I mean, you're pretty and all, but I'm not trying to make a move on you."

It had been a long time since this forty-five-year-old had worried about a teenage boy getting fresh, and anyway, I'm not comfortable about physical closeness with people I don't know. Besides, this would be inappropriate. I smothered a smile and said, "Thanks,

Frank, but I'm okay. It can't be too long before the cops get here."

Ten minutes later, a Skagit County Sheriff's patrol car pulled up, lights flashing. A trim uniformed deputy got out of the driver's side and a tall broad man climbed out of the passenger side. The deputy's baseball cap showed a handsome young face with blue eyes and a blond mustache. The other man's poncho shadowed his face so that I saw mainly a wide downturned mouth.

As though we were all orchestrated, everyone stood up at once and converged silently on the patrol car. I was reminded of zombies in a movie, except that no one was yelling "brains!"

"I'm Harold Workman from the Skagit County Sheriff's Office," the man in the poncho said as we gathered around him without speaking. "More cars are coming, and we'll take you all to the police station in Concrete to ask you a few questions. I'll talk with each of you after I check out the location of the body and videotape the scene."

Our reactions to his promise of warm dry cars and a warm dry police station dispelled my notions of the undead. Little Angie Rimbaud's face lit up, while her parents put their arms around each other's waists and their other hands on Angie's shoulders. The two older women smiled for the first time since we landed on the sandbar, and Walt hollered, "About time!" as he slapped Frank on the back. Frank winced as he grinned at me and held a thumb up. Even Abby stopped looking so worried, and I know my shoulders dropped farther from my ears. Never thought I'd be grateful about going to a police station, but I guess there's a first time for everything.

"I'm going to ask you not to talk to each other about this," Workman continued, "until after I see each of you separately. I appreciate your cooperation."

A large police vehicle towing a motorboat pulled up as the car I was in drove away.

The Concrete police station was empty and dead on a winter Saturday afternoon when we first entered, but it was dry and warm—too warm, in fact, even after I took off as many layers as I decently could. Another good-looking uniformed deputy took our names and addresses, then left us on our own. He was older than the driver of the first car that had met us, and his hair was dark but thinning. He looked sharp and fit in his uniform, though, and moved quickly and gracefully. I mentally dubbed him "Eye Candy," as the best looking of a handsome lot. A few other uniformed deputies and police officers—all men, I noticed, and mostly trim in their uniforms—came in later and moved throughout the room as I tried to keep awake by admiring the scenery.

Workman came in thirty minutes or so after we arrived. He pulled off his rain gear and draped it over a folding chair. His khaki shirt was tucked into khaki pants soaked from the knees down. A wide gray streak ran across the front of his full head of dark, gray-flecked hair. I noticed again his wide mouth, slightly turned down at the corners. Claude Akins. That's who he reminded me of, the actor and country singer Claude Akins. Tall and broad without being fat, and with a mellow concerned look on his face. Looked like he ought to be driving an eighteen-wheel rig around the country with a buddy, rescuing damsels in distress, or behind a guitar singing about losing his sweetie and his dawg.

"Eye Candy" handed him the list of names. Workman glanced at it, then looked around the room, taking note of each of us. He spoke calmly, but loudly enough to make himself heard. "Again, I appreciate all of you cooperating with us and I'll get you out of here as soon as possible." He pointed at the list and said something to the deputy, who looked in my direction. "Ms. Tierney," Workman said, looking at me, "Your guide told me you might know something. I'll speak with you last, if you don't mind."

Abby, our guide, went off with Workman first, while the rest of us settled down to wait. One of the officers offered coffee. Walt took his offer, but grimaced and almost spit it out before setting down his almost-full cup. None of the rest of us took any. Angie Rimbaud, the little girl who had sat next to me on the bus, stared at me, then smiled. I smiled back. Her silky-fine brown hair had dried to a tangled mess. She and her parents had talked for some time before lapsing into silence. Now, though, Angie glanced at her parents before coming across the room to me. "Was she your friend?" she demanded, putting a hand on my arm.

"No," I said. "I just talked with her once. But I care."

"Then you were her friend. I think she needed some."

"Angie, you stop bothering Ms. Tierney," Rose called in a tired voice. "Get back over here this minute."

Angie ignored the order, reached into her pocket, and handed me a plastic bag full of candy. "That man said you have to stay 'til last. Here, you can have my M&Ms—and my bubble gum. You might get hungry."

Pete came and put a hand on her shoulder. "Come on, Angie. Don't be a pest." He gave her a gentle shove toward her mother and she scampered away. "Not quite the trip we expected, huh?" he said. "I don't know how we're going to explain this to Angie."

I spread my hands and shrugged. "It won't be easy. Maybe she felt for the other girl. You're evidently raising a caring child."

His face lit up. "Yes, she's an only child and we didn't want her to turn out selfish and self-centered. She really does feel for others. That's part of why this is going to be so hard." He shook his head and walked back toward his family.

Workman finished interviewing Abby and the two older women, then sent them off with one of the deputies. He questioned Pete and Rose Rimbaud separately and had Angie join him and Rose for a few minutes before he sent the family off with another deputy. Angie waved at me as she went out the door. I hoisted the bag of candy, saying, "Thanks again," and Angie rewarded me with a smile that seemed to linger in the doorway after they had gone.

Walt was with Workman for less than five minutes, then sat across the room and glared at me when Workman called Frank in.

As I waited, the room felt increasingly stuffy and overheated, especially in contrast to what we'd had outside. Most of the deputies and officers were no longer in sight, and "Eye Candy" had left, so there was nothing pleasant for me to focus on. I studied the room more carefully. Openings in the back wall were sealed off with concrete blocks—or was that cement blocks? I never could remember which was which. Marilu would have said they must be concrete here in Concrete, I thought, slumping in my hard metal chair.

When Frank finally came out he ducked his head in my direction and mouthed, "You're next."

I jerked upright and grinned at him. "Bye, Frank. Better eagle watching next time."

He and Walt made for the door, and Frank called back, "Bye, Sarah. Give me a call if you learn anything. Dad's in the Tacoma phone book under Walter Randall."

"You can call me, too. In Tacoma under S. J. Tierney."

Frank waved and was out the door with his father and a deputy. Another deputy brought my car keys over, saying, "We brought your car here. We didn't want it to be alone at the staging area."

Workman loomed in the doorway. "Ready for you, Ms. Tierney."

I stood up, stretching to unkink the muscles in my back, and followed him into the inner office. Workman gestured me to a seat beside a shabby metal desk before taking the chair behind the desk.

"You kept Frank a lot longer than the others," I said after he sat down. "I'm wondering why."

"Funny you should ask," Workman said. His dark brown eyes looked out from a deep network of wrinkles. As he spoke the creases on his broad corrugated forehead deepened. "Basically I had two reasons. The main reason was that the guide said you and Frank talked while you were waiting. I figured you might have told him whatever you knew and maybe I could pick up something you maybe would forget to tell us."

He made a noise like a deep purr, and the corners of his mouth turned up. "The other reason is I was once sixteen years old myself. Now that he's been questioned at length by a cop, he has a better story for his friends once he's free to talk about it. I've asked everybody to keep quiet for now with their friends and especially the press, but at least he'll have something to talk about later."

That tickled me, a deputy paying attention to the feelings of a teenage boy. "That's good! That's really great! He's a good kid and he seems mature for his years. And I did tell him a lot before you asked us not to talk with each other."

Workman grinned at my reaction, but immediately turned serious. "I'm sorry I have to keep you so late. Would you like something to drink—or eat—before we get started?" he asked.

"I could sure go for black coffee and a sandwich." I pulled out the bag of candy and bubble gum and plopped it on the table between us. "I couldn't refuse little Angie's sacrifice, but this wasn't my first choice for lunch or dinner. Dessert, maybe. Feel free to take whatever you'd like."

He grinned again and grabbed a couple of M&Ms before glancing at the coffeepot and the used plastic foam cups around the room. I saw a ring of milky mold in the cup nearest me, making its own contribution to the room's ambiance. "The stuff here was probably brewed yesterday—or last week. I'll ask one of the guys to get something from the Ti-Pi Inn down the street. I could use some, too." He strode off, and when he rejoined me in a few minutes I excused myself to go to the restroom.

"Eye Candy" was back with food and a Thermos of coffee from the restaurant when I returned. After Workman and I wolfed a couple of sandwiches and drank some coffee in silence, we both reached for the M&Ms at the same time. "Nothing like some dessert," I said, gesturing for him to go first. He took a hefty handful, then picked up a small microphone and turned on a tape recorder on the desk.

"For the record, I'm talking with Sarah Tierney regarding her knowledge of the body found on a gravel bar in the Skagit River between Marblemount and Rockport. Ms. Tierney, we'll get all the specifics in writing, but please tell me now who you are, where you're from, and what you do."

He pointed the mic in my direction, then popped some candy in his mouth. I swallowed my candy in a hurry, conscious that I was giving a formal statement. "I'm Sarah Tierney from Tacoma," I said. "I'm single, forty-five, and I opened a freelance writing and editing business in September. Before that, I was dean of admissions at Tacoma's Commencement Bay College." I paused and waited for more instructions.

"Please tell me how you came to be at the Meeting Ground Motel last night."

Workman smiled, and I relaxed a little. "A friend and I signed up last fall for a RiverRafter eagle trip. She chose the motel and made reservations. She figured it'd be quieter than the other choices and maybe have more character. And it was a lot less expensive." I paused.

"Tell me more about your friend. Where is she?"

"She's starting to get serious about a new guy. They don't get enough time together because he's a state legislator, but he was free today. When she backed out at the last minute, I decided to come alone."

"Okay. Keep going."

"Do you want all this extraneous stuff? Shouldn't I be giving you 'Just the facts, ma'am'?"

"No, I like the embellishment," he said, reaching again for the bag of candy. This time he pulled out a big piece of bubble gum and unwrapped it. "Takes longer, but it helps me evaluate what a witness notices and how well she presents it, all that kind of thing. And sometimes I think a detail's important even when the witness doesn't. You drove up yesterday?"

I nodded, then remembered the mic wouldn't pick up my gestures. "Yes, I drove from Tacoma yesterday."

"Why don't you tell me what happened from the time you started out?"

"But none of it has anything to do with the girl until last night," I protested.

"Just humor me, huh?"

"Okay, but it seems odd," I said. I reviewed the previous day in my mind before starting talking again. "It's only about 150 miles, but I'd planned an early start since the days are so short. Stayed up late Thursday night and just couldn't wake up when the alarm went off, though. I got the car loaded about 11:00 and headed straight down the 30th Street Hill to Old Town."

I glanced at him. He was listening, really listening, to what I was saying, but he had also started working on the bubble gum. When our eyes met he smiled.

I picked up the narrative. "It was foggy and gray as I drove along Schuster Parkway, with big white clouds rising from the pulp mill at the head of Commencement Bay. I couldn't even see Puget Sound just beyond the railroad tracks and old warehouses."

Workman blew a small bubble, but he was still listening intently. He shook his head when I asked if he knew the city.

"A lot of people don't like Tacoma," I continued. "They say it's a smelly blue-collar town, and they're partly right, although there's not much smell anymore. But that's not all it is. If people can't see past the problems, I hope they'll go away and leave my city small enough for me to feel I'm an important part of it."

I dropped some of my exaggerated style and spoke in a more normal manner. "Even a supporter like me would have had a hard time liking downtown Tacoma yesterday morning. The new freeway spur isn't finished, so Pacific Avenue—the main street—was the fastest way from my house to I-5 heading north. All the fake Christmas greenery and lights along Pacific Avenue looked desolate.

"Hardly any traffic was downtown yesterday, although it's generally pretty busy since the city's been growing. People still hang on to their old ways, though, and they jaywalk even in the middle of the block on Pacific. Often some street people are milling around just beyond the main business district, but yesterday the rain must have kept them in the shelters. I was glad they weren't out where I could see them."

"Why didn't you want to see street people?" Workman asked. His eyes were focused on my left hand. Glancing down, I realized I'd been circling my second finger around my thumbnail for some time. I clasped both hands in my lap. They seemed large and awkward, and I was conscious of my short, functional, unglamorous nails. Workman looked back at my face as I started talking again.

"I've been studying homelessness in Pierce County for the past several weeks." He raised a thick eyebrow but didn't speak. "It's for a freelance assignment, a grant proposal to raise funds so the Martin Luther King Center can set up another shelter. I have to care about the project or I can't write a good proposal. And then, talking with a lot of people who live on the streets has dredged up some powerful feelings. I've just been feeling drained."

"What kind of feelings?" He looked as though he really wanted to know, and I found myself opening up more.

"About families, poverty, substance abuse, the government's policies, you name it. The street people are just part of it. I always get a little down this time of year anyway, so between the assignment and pre-Christmas blues, I needed to get away."

"Lots of people are depressed at Christmas," Workman said. "Why do you get that way?"

He seemed so sincere that I was starting to warm up to him, but I surprised myself by how much detail I was telling him. "Oh, every year I get sad about not having an old-fashioned family Christmas. And every year I remind myself I've never had a Christmas like that. My parents meant something different by 'old-fashioned' Christmas," I said with heavy sarcasm, tipping an imaginary glass.

He nodded again, as though he understood. "Okay, go on."

"I got on the freeway heading north, but traffic was so bad because of the rain I got off as soon as I could and took the back roads."

"Do you know what roads?"

"Not offhand, but I could probably find them on the map."

"We'll look into that later, if we need to."

"I went in some antique and junk shops on the drive up, then stopped at Snohomish for dinner. It was about 8:00 yesterday evening when I saw the sign for the Meeting Ground Motel. I followed the arrow pointing away from the river down a graveled road to the motel entrance. There was a phone booth next to the motel sign, and a log church across the drive."

I paused and took a gulp of cold coffee. Workman held up the Thermos bottle, but I shook my head. "You're doing great," he encouraged me. "I'm interested to hear what you think of the motel."

"You're probably familiar with it, but it wasn't at all what I'd expected. All those log cabins! And it certainly wasn't the most businesslike office I'd ever seen."

Workman chuckled. "Uh-huh. Homey."

"I opened what I thought was an office door and stepped into a living room—all frilly pastel blues and pinks. A sweet old German shepherd came over and sniffed my leg. He lifted his face toward my voice when I spoke to him, but he probably didn't see much through the white cataracts covering his eyes. I scratched behind his ears and waited a minute, then called out."

I paused to think a little further ahead. If Workman wants detail, I'll give him detail, I thought.

"A short, rotund man came in. He had bright blue eyes, a florid complexion, and a fringe of white hair around a nearly bald scalp. Blue-and-white-striped overalls covered a prominent stomach. 'I'm Harry Burton,' he said. 'You must be Miss Tierney from Tacoma. Everybody else with a reservation has already checked in.'"

Workman interrupted me. "Is this verbatim, or are you making up dialogue for my benefit?"

"I have a good memory for conversations. It's probably pretty much word-for-word."

"Okay. Go on, then."

"Burton grinned when he saw me rubbing the dog's ears. 'I guess Tramp's already got you conned into scratching where he itches,' he said." I tried to imitate Burton's speech, feeling I was doing a credible job. "'He purely loves attention, but he don't let just anybody do that.'" Workman grinned, and I wondered if he knew Burton and Tramp well.

"'He probably smells my dogs on me,' I said.

"'I don't think he's smelled anything for a couple of years, but he knows when somebody likes him. Come on in the office and fill out the top three lines of this card for me so everything's nice and legal.'

"We talked about the motel and the Meeting House, and then I asked if many others were there for the eagle watching trip.

"'A family from Gig Harbor is in Number Six and a couple of older women are in Eight,' he said. 'My wife, Madelyn, turned away a group of hippie-looking types on motorcycles, but they probably weren't here for the eagles anyway. We don't like loud goings-on here and we don't like trouble.'

"I told him I like it quiet. Then Burton asked Tramp if he wanted to go for a ride, and the dog moved away from me, bouncing in excitement. 'I'll drive to your cabin and show you around,' Burton said, looking my way. 'Follow me.'"

I stopped my narrative again and picked up my cup. It was empty, and when Workman lifted the Thermos bottle, I nodded. "You still want all this embellishment?" I asked yet again as he poured.

"Yeah, I'm enjoying the performance. We don't get much theater up here."

I looked to see if he was amused at me or with me, and decided it was with me. Taking a swallow of coffee, I went on.

"Burton moved quickly to the small pickup next to the office. When he opened the passenger door, Tramp put his front paws up on the seat and waited. Burton grabbed the dog's back legs and helped him scramble onto the seat, then had his truck halfway down the drive by the time I got in my car, shifted the gears, and took off after them."

Workman started laughing, then. "I must have seen him help Tramp up a hundred times."

"I thought you might know them," I said, laughing with him. "Tramp waited in the cab," I continued, "while Burton opened up the cabin. 'Sorry to be in such a hurry,' Burton said, 'but I just realized the "M*A*S*H" rerun will be on in a few minutes. Hope you enjoy yourself.'

"It was far too early for bed, and I wasn't ready to settle in to read or watch TV. It took only a few minutes to unload the car and unpack. Then I picked up the folder about the Meeting House and walked through the rain toward the church."

I paused once more, noticing my finger was circling my thumbnail again. "Look, I'm sorry, but I can't go on like this," I said.

Workman's posture switched from relaxed watchfulness to full alert. He removed the bubble gum and threw it in the wastebasket, but didn't say anything. The silence lengthened until I felt I had to continue.

"I can't keep up this light tone. The way I'm making a production out of this. I mean, it was light up to now when it was happening, but from this point on, it's not amusing."

He relaxed again, letting his bones and muscles settle back into his skin, then ran his hand over his hair. "Okay, then treat it seriously. You tell it the way you want to."

I told about the encounter in the church much as I had told it to Frank. I told just the facts, not what I had thought. Marilu was in my head only; she hadn't been in the church, and I left her out of my story.

"Why visit the Meeting House?" Workman asked. "You're on a holiday, at a motel. Do you always stop off in churches?"

"Not always, but the brochure said this was a historical and tourist attraction, and Burton seemed really proud of it. I was curious and thought I might as well visit it. Besides," I added, "I figured it wouldn't hurt to talk with my higher power in a church setting."

He glanced up. "AA, huh?"

"No, ACOA—Adult Children of Alcoholics. Same twelve-step program, though."

He nodded again. "That group pretty important to you?"

"It helped pull me out of a kind of hell."

Suddenly I didn't want to explain to him. "Will you excuse me?" I asked, standing up and heading toward the restroom again without waiting for an answer. Workman clicked the recorder off as I rose. ≠

Chapter 3

I should have known better than to look at my face in the mirror as I washed my hands. The sight hadn't bothered me on my earlier visit to the restroom, but now my freckles and frizzy reddish hair made me feel childish and at a definite disadvantage with the officer.

He was reviewing his notes when I came out a few minutes later. "You okay?" he asked, glancing up.

I nodded. "Uh-huh. Just too much coffee."

"You're nearly done," he said, turning the recorder back on with a no-nonsense snap. The atmosphere seemed to have changed somehow while I was away. "What happened when you left the Meeting House?"

"I walked back to my cabin and went to bed. This morning I showered, packed the car, had breakfast at Mountain Song Restaurant, and went straight to the staging area at Miller Park." I finished with a brief, straightforward account of the raft trip, finding the body, and waiting for the deputies.

Workman looked straight at me. The broad face that had seemed so sympathetic and friendly a few minutes earlier was transformed, much as one of my dogs, Jesse, changes from a goofy pet to a hunter when he sees a cat. It's mostly in the eyes, a narrowing and an intensity. For the first time I felt as though he might not think I was trying to help.

"Exactly why did you volunteer to stay with the body, Ms. Tierney?"

"I told you," I said, defensive. "I met her last night and felt kind of responsible."

"Most people wouldn't feel *responsible* for a stranger they'd seen only once. You just talked with her for a few minutes, you said. That's hardly enough to make you want to sit with her body in the cold and rain." The voice wasn't unfriendly, but the eyes remained intent.

"I didn't want to just *leave* her," I said. "She was all alone."

"She was dead," he said in a flat, cool, voice. "She wouldn't have noticed she was alone. Did you have some other reason for wanting to stay?"

The heat went out of me. "She looked so much like my sister," I said, looking at the floor. I put my ankle on my knee, grabbed the bootlace, and started poking the tip into the holes. "Marilu died when I was away at college. She wasn't even sixteen, about this girl's age. She crashed, drunk, while driving a stolen motorcycle. ACOA helped me realize I wasn't responsible for my parents' drinking, but I still feel I could have helped Marilu if I'd tried harder instead of escaping as soon as I could. I've always hoped somebody stayed with her."

He shut off the recorder. "I'm sorry," he said. "Sorry about your sister and sorry I bullied that out of you. I knew there was something else, and it might have been important. That's enough for now."

He stood up while continuing to speak. "I'd like to walk you through your story tonight, while it's still fresh in your mind, at the same place you talked with the girl. Being there might help you remember something else. It's already late, so I'll go with you to the Meeting Ground and we'll arrange for you to stay there again. Then tomorrow we might have more information from our investigation. I'll talk with you again, get you to sign your statement, and let you go home by midafternoon."

The sharp burst of pain in my heart when I told him about Marilu had subsided, along with my defensiveness. Still, I didn't want to relive the meeting with the girl who looked like Marilu once again. Despite my feelings, I had to help however I could.

I nodded. "I'm glad to help, but I'll have to find out if my dog sitter can stay."

"You can use this phone. Do you have a backup if the sitter has to leave?"

"Yes, a friend has a key and I'm sure he can help."

"Good," Workman said. He busied himself at the desk, but stayed in the room while I called.

Hazel, my dog sitter, answered on the first ring. As usual, she chattered without pausing for answers or even for breath. "Hi, Sarah. What's up? You just caught me. Jesse and Golda and I went for a walk in the rain earlier, but I didn't want to take them out again in this downpour. We've been sitting around all afternoon with a fire going. It's a lot cozier than my apartment! I just fed the pups and finished packing up. I was about to leave when the phone rang."

"Could you stay another night? Something's come up, and I can't get home 'til tomorrow evening."

"Yeah. No problem. The dogs and I will have a fine old time. You just stay there as long as you want, just let me know. I'll pop a movie in the VCR and send out for pizza. Hope whatever's come up is handsome, single, and rich."

"Don't I wish? Thanks, Hazel, you're an angel."

* * *

I ached as I got in my car a few minutes later. The deputy who had brought the car had adjusted the seat for his height. I moved it back to the position fitting my legs. The strain of finding the body, sitting in the rain, and drowsing off in a chair had taken a toll on this not-so-young body. And the interview had taken a toll on my emotions. Despite the coffee, all I wanted to do was sleep. Not a good idea while driving.

My stash of sunflower seeds helped. Putting a seed in my mouth, moving it around so I can crack it with my teeth and extract the nutty kernel, then depositing the shell in the litter bag helps keep me awake when I'm driving. It worked fine this night.

The road streamed with water, and my lights illuminated only a small area ahead of me. Once I left Concrete, the road ran alternately between wide-open areas and tree-lined tunnels. I saw the turnoff to Howard Miller Steelhead Park, where we had boarded the bus for the raft trip this morning. It seemed a long time ago.

The dark, the heavy rain, and my tiredness kept me driving between forty and forty-five. No cars came toward me, and the only lights in my rearview mirror were those of Workman, who followed at a comfortable distance with the lights of his jacked-up truck on low beam.

I turned off Highway 20 at the motel sign, then stopped by the Meeting House. Workman parked next to me. The light over the phone booth shone bright on the sign I had noticed before: "Meeting House Always Open. All are Welcome. I Will Give You Rest." The last sentence struck me as ironic now. What kind of rest did the little girl have? What kind of rest did I have now that I was involved in a murder?

I fumbled in the car pocket for an umbrella. Opening the door just wide enough to get my hand out, I stuck the umbrella up and pressed the automatic button.

"Whoa," Workman said, stepping backward and putting up his hands. "You almost got me. A concealed weapon is a serious offense."

I hadn't realized he had come to my car door. "I'm sorry," I said, flustered. "Are you okay?" Getting out of the car, again I almost hit him with the umbrella.

"You didn't quite get me, but you will if you keep trying." He grinned and backed away, brushing off my repeated apologies. "That's why I like ponchos. No spokes."

He took my elbow as we started up the stairs, careful of the slippery moss-covered steps. The top of my head came just up to his chin.

"You'll have to check all weapons at the door," he said, taking my umbrella and putting it in a corner. His voice grew more serious. "I'll stand back here, and I want you to do exactly what you did last night. You can condense time, but try to repeat every single action and tell me what you're thinking. Don't try too hard, though. Just let it flow."

He slouched against the doorframe to watch.

The room was as serene as it had been the night before. Standing just inside the entrance to the sanctuary for a few moments, I tried to get back into the previous evening's mood. Workman was silent and unobtrusive as I walked to the front, looking at the heavy metal cross, the crèche, the pulpit, and the room's few other features. As I walked I started talking about my actions.

"I sat down here to sort of soak up peace, just sitting for a few minutes," I said, gesturing to the pew. "Didn't have my eyes closed or anything, and I wasn't drowsy. I heard an extra noise—more than the rain and wind like we're hearing now—and it registered that a car had pulled in across the drive."

I sat in the same place as on the previous night and resumed talking. "I resented it when the door opened. It had been so peaceful, and I didn't want to be bothered. Then I felt bad about being resentful." I repeated my conversation with the girl as I had already told Frank and as Workman had taped earlier, but this time I included my feelings about Marilu. It didn't hurt as much as I thought it would.

"One thing I thought about later," I said, turning back to face Workman. "She mentioned colored glass and pretty pictures and statues at Holy Rosary. I'm sure half the towns in the state have a Holy Rosary Catholic Church, but I wondered if she might mean the one in Tacoma. I've never been there but I've heard it's pretty ornate."

Then I brought up what I'd been thinking ever since I first saw the girl's body. "Haven't most of the Skagit River Killer's victims been from Tacoma? Holy Rosary church isn't much of a clue, but it may help you. Also, the victim and the place seem to fit what I've read, but the method isn't like what's been reported in the paper. And none of the victims were found so soon after they were killed, were they?"

"Don't theorize just now, huh?" Workman said from the back of the room. "We're thinking along the same lines, but let's not follow it up until after you finish here."

I disliked his cutting off my questions, but he was the law enforcement expert. "Okay," I said, turning to face the pew where the girl had sat. "When the car beeped, she jumped up and said, 'Gotta go. He told me to stay in the car,' and she went out the door without quite closing it. The wind was sharp and damp, so I got up to shut the door. Then I heard a man's voice demanding, 'What were you doing in there? Get in.'"

I got up and walked to the door at the back. Workman stepped to the side. I opened the door, then started to close it. Just like the night before, the wind came in, bringing rain with it.

"I just remembered. Something about his voice irritated me just a little. He spoke precisely. Not quite as though English was a foreign language, but more like he came from a poor background and tried to improve his pronunciation. Like some speech teacher kept drilling into him that he had to enunciate every syllable. They did that with me when I went to college up North, in Minnesota, 'cause they couldn't understand my Southern accent; that's part of why I listen so carefully to speech patterns. And he put equal stress on each syllable. With slight spaces between words. It wasn't an uneducated voice, like hers."

I thought a little more. "I guess each word *was* only one syllable, except for 'doing.' But he said '*What* were you do-ing in there.' He didn't put a proper inflection on the question at the end, but put a lot of emphasis on the 'what.' When he said, 'Get in,' each word had equal value, and there weren't any inflections. I could almost see him moving his lips a little too exaggeratedly and projecting each word with his teeth and tongue. He didn't use everyday informal speech patterns."

"That's good," Workman said. "That might help us. Anything else?"

"No; I just heard one car door slam and the sound of the motor revving and tires crunching on gravel as the car took off. No bad muffler. No peeling rubber. I don't know which way they went. When I left to go back to my cabin, the phone booth across the way suggested the man had been making a phone call."

"We'll check that out," Workman said. "Right now, let's go to the office, then I'll see you to your cabin."

"There's one other thing," I said as we walked in the rain toward my car.

"What?" Workman asked.

"He wasn't really young or old—the man, I mean. His voice was mature, forties or fifties I think, but I can't judge closer. I have a sense he could be a teacher or a salesman, but that might be pushing it too far when I heard only a few words. Anyway, he wouldn't be dynamic, but he would be clear and precise. And I think I'd know his voice if I heard it again." ≠

Chapter 4

I drove toward the office where I'd registered the night before. Again, Workman followed in his jacked-up Blazer. He stood well out of the way when I opened my umbrella, and he kept his distance as we walked to the porch.

Opening the door to the room with the frilly pastels, he called, "Maddy! Harry! You here?" Tramp pulled himself up from his bed with effort, then went straight to Workman, wagging his tail. I felt hurt, after all the scratching I'd given him.

"How you doing, old boy?" Workman said, bending to rub behind the dog's ears. "Tramp and I go way back," he said, looking at me as though he were reading my mind. "In fact, I brought him to Maddy and Harry when he was just a stray pup. He doesn't forget old friends."

Seeing how familiar Workman was with the motel, I felt silly about how I'd described it and its inhabitants to Workman. The dog leaned into Workman's scratching and didn't budge when a rotund woman came in. With her white hair, blue eyes, and ruddy complexion, she could almost have been her husband's twin. Her small-print dress would have looked odd on Harry, though it suited her well. It reminded me of the flour-sack dresses many older country women still wore around Turtle Creek when I was a kid.

"Hi, Harold," she said, nodding and smiling at the deputy. She put a plump hand out for me to shake. "You must be Miss Tierney. I'm Maddy Burton. Sorry I didn't get to meet you last night, but I'm glad to have the opportunity now. You're in the same cabin again. Hope that's all right."

"That's great! I liked it a lot," I assured her.

"Charge it to the Sheriff's Office," Workman put in.

"You hush, Harold," Mrs. Burton said. "I want this killer caught as much as you do, and we can afford to let Miss Tierney stay on the house tonight."

"That's nice of you, Mrs. Burton," I said.

"Maddy, please. Mrs. Burton was my mother-in-law, and she's been dead for years. You just call me Maddy."

"I'll be happy to, if you'll call me Sarah."

"I'll do that. Now, do you need anything tonight, Sarah? Food, a book or pack of cards, a bottle?"

Obviously she was more modern than she looked. "No thanks. I think I have everything I need."

"Sure you wouldn't like something to warm your insides?"

"I appreciate the offer, but I'll pass. I may have a cup of herb tea when I get to the cabin, but I brought the fixings."

Workman had been scratching Tramp's ears and chest all that time, but now he stood up and stretched his long legs. "Oof, knees can't take so much deep bending anymore. Maddy, you and Harry need to get a table for Tramp to stand on so I can scratch him as much as he wants."

"He couldn't get up on it if we did get him one. And it's not possible to scratch him as much as he wants! You sure spoil that dog, Harold. If you hadn't always been this bad, I'd say you were just missing Alex. Never saw anybody as attached to a dog as you were to him—and him to you!"

She turned and gave me the key to the cabin, holding my hand in both of hers for a moment. "No need to fill out another card," she said. "We know who you are, and I'm sure it's all legal, what with Harold bringing you here. You just get a good night's rest. You can leave the key in the cabin tomorrow."

"That's right, Maddy, it's all legal," Workman said. "And I'll see Ms. Tierney to her cabin. Thanks a lot for putting her up tonight."

I thanked Maddy again for her kindness, appreciating her warmth more than I could tell her.

Workman took the umbrella from me and held it over my head on the way to the car, then closed my car door. "If I hold on to this, you can't stick me in the eye with it. See you at your cabin."

He sheltered me with the umbrella again from the car to my cabin. He also took the key and opened the door, then turned on the lights in each room and pulled down the shades. He even checked the shower stall and under the bed before handing me the key.

For the first time I felt concerned about my own safety. "You don't think the Killer would come back here, do you?" I asked, noticing I thought of "Killer" as a proper name.

"No, but there could be a squirrel or a field mouse, and I figured you might be a little more alarmed than usual if you heard noises tonight. Didn't mean to scare you. Just thought we both might feel more easy if I checked."

His thoughtfulness made me laugh. "I *am* relieved. Thanks."

Workman helped unload the trunk, grumbling about the amount of stuff I'd brought.

"I know! I've packed less for a month abroad than I pack for a night away when I'm traveling by car. Besides, I wasn't sure what the weather would be, so I kept all my options open. I didn't really throw in *everything* I own."

"Coulda fooled me," he said, putting the cooler on the kitchen counter. "Even with all this, are you sure you don't need anything else? TV reception's pretty good, but I have some paperbacks in the truck if you'd rather read."

"Thanks, I have a couple of books with me. I'll probably just take a shower and go straight to bed."

"Okay. We should know something by early afternoon. I'll check back about 1:30 to let you know if we have more questions or know anything new. If the freezing level drops any lower, we might get snow, but Harry'll make sure you don't get stuck."

He hadn't said anything more about the Skagit River Killer, but he didn't really seem to be hiding anything either. Again, I blurted out what I was thinking. "Look, I'm too tired to comprehend much tonight, but tomorrow can I get some answers, or at least some information?"

"Sure, but I want to ponder this before I tell you what I think.

I'll tell you now this is the closest we've gotten to a break with the Killer." He seemed to capitalize the word as well. "We didn't have *anything* to go on 'til now, and we don't want to mess this up. I hope we'll know more by tomorrow. We'll talk about it then."

"I appreciate that, Deputy Workman," I said. "And I'm not in shape to talk about it now, anyway. Besides, I'm sure it's been a long day for you, too. You'd better get home, before your wife gets really upset."

"Thanks, Ms. Tierney. It's *Detective* Workman, not deputy. Or it was. I turned in my resignation a month ago, but I guess I'm still official until I've finished using up my vacation. They called me in because I worked on some of the other Skagit River murders."

He walked to the door and fixed it to lock automatically. "Also, there isn't any wife. Be sure to put the chain lock on. See you tomorrow." He closed the door behind him and strode toward his truck, his boots clumping on the porch floorboards.

Okay, I thought. *Must have touched some kind of nerve, there. About the job, the vacation, or the wife? I'm sorry I upset him. He's a nice man.*

I was surprised he wasn't married. He looked cared for, clean-shaven, hair neatly cut, clothes clean and ironed, properly fed. A lot of middle-aged unmarried men get sloppy about those things.

Also, like someone in a long-standing relationship, he had the kind of comfortable self-respecting manner that's one of the reasons married men are often so much more attractive than those who're available. Maybe he didn't have a wife, but he probably had a significant other. He wasn't handsome, but was appealing—too appealing to be unattached.

I pushed thoughts of Detective Workman aside as I prepared for another night. I had been delighted with my cabin the night before. That pleasure seeped back as I put a kettle on to boil and hung my still-damp outer clothing in the shower.

When the water boiled, I made herb tea and took it into the living room, breathing in the tea's minty scent. Friday night I had chosen the pale greeny-gold plush rocker over the sofa or straight wood chair. It was a good choice and I sat there again, sipping my tea and settling in. Glancing at the magazines piled on a table next to the sofa, I wondered what kind of books Workman read. *Probably shoot-'em-ups and spy stories*, I thought. *What does it matter what he reads? He was nice to offer his books.*

I still felt jumpy, so I tried to situate myself in the cabin as a centering technique. I don't use meditation techniques often, but anyone who went to college when and where I did has tried some of them. They help when I'm especially tense. And I certainly had reason to be tense now.

To help calm me I focused on the chenille spread, the small pot of ivy on the kitchen windowsill, the strips of green Formica separating the appliances and sink, the honey-colored paneling covering the walls, and the several dog pictures in inexpensive frames. New-looking cotton curtains in an old-fashioned flower pattern hung at the window and door. I hadn't seen anything like these curtains in years. They were ironed, and even starched! No wonder I felt in a time warp.

All the inexpensive homey old-fashioned touches had a soothing effect. I moved to sit in one of two chairs at the small drop-leaf wooden table. The pattern of the faded tablecloth matched that of the curtains, but the worn fabric contrasted with the fresh material in the windows. Other than an old cigarette burn, the tablecloth was immaculate, starched, and ironed. Its scent recalled my childhood.

We had been poor, but we had a home. Until Mama started drinking along with Daddy, it was as clean and comfortable as she could make it. After that, Marilu and I tried, from time to time, to keep it nice. I wondered what kind of home the dead girl had come from, back when she had a home. I wondered if she'd ever had a real home.

I shook myself back to the present and put the kettle on for another cup of tea. This year's Norman Rockwell calendar hung over the table, advertising Vaux Pharmacy in nearby Mount Vernon. The November picture showed a barefoot boy holding a pumpkin and looking up as geese flew overhead. Someone had forgotten to update the month, so I flipped the calendar to December: A girl and boy sledding down a hill with a dog running beside them.

Another dog picture hung beside the calendar. I wondered if all the cabins featured dogs, or if they had different themes. Maybe this was the dog cabin, another had cats, another, horses. Whatever. I was in the right place. How were Jesse and Golda doing at home? I wished I could hug them right about now. They were always a great comfort when I was low.

Jesse's a big chocolate lab I got at the pound, tall enough to rest his muzzle on the dining-room table. Golda, a medium-sized vanilla mutt, is quieter and always anxious for affection. The dogs have a dog door between the back porch and the fenced-in back yard, so my last view of them the day before was when they came out and stood in the pouring rain to give me a maximum dose of guilt. It worked, but I've learned to dump dog-induced guilt as soon as the dogs are out of sight.

Come on, Sarah, I thought. *Back to here and now.*

I thought about the "poem" over the toilet in the en-suite bathroom, *Ode to a Septic System:*

All us folks with septic tanks

Give to you our heartfelt thanks

For putting nothing in the pot

That isn't guaranteed to rot.

Hair is forbidden, matches, too,

And cigarette butts are taboo.

For all these things

Please use the basket.

There's a darn good reason

Why we ask it.

I've always memorized doggerel and song lyrics without trying, so I already knew this "ode" by heart. I was sure it would stay with me for days.

The kettle whistled, and I pulled out my assortment of herb teas again. "Sleepytime" seemed a good choice. I glanced at my watch. Barely eight o'clock. Earlier than when I went to the Meeting House last night. No wonder I wasn't ready for bed, even though I was so tired.

I sat down in the living room again, holding the cup to my face and breathing in the soothing chamomile scent. I had tried to avoid thinking about Marilu, the dead girl we found in the river, and all the other dead girls found in or near the Skagit. It wasn't working. Maybe I'd better face what bothered me so.

And maybe I'd better use what ACOA taught me about dealing with problems. The twelve steps talk about believing in "a Power greater than ourselves" and turning "our will and our lives over to the care of God *as we understood Him.*" I still haven't figured out what—if anything—I understand about God; all I'm sure of is I don't believe most of what I learned in Sunday school. And my higher power doesn't seem to have much to do with organized religion. But I use the AA prayers and I "act as if" I believe, and I function a lot better than I used to.

Getting comfortable, I took a couple of deep breaths. Out loud I said, "Please, grant me the serenity to accept the things I cannot change, courage to change the things I can, and the wisdom to know the difference. If you're there, please keep Marilu close to you, along with that poor girl I met last night. And help me do whatever I can to help find the girl's killer. I've been trying to think about everything else, but now I ask for help in concentrating on what I might have learned last night. Thanks."

My mind didn't go straight to anywhere in particular, but seemed to swoop in big circles, somewhere on each trip around touching on Marilu, the Skagit River Killer, and his victims.

Putting Marilu aside, the girl last night certainly seemed to fit the profile. She was young, short, and probably a prostitute. She might have been from Tacoma. She was definitely dead. ≠

Chapter 5

I didn't get a hot shower that night, nor did I spend much time thinking about the murders. As soon as I let go and stopped trying to empty my mind, it emptied itself in a sudden burst of tiredness. It was all I could do to brush my teeth and take my clothes off before falling into bed. A thought of the Killer flitted through my mind, leaving just as quickly as it came while I dropped into a sound sleep.

At eight the next morning, I awoke refreshed. Blue sky was overhead and the sun showed above the mountain peaks surrounding the cabin. I slipped on a warm robe and loafers and stepped onto the small porch. The yard was sodden, and moisture hung heavy close to the ground, but it looked like this would be one of the glorious Pacific Northwest days that come unexpectedly to the wet side of the mountains in the middle of winter.

I closed the door and stepped off the porch. Holding my long blue robe so the hem wouldn't get wet, I walked into the yard, smelling the clean, fresh, cold air. A movement to my right startled me. I jerked my head around. Then something moved on the left, just visible out of the corner of my eye. I jerked around again, and for a moment had the disorienting sensation the entire field was undulating in front of me. Then the scene resolved into a calm, pastoral one where dozens of rabbits of all sizes and colors crept and hopped through the wet grass. Three moved in my direction, one a large, somewhat moth-eaten brown rabbit, one a medium-sized black-and-white piebald, and one small solid black bunny. The large one reached me first, then sat up on his hind legs, forepaws hanging in classic bunny fashion, and wiggled his nose. The fur on his nose was raggedy, as if it were worn down from too much petting.

I laughed, then talked to him and the other two who had drawn up next to him and had struck the same pose. "Sorry I don't have anything for you this morning," I said. "I'd definitely offer you something if I could." Other rabbits started converging on me as I talked. I giggled at the thought of how Alfred Hitchcock could make a new movie, *The Rabbits,* in which a hapless tourist is overrun by hungry bunnies. But my tragedy was averted as the lead rabbit dropped to all fours and scuttled away and the rest of the advancing horde moved off, searching for more promising food sources.

I looked up to see Maddy and Harry walking up the drive toward me. "Good morning," Maddy called.

"Good morning. How are you, and where's Tramp?"

"We leave him in the cabin in the mornings," Harry said. "He can't move too well when he first gets up and it kind of gets to him that he can't play with the rabbits like he always used to. This time of day we go out without him and check the grounds and make sure everything's okay. Did you sleep well?"

"Like a top. And it's beautiful here this morning. But what's with the rabbits? I feel like I'm in a dream!"

"It's the real world, but it's still a pretty sight," Maddy said, putting her hands on her plump hips as she looked around her domain with satisfaction. The cabins were neat, the grounds tended, water sparkled on every branch, and snow clung to the tops of the mountains. Dozens or hundreds of rabbits grazed throughout the clearing.

"My dad bought ten rabbits for me and my brothers back when we were kids living here," she explained. "They were supposed to be livestock, but Mom couldn't bear to cook them and none of us would eat them—and I don't think Dad could bear to kill them, either—so ultimately he turned them loose. I think other people released their pets here as well. They bred with the wild rabbits, and now we have all these almost-tame rabbits in all colors and patterns. We just enjoy them, along with the scenery. They're part of why I wouldn't want to live anywhere else."

"Right now I'm glad I'm here myself," I said. "Except I'm starting to get cold. Is there a service in the Meeting House? I feel like being around people today."

"Nothing's in the Meeting House, but there's Assembly of God and Marblemount Union Sunday School in Marblemount and an Episcopal church a couple of miles up Highway 20. I can get the times of the services for you."

"Episcopal!" I said, delighted. If I was going to church I wanted it as different as possible from the kind I grew up in, one with some of the order and ritual so lacking in my childhood. "I've never been to an Episcopal church. Will they mind if I wear jeans?"

"Honey, this is a tourist area. They should be used to anything. Besides, they aren't being Christian if they mind what you wear. Most likely they'll just be glad you came. I've never been either, but I know their service is at noon."

"Good, I'll go, then. But I'd better get inside and warm up right now. Good talking with you two again. I really like your place."

"Thanks," Harry said. "We've enjoyed having you. Do you think you were able to help Harold?"

In this peaceful morning, the murder had slipped to the back of my mind. "Not much. But we're meeting again this afternoon. Maybe he'll come up with something then."

"If anybody can make sense of it, it's Harold," Maddy added. "We're real sorry he decided to retire. He's solved some tough crimes for the Sheriff's Office and been a good neighbor at the same time. You get on inside," she said. "You're starting to shiver."

I went in and shucked the soaked loafers just inside the door. Now was the perfect time for a shower. The strong, hot flow of water felt luxurious on my chilled body, and I stayed in for a long time.

Church seemed to call for looking as good as I could. My dark blue jeans and gold turtleneck shirt were wrinkled from being crammed in the suitcase for a couple of days. I hoped they'd smooth out with wear. I'd omitted my usual lipstick and mascara on the raft trip yesterday, and because of my freckles I never wear any other makeup. Today, though, I had a chance to look decent. My hair came out wavy, rather than frizzy, and I paid special attention to fixing my face. By the time I was ready and had packed my clothes, it was 10:00

and I was ravenous!

My yogurt and instant oatmeal left me longing for the previous day's bacon and scrambled eggs, but what I missed most this Sunday morning was strong, bitter restaurant coffee. Neither the instant coffee provided in the cabin nor my herb tea was what I wanted now. I held firm, though. No use hauling a cooler and food around if I was going to eat out all the time. I finished my breakfast, cleaned up, and finished packing everything in the car.

At a few minutes before noon I drove up to St. Francis' white clapboard church. It stood alone in a clearing by the side of the road rather than in a town, and I parked among several other cars and trucks in the semicircular gravel drive. Jacked-up vehicles were popular out here in the hinterlands, I noticed. Two high Blazers and a Jeep with big tires sat next to several high-riding pickups. My ancient—and low-slung—blue Saab seemed out of place.

I slipped into an empty pew in the middle of the church. Promptly at noon, a young girl in white robes walked in carrying a cross, followed by Detective Workman in a white robe. I was surprised to see him there, but now I knew why the cherry-red Blazer in the drive looked familiar! A tall, thin woman priest in a white robe and a purple sort of long scarf followed Workman.

O Come, O Come, Emmanuel burst from a small electronic organ, and I joined in, singing enthusiastically, if not musically. The priest opened with prayer and Workman read the scripture lessons in a clear, calm voice. I was conscious of the cadence more than the words, now and then letting a phrase enter my mind and stay there while other words flowed on unheard.

The priest delivered her short sermon with spirit and conviction, but my mind was back on the events of the last couple of days. As my thoughts wandered, I looked through the arched clear glass window behind the altar at barns, a meadow, and dark clouds massing behind the mountains. An eagle soared in the middle distance, then dipped and disappeared from view. *I wonder if I'll ever see an eagle without thinking of the girl*, I thought. Cattle with white faces and black bodies moved into my view, providing a counterpoint to my thoughts.

It wasn't exactly revenge I wanted; I had no connection with the girl other than her resemblance to Marilu, and certainly no reason to avenge her. But I felt rotten that she had probably had a lousy life and an even more lousy death. The other Skagit River victims had been abstracts to me, but she was real, had been a living human being when she talked with me only a short time before she was killed. I wanted peace for her, and I wanted to keep others from being killed. And maybe, if I could put her to rest, I was ready to put Marilu to rest as well.

A hugely pregnant young woman seated in front of me led the congregation in prayer. My eyes filled with tears when she said, "We remember especially the stranger who was found dead yesterday not far from here. May she find peace and rest." I groped in my pocket for a tissue as the tears spilled over, then had a hard time finding my voice to participate in the rest of the service.

I stood along with everyone else, and the priest said, "The Peace of the Lord be always with you."

The congregation responded, "And also with you," then started shaking hands and hugging one another. This was *not* like the church where I grew up! The couple in front of me hugged each other, then the pregnant young woman shook my hand and wished me, "The peace of the Lord. We're glad you're visiting with us this afternoon. I'm Connie Harrelson, and this is my husband, Jim."

"I'm Sarah Tierney. Glad to be here."

Connie looked into my face and asked with evident concern, "Are you all right? Is something the matter?"

"I'm okay. It was just your prayer about the murdered girl. I've been pretty upset about her."

"I understand. My dad is really bothered, too. He asked me to put in that part."

Other hands reached out to shake mine, and Connie let go. I was surrounded as members of the congregation moved around, everyone greeting everyone else. It seemed an elaborate dance, with some people remaining stationary and others, including those leading the service, moving from pew to pew.

My tears were done with, although I was sure my mascara had washed off and my eyelids were red and swollen. Pleased with the friendly greetings, I turned again to face the front just as Workman hugged Connie and gave her a kiss on the cheek.

"Afternoon, Dad," she said. "This is Sarah Tierney. You'll tell Judy?"

"I've met Ms. Tierney," Workman said, enveloping my hand in both of his warm hands. "We're glad you joined us for worship. The peace of the Lord be with you."

"And with you," I murmured. The noise level had dropped and people were finding their seats again. Workman turned and walked back toward the altar.

As the service continued, I lost myself in trying to follow the unfamiliar ritual. The priest said communion was open to everyone, so I went forward with the other worshippers. Kneeling at the peeled-log rail, I held up my hands like the person next to me. The priest approached, greeting each person by name. "Sarah, the body of our Lord Jesus Christ keep you in everlasting life," she said, breaking off a piece of bread and pressing it into my hands.

I put the bread in my mouth, wondering how she knew my name. Workman followed her, holding a cup. "Sarah, the blood of our Lord Jesus Christ keep you in everlasting life," he said, lifting the cup to my lips. *Real wine*, I noticed, *not Welch's grape juice like my church had in Turtle Creek.*

Back in the pew, I realized the priest must be "Judy," and Workman had told her my name. I liked hearing my name spoken when receiving communion, just as I had liked it when almost everyone in the church welcomed me. I hadn't expected people to be so warm to a stranger.

The service was nearly over. Again, in the final prayer, I was struck by certain phrases and let the rest wash over me: "And now, Father, send us out to do the work you have given us to do . . . ."

A number of people spoke with me as I waited in the aisle to go out. Workman disappeared, but showed up next to me in a couple of minutes. He looked better in pressed khaki; he really was too broad to look his best in a white dress.

"Good afternoon, Detective Workman."

"Just Harold, here," he said in a low voice. "Hope you slept well last night. I was going to stop by the motel and see you on the way home from church. Meant to tell you the Sheriff would reimburse you for your lunch, but now I have a better idea."

Connie and Jim came up behind Workman, who put an arm around Connie's shoulders. "Is that kid coming today, sugar? You're as big as a house!"

"Yes, Dad, as big as a house and twice as clumsy. Don't worry, you know it's not due for another two weeks. It's Dad's first grandchild," she said, turning to me. "He's getting pretty bad."

"It's *our* first kid," Jim said with a grin, "but we're handling it better than Harold."

"Can you come over for dinner this afternoon, Dad? It's roast chicken, and Jim's cooking."

"Can't, Connie, Jim, but thanks for asking. I've got to work on this case."

"Okay, maybe next week. Sarah, it was good having you here. Hope you can come again."

Both the young people hugged the priest before slipping out the door, then Workman introduced me. "Judy, this is Sarah Tierney. She came up for an eagle rafting trip. Ms. Tierney, this is our vicar, Judith Goudge."

The thin priest's face was shadowed as she took my hand. "Harold told me someone was helping," she said quietly. "I'll be praying for you, as I already am for Harold." We chatted for a few moments, then she moved us out the door so she could speak to others behind us.

Sunlight struck the cross atop the church and brightened the mossy trees encircled by the drive, but clouds were moving in fast. I looked up at Workman, zipped my jacket, and asked, "You were saying something about a better idea for lunch?"

"I thought you could come to my place. I'm a fair cook, we'd have a chance to talk, and you could be on your way home while it's daylight."

"I'd like that," I said, surprised at his offer. I didn't think a city detective would have asked me to ramble on the way he had the day before, and I was sure a city detective wouldn't invite me to lunch at his place, especially with him cooking!

"If you're all packed up, you'd better ride with me," Workman suggested. "I live on the other side of Marblemount, and you'll have enough driving later without backtracking. Also, it's rough getting to my house. I'll call Maddy and Harry so they won't worry about us connecting."

"Is my car okay here?"

"Ought to be. We haven't had a car break-in for several years."

"You should know. Let me get my umbrella. Those clouds are coming fast."

"Oh, no, you don't! I'll make sure you stay dry without putting my eye out."

I laughed and followed him to the high red Blazer remaining in the drive. It wasn't easy suddenly to think of him as Harold. Or maybe he had meant me to call him that only at church. Now I supposed we'd get back to detective-witness roles. That was okay with me. He was a cop—and a religious one too, not my type anyway.

I've been paranoid about cops ever since I was a kid and they were either bringing Daddy home, morosely drunk, or taking him away, belligerently drunk. I got even more distrustful of them when they were on the other side of demonstrations against the Vietnam War when I was in college. Besides, Workman was probably involved with someone anyway, maybe the priest. She wasn't wearing a ring, either.

Whatever my role, I was glad I had on jeans when Workman had to help me climb in the truck. A skirt would have been up to my waist as I stepped up. I laughed as I fastened the seat belt.

"What's so funny?" he asked, settling into the driver's seat.

"That reminded me of the way Harry Burton helps Tramp into the truck."

He chuckled. "I guess there's some resemblance, but I wouldn't be so indelicate as to hoist you by your hind legs."

"No, but why's the truck so high anyway? I thought trucks like this were all driven by showoff teenagers. Or is this standard sheriff's-type gear?"

"Yeah, the Sheriff's Office has a few of this kind of truck, but this is mine. It's four-wheel drive, and it's jacked up and has big tires so I can get around in the back country when I need to. Bought it from my son Al when he got shipped overseas. The view sure is different from up here, isn't it?"

He was right. I could see a lot more from the high cab than from my car, including frequent views of the Skagit River on my right.

"You sure it isn't just to impress the women, huh?"

"Probably was at least half of why Al got the truck, but not for me. My ex-wife and I had a Dart and a Ram pickup. I was used to fairly large pickups and little cars at home and high trucks at work. I like high better. She got the Dart and I got the pickup, but that truck fell apart just about the time Al left."

I glanced around the cab. Clean, but cluttered. Some books and tapes in a box within easy reach behind the passenger seat; a litter bag hanging from the dash; newspapers, mail, and tools on the floor; a can holder on each door, with an open Diet Pepsi can next to Harold. A faint doggy smell came from the back seat. A gun rack along the side window held only fishing gear.

"What, no shotgun or rifle?" I asked. "I thought everybody out in the country hunted."

"I don't, not anymore. I've seen too much on the job about what guns can do. You hunt?"

"Never got into it, and I hate guns. I prefer walking my dogs or reading. And I travel, at least when I can afford it and can take the time off from work. Actually, I haven't taken any real trips for a while, but I want to start traveling again."

"Yesterday you said you're a freelance writer and editor, but that's about all I know," he said. "Do you do other kinds of writing besides grant proposals?"

"Oh, don't get me going on my work or you'll never hear the last of it. It'll be worse than yesterday. Besides, I'm supposed to be on a holiday." *He's just being polite*, I thought, *he's not really interested. Better get back to business.* "Did you find out anything more about the girl? Or did you think about anything else I could help with?"

"I'd just as soon postpone that until later. I'm expecting more information by phone, and we'll have enough time to discuss it after I talk with the others. Also, your statement is typed up and I have a copy, so I'll get you to sign it before you leave."

What do we talk about now? I wondered. *I quashed talking about my work, and he quashed talking about his.*

I reached back and grabbed a couple of books from the box. "Are these the ones you were going to lend me? Dillard's *Pilgrim at Tinker Creek* and Fuentes' *Old Gringo*? I would have thought you read detective fiction."

"Some mystery novels are in there, too," he said. "I read just about anything, especially when somebody I like recommends it. That way I try things I might not think of on my own."

Again, I couldn't think of anything to say. Everything he said and did intrigued me and frustrated me at the same time. It had been a long time since I'd met a man as interesting as this one.

"You said something about getting this truck from your son," I ventured. "How many kids do you have?" *And tell me more about your ex-wife*, I wanted to say.

"Three. You met Connie. She and Jim got married right after she got her degree from the university. She works for the Forest Service, but she's on maternity leave now. Alan's in Germany with the Army. Not married yet and not serious about anybody. And Nancy has a fellowship to grad school at MIT. She's really good in mechanical engineering."

"Did she get that from you or her mother?"

"Neither. It's all her own. Alice, my ex, is strong in financial stuff and sales. After we split she went to Denver as a broker at Merrill Lynch. Me, I'm a pretty good law officer, but my real talents are working with my hands and with words."

"And getting people to talk. You sure got me to draw out my story yesterday. Do you always get people to talk so freely?"

"Well, it helps that I'm interested. If I hadn't gone into law enforcement, I might have become a shrink—or a priest. Both have to listen a lot."

"I'd feel sorry for the priest who had to listen to such longwinded confessions."

"Cops listen to confessions, too. And sometimes the more longwinded they are, the better we can check them out. People sometimes confess for strange reasons and in strange ways."

He stopped talking to concentrate on a sharp turn away from the river. I watched his hand fighting with the gears before slamming the gearshift into place. It was a nice-looking hand, big, long-fingered, and clean. I liked his competence in handling the truck. And I liked him. Too bad he hadn't said anything about women friends. Undoubtedly he was attached. Again, I reminded myself he was religious—and he and the thin priest seemed very much at ease with each other.

My growing interest in him surprised me. I hadn't been with any man who appealed to me so in a long time. Those who liked me didn't interest me. Those I liked were invariably married, attached, gay, or just not interested. Why should I think he might be different?

The silence felt more comfortable now. After a mile or two Harold turned the truck uphill again. As we climbed, I saw traces of snow around us. The rough driveway was adequately graveled but overgrown, so brush hit the truck on both sides. He grinned at me when I flinched from a branch slapping the windshield. "I like my privacy. Helps keep the tourists and hikers out."

The drive opened into an orderly clearing. A large shed stood in front of us, connected to the rough-boarded brown-stained house balanced on a small knoll to the right. Overlooking a lively creek, a large balcony jutted from the house. Although sunshine filled the clearing, nobody had bulldozed this place clear. Instead, trees had been judiciously removed to give the sense of a natural clearing within the forest.

"Nice!" I exclaimed. "How did you ever find it?"

"I didn't *find* it," he said, sounding offended. "We cleared the lot ourselves and *built* the house, over several years. Alice and the kids and I all worked at it, with help from friends at church and a lot of the guys from the Sheriff's Office. We had a regular barn-raising to get it started and a lot of work parties after that."

He pulled into the shed. I leaped down before I noticed he was coming around to open my door.

"Hope you don't mind going in the back way," he said, unlocking the house door and showing me to a cedar-paneled flight of stairs. At the top was a large, sparsely-furnished room. Horizontal natural cedar walls and exposed beams blended with the wood tables and bookcases throughout the room.

"Bathroom's down the hall to the left," he said.

Like the main room, the bathroom was clean but lived in. Harold seemed to be comfortable within himself and within his home—and to take care of both. I wished *I* looked a little more cared for right now. My hair still looked okay, but the tears had washed my mascara off and my sandy lashes were as stubby and unglamorous as if I'd just gotten out of the shower. I realized that when I'd dressed I'd subconsciously thought about looking nice for Harold. Maybe I'd better work on getting less interested in him.

"Can I do anything to help?" I asked, finding him moving around the kitchen.

"Thanks, no. I decided to cook up a big batch yesterday, before I got called out, and stuck all the fixings in the fridge. Just have to sauté the onions and garlic and put the whole mess on to cook. You do like onions and garlic?" he asked.

"Love them. What are we having?"

"Ratatouille. It's easy, and I often fix a big batch and eat it for days. We'll have garlic toast too."

"You *are* domestic, aren't you? That's wonderful! Do you do your own cleaning, too?" I didn't like the edge in my voice. He looked like Claude Akins, worked a job that took courage and intelligence, and here he was acting like Alan Alda: every woman's dream of a well-rounded, sensitive man. So why did I sound like I was sneering? *Damn, that's no way to act. He doesn't deserve this.*

He pulled the heavy cast-iron pot off the hot element and stood looking at me. "Yes, I do," he said. "Look, Sarah, if I'm doing something wrong, I can fix a couple of microwave dinners, finish up down at the station in Concrete, and let you get on your way."

I felt as though the teacher had caught me misbehaving in class and called me up short. Or, more likely, as though the cop was about to arrest me for some infraction.

"I'm sorry," I apologized, eager to head off his anger. *Watch it, Sarah*, I told myself. *Overappeasement is typical ACOA behavior.* "I'm upset about the girl and I don't know what to do to help in that situation. And then you keep surprising me. I don't know what to expect and don't know how I fit in."

"And you're probably upset because of your sister," he said, letting out a long breath. "Look, we'll get to what you can do to help. Meanwhile, don't worry about the surprises. You seem to expect me to be someone else or act differently from the way I am. I'm not the personification of Mr. Detective or Mr. Rural America, or whatever stereotype you seem to expect! I'm just Harold Workman, with about as many different sides to me as most people have once you get to know them."

He let out another deep breath and put the pot back on the heat. "I'm sorry I snapped at you," he said as he stirred the onions and garlic. "The guys at the Sheriff's office have been ragging me for not being macho enough, especially since Alice and I split, and you seemed to be doing the same. Guess I've gotten thin-skinned about it. You also got the brunt of my being more than a little tense about the Killer."

He's not acting like a cop, I realized. *He's acting like a person who's been teased too often.* "Truce?" I asked in a small voice.

"Truce," he said. "Let's both try to relax. You can set the table if you want to help." ≠

Chapter 6

We were silent as I set the table. I felt the need for some sort of peace offering, but Harold beat me to it.

"How about a glass of white wine?" he suggested as he put the lid on the bubbling red mixture. "This will take about half an hour, and we can talk while it cooks."

"Sure, sounds good," I responded, after a moment's hesitation.

Harold poured the wine into fragile long-stemmed glasses, then moved into the living room and lit the already-laid kindling in the fireplace. Turning on a couple of lamps, he gestured toward the thirties overstuffed plush furniture flanking the fireplace. "Sit wherever you want. They came from my grandparents' home and they're all pretty comfortable."

I surveyed the room before choosing. It was both sparsely furnished and richly textured, with many carvings and books. A threadbare burgundy oriental rug defined the seating area in front of the fireplace. I guessed the big green chair was Harold's usual seat. A reading lamp was tilted to hit it just right, and the table next to the chair was covered with books and papers, some spilling over to the floor. A large smudge on the wall nearby showed that a dog had often slept there.

"Maddy said something about your dog," I said, sitting back on the maroon sofa and gesturing toward the smudge. "Was that his spot?"

"Yeah, close to me and the fireplace, his favorite things," he said, sitting in the green chair. "Alex died a couple of months ago, but I still expect him to be there when I look up."

"What kind was he?"

"Irish setter. He'd been mistreated, and one of the deputies thought he'd make a good dog for my family. He was a one-person dog, though, and I was the person. Had him almost twelve years. I gave notice a week after he died. It wasn't just his death, of course. Judy and I had been talking about my changing careers."

He poked the fire while I sipped my wine. Then he leaned back in his chair and became businesslike. "We can talk about that sort of thing while we eat. Right now I want to tell you what little we know about the girl. You already know she was strangled. She may have been raped, but we can't be sure because we think she was a prostitute and because the river washed a lot of the evidence away. The pathologist said she had some internal bruising and slight lacerations, but that could have been from a john. She also had recent bruises on her body, not necessarily from the guy who killed her."

He leaned back and closed his eyes, reciting. "After she died, she was dumped from the Marblemount Bridge. We found the heel from her shoe on the bridge deck and fuzz from her coat on the railing. There was no sign of struggle on the bridge itself. We're guessing she was murdered somewhere else, brought to the bridge, and hoisted over. Even on a cold winter's night, the Killer would risk being seen if he was on the bridge for long."

As I listened, I thought again of the slight girl who had spoken to me in the church, and of the violence that had left those marks on her body. Revulsion hit me as I realized what her last hours must have been like.

"Also, her purse was found near the road on the other side of the bridge," he continued. "The outside had been wiped, and the only prints inside were hers. The purse held some names and addresses, mostly in Tacoma, but no I.D. One of the Task Force guys is checking out each address and trying to get a positive identification."

"I'm surprised you know so much this quickly," I said.

"The Task Force has a lot of people working on it. Also, the coroner shipped the body to the King County Medical Examiner's Office right away, since they're better equipped than our Skagit County Coroner's Office and they've handled most of the Skagit Killer victims. Of course the Task Force and the Sheriff's Office share information. As I told you last night, this is the first time we've gotten *anything*. It's also the first time the victim was found less than 24 hours after she died, and we're working fast so these leads don't get cold."

"Does it help much to know the murderer may have stopped at the Meeting Ground so recently?"

"Maybe, but he evidently brought the girl up from Tacoma, and he might be from anywhere within the Puget Sound region. He most likely isn't near here now." Harold stood and poked the fire again, then held on to the heavy wrought-iron rod as he turned and faced me. "What is it that's so good about heating the backs of my legs at a fire?"

"Probably a reminder of our cave-dwelling past," I replied, joining him at the fireplace. "Too bad the Killer doesn't seem to have put *his* cave-dwelling ways far enough in the past." We stood warming ourselves at the fire for a few moments. Harold's information had chilled me all the way through. The fire seemed to help.

"Harold, from what I read in the papers, the Killer's always been careful not to leave any clues, or at least not any that were discovered. I know the Task Force might have kept something hidden, but this killing seems pretty sloppy for him. Could it be the work of a copycat?"

"We don't talk about 'clues,' you know," he corrected me. "We just want 'leads' we can follow or 'evidence' that will stand up in court. But to answer your question, we're reasonably sure it's him. I think he might be running scared. Maybe he knew the girl talked to someone in the chapel and that spooked him. Or maybe something else happened, and he didn't like having his plans messed up." He lifted his head and sniffed. "Hold on a sec while I check the food."

He headed for the kitchen, moving lightly, as many large men do. An almost irresistible odor came at me when he lifted the lid; I was going to be glad when our meal was ready.

"Does that mean I might be partly responsible for her death?" I asked as he came back into the living room.

"What do you mean?"

"If he got spooked because she talked to someone . . . ."

"No!" he said. "He would have killed her anyway. What her talking to you might have done is to get him to make a mistake. And that's good."

"Good because it left some 'evidence'?"

"No evidence, exactly, but leads, something to follow up. We got hold of the telephone guy this morning. He lives in Sedro-Woolley and was willing to come out when he heard what for. Turns out he collected the coins just last Thursday and there were only four quarters in there today. None of them has usable prints, but it tells us only four local calls were made from that phone between Thursday and last night when we sealed it."

"Harold, I'm not trying to tell you how to do your job, but do the four quarters necessarily mean four local calls? Couldn't it be maybe one long-distance call that cost a dollar, or one local call and a seventy-five-cent call, or some other combination?"

"We'll find out. The phone company is checking for credit-card calls, too, but it'll take a few days to get the complete record and see if there's a pattern. If he's used that phone before, we might be able to start tracking him down from that. At this point, we have no way of knowing who he is or who he called. And there aren't any prints on the phone; it was wiped."

"Could he maybe have called about weather conditions? If he dumped her from the Marblemount Bridge, he was headed toward the mountains when he stopped at the Meeting Ground. Maybe he wanted to know about the passes."

"That couldn't be it," he said. "Highway 20's closed at Thunder Arm all winter because of snow. It's been closed since late last month. He evidently knows this area pretty well and he'd know better than to try heading over the pass."

"But he could have been going to somewhere higher than the motel and wanting to know if he could get there!" I said. "Wasn't the freezing level lower than usual? Maybe he called the State Patrol for an up-to-date report."

"That's an idea, but it wouldn't be the State Patrol. The Department of Transportation keeps track of pass conditions."

"That's never up to date! Everybody I know calls the State Patrol if we want the latest road conditions."

"What's your point, Sarah?" He hadn't caught my excitement.

"If he's like a lot of people, he probably called the Patrol. Why don't you check with both the DOT *and* the State Patrol to see if they keep records of calls? If he talked to a person, you might be able to get an idea of where he was heading!"

Harold strode to the kitchen phone and dialed. I followed him and took a seat at the white enameled kitchen table. While he waited, he looked up another number in the phone book. "Harold Workman here. Sorry to bother you, but would you have any way of knowing if someone called the live line for road conditions Friday night about 9:00? It's important. Yeah, I'll hold."

He looked over at me. "Friend in the Patrol," he mouthed, then spoke into the mouthpiece. "Yeah. You keep tapes of all calls, just like we do, huh? Can you check that and get back to me? I'm at home. Thanks. Appreciate it."

He dialed another number, then slammed the phone down. "It's a recording!"

"DOT?"

He nodded.

"Then he didn't call that line. Is any other number listed for the DOT?"

"That's the only one open outside of office hours. So the Patrol is the only place he could have gotten updated information!"

"*If* that's why he was calling."

The phone startled me. Harold snatched it up. "Workman here. Yeah, what do you have? Nicole Turner. Tacoma. This is positive? Uh huh. Her uncle? How old? *Twelve!* Oh, Larry." He sagged. "No!" he exploded. "She was not 'just a hooker.' She was a twelve-year-old human being. About the age of your daughter, if I remember correctly. Okay. Okay. Call me if you get any more."

He put the phone down and slumped into a kitchen chair across from me. "You heard, of course. Christ!"

It wasn't a curse. Maybe a plea.

"Somehow her age makes it even worse," he said. "Probably raped, definitely strangled, and dumped in a cold river—and only twelve years old! She's the youngest one yet! And what kind of life was Nicole Turner having before that, anyway? Hoping for a warm place to sleep and that her pimp or a john wouldn't beat her?"

My tears were back, for the girl, for the pain Harold was feeling, and because I saw Marilu's face when I thought of the girl. I put a hand on Harold's shoulder. "The Task Force is trying, and you're doing your best to catch the person who did it. That's all anybody can do—their best." My brave words died away in a loud sniff. "Where's some tissues?" ≠

Chapter 7

Harold's eyes looked damp as he glanced up at me, then he turned his face away. "On the windowsill. Ah, Sarah. You're right, of course. Judy's been telling me the same thing. I'm sorry I ranted. Twenty-three years in the department and I never let myself hurt too much for anything I worked on. I give notice, and it's like I turned a switch and allowed myself to feel."

He heaved himself out of the chair and busied himself at the stove. "No, that's not totally so; all the Skagit River killings were starting to get to me anyway. That's part of why I quit."

I debated handing him a tissue, but decided his sudden busyness was to avoid needing one. I wiped my eyes, then blew my nose. "What were your other reasons for leaving?"

"Oh, a lot of things. I turned fifty and was eligible for retirement. I wasn't responsible for Alice or the kids anymore. Didn't even have to worry about my dog maybe not adjusting to a change. Also, I had inherited a little money when my mom died a couple of years ago and saved up some more. Mostly, I guess, it was just time for a change."

He lifted the lid on the ratatouille and stirred the mixture. "When I joined up I thought I could do more to stop the bad guys. To protect the good folks. And just to help people. Lately I've been working with Judy on figuring out what to do next. But it bothers me that I didn't do too well on stopping the Skagit River Killer. That's why I said I'd work this case when the Sheriff called."

"Figuring out this murder seems to be the *immediate* thing to do next," I said. "We were doing pretty well in finding things to check out. If it's okay, I'd really like to work on this with you some more."

He gave me an appraising look. "Maybe I'd better get on with cooking, first. Let's finish brainstorming after we eat. I just need to sprinkle mozzarella on the ratatouille and put it under the broiler for a few minutes. And are you up for several pieces of garlic toast?"

I was happy enough to back off from such intense emotion. I never let myself feel that much except with my closest friends and sometimes at twelve-step meetings. And I wasn't used to strange men revealing so much of themselves to me. How was I supposed to react, anyway? I could hardly hug him and make the hurt go away, and we didn't know each other well enough to cry literally on each other's shoulders.

Our meal was wonderful! The zucchini and onions and peppers and tomatoes and eggplant were balanced with just enough garlic and other seasonings. The browned mozzarella added a chewy texture and a wonderful taste. It was echoed in brown sprinkles of mozzarella topping each piece of heavily buttered and garlicked toast.

The conversation was excellent, too, casual and generally about ourselves. I liked the way he spoke about his divorce, without either the bitterness or longing I'd heard from all too many divorced people.

"Alice and I both did a lot of growing throughout our marriage," he said between bites. "Unfortunately we grew in different directions. She found out she didn't like being a cop's wife; worrying I might be shot kind of got to her. And then she got tired of living out here and wanted a more high-powered life. I was going just the other way. I wanted a slower, more interior life. I was getting more introspective while she was wanting the career she'd postponed. We're still friends, at least as much as we can be, but there's an edge to it."

We talked, too, about the aborted eagle-watching trip and how much this city dweller had looked forward to it. "I can imagine!" Harold said. "This time of year I see eagles almost every day, but it's always a thrill. Maybe you can come back and finish your trip some other time."

"Maybe," I said, "but I'm not sure I want to."

"I hope you will. It would be a shame to have eagles ruined forever for you. A normal trip—preferably in sunshine—probably would help erase some nasty memories."

"Maybe," I said again, not wanting to pursue the idea now.

I responded more eagerly when he asked about my life and interests. He was a comfortable man, even if he was bossy about when we talked about the murder and when we talked about other things. And, I was beginning to think, an honest and direct one. He wasn't asking just to be polite. He listened with interest, yet maintained a reserve that left me thinking, with disappointment, that he was interested in people in general rather than me in particular.

I told him about my recent work on the Martin Luther King Center proposal and how it had left me especially sensitized to those without homes. "One scene keeps coming back to me. I'm not sure why, but it says a lot to me about street life. I was in the downtown library doing some research. It was cold out and had been pouring all day.

"Two tables down from me was a man wearing several layers of dirty, stinking clothes. He was asleep with his head on the table, twitching and making scrabbling sounds like a dog. After several minutes he jerked awake and looked around like he expected to be chased out. But the room wasn't crowded, and everyone just gave him a wide berth.

"About an hour after I first saw him he got up and shuffled toward the restroom. He hunched into himself, either in pain or not to be noticed, I thought, and he drew his heavy old-fashioned coat around him, although the library was quite warm.

"A few minutes later he shuffled back toward his spot at the table. Someone else had sat down there, and he straightened a little in surprise. A bottle dropped from inside the coat and smashed on the marble floor."

I grimaced. "Glass fragments everywhere and the strong smell of Ripple throughout the library. And the look on his face, like he'd lost his last friend."

"Well, he had. At the least the last friend he knew about."

"He'd tried so hard to be unobtrusive and to coexist with the rest of us, and he'd failed so miserably. Of course the staff hustled him out in the cold rain again, blocks from the nearest day shelter."

I noticed I'd been leaning forward, elbows on the table as I told my story. Abashed, I sat back in my chair. "I can't really explain why that hit me so hard. In fact, I haven't told anyone else, but it's bothered me ever since."

"I can see why it sticks with you. He was a specific person to you, just like this girl is for both of us. You were thinking about what his thoughts and hopes were. And feeling his pain instead of judging his lifestyle."

"That's probably a lot of it," I said. "Because I empathized with him, I didn't condemn him for disturbing me and all the other patrons. And the contrast between his living arrangements and mine were so apparent when I went back to my comfortable, dry home." I paused, then continued. "The alcohol's a factor, too. If my parents hadn't died early or if Marilu had lived, would they have wound up like him?"

Harold didn't say anything for a minute or so. "Does dying young solve the problem, then? Is it preferable to winding up like that man?"

"Oh, no!" I said, shocked. "Dying cuts off any chance of change, of redemption, if you will. If Marilu had lived, she might have gotten sober, might have had a worthwhile, satisfying life. She would have had a chance, anyway, to break away from the alcohol."

"Is your family why you hesitated when I offered you wine?" he asked.

"Probably." I gave a brief laugh. "You don't miss much, do you?"

"I hope not. On the job or when making new friends."

He rose to clear the plates. "All I have for dessert is fruit—apples, oranges, or bananas," he offered. "And I can give you a caffeine fix for the drive home, either coffee or tea."

"Black coffee and an apple sound great. May I help?"

"Sure. You wash the apples while I fix the coffee."

I rummaged in the refrigerator and came up with a couple of

Fuji apples while Harold filled the glass pot. When the phone rang, he turned off the water and answered immediately. "You *did*? Eight forty-seven on Friday night and he asked about the freezing level? Anything else? Do you have the tape there? Great! Could you play it over the phone? I have someone here I'd like to listen to it. Just a minute."

He handed me the phone. "Sarah, you listen here. I'll pick up in the bedroom."

He moved down the hallway, then came on the phone. "Tom, this is Sarah Tierney, who may have heard the same man on Friday night. Sarah, Sergeant Tom Prine. Tom, you can run the tape anytime you're ready."

There was a brief staticky silence, then a slow, precise voice came on. "I would like to know the freezing level and road conditions near Marblemount."

Another voice came on, speaking more quickly. "Well, the freezing level has moved down to around twelve-hundred feet. We're advising everyone to stay off secondary roads above that level. It's snowing heavily and the plows won't be out until it stops. Route 20 is clear to Newhalem, but the rain has caused a rockslide just beyond there."

"Thank you, thank you very much," and the conversation cut off.

"That's all," Sergeant Prine's cheerful voice came on. "Is it the voice you thought?"

"Yes, it is. But I think he tried to disguise it. It seemed muffled, and not as high as I remembered."

"Would you make two copies of that and get one to Larry at the Skagit River Task Force and one to me?" Harold asked Prine. "Could be important."

"Task Force, huh? I heard you had another body. Sure, I'll get these right out in the next cars heading your way. Why are you working on this, anyway, Harold? I thought you quit and were buying a newspaper."

"You thought right, but I've got to find the right paper, first. I'm still officially using up vacation, and Sheriff Potter asked me to help. One of the guys is out with a broken leg and another just had an emergency appendectomy, so they're shorthanded. And I'd worked on the earlier cases."

"Well, it's good to talk with you again. I sure hope this helps."

We hung up the phones and Harold came back to the kitchen, elated. "You were right! Now we have the first concrete lead! He was trying to get to a higher elevation near Marblemount. We'll check every cabin, every side road, every turnaround. And if we find a suspect, we can use the tape for a voiceprint!"

"I was a little off on the voice, though," I mused, intent on my analysis. "He didn't space all the words evenly. He clumped them, with spaces between, and the spaces aren't as pronounced as I thought. And did you notice the way he said 'thank'? It was more like 'thenk,' like Ed Sullivan used to say it. And his 'I' was an exaggerated 'eye' sound. Maybe I'll pick up something else if I hear it again."

"You will, and so will the voice experts we'll put on it." He put a hand on my shoulder and gave a quick squeeze. This is wonderful! Thenks, yourself!"

"I don't understand why he'd drive off the main road to call from the Meeting Ground, though," I continued thinking out loud. "Wouldn't it be out of his way?"

"Not much. You probably went in and out the same way, but the road to the motel is just a big shallow loop off the main road. It wouldn't take but a few minutes more than calling from a phone on Highway 20—if there were any—and he'd be less likely to be noticed."

"And he'd know that. As you said, he knows this area well."

"Far too well," Harold said.

We were both on a high as we finished our coffee and fruit. Although we chattered about the tape, there really wasn't much more to say about the girl. Harold brought up facts about past killings, but nothing I hadn't known from the papers.

All the thirty-three known victims were street prostitutes who had worked lower Pacific Avenue, the Tacoma city limits on South Tacoma Way, or the SeaTac strip near the airport halfway between Tacoma and Seattle. Many were black, but some were white or Asian. All were young and small. The tallest of the bodies found to date was just five feet two, and the oldest was sixteen.

"They don't all look similar, like Ted Bundy's victims," I commented. "I mean, they aren't all in the same racial group or with the same hairstyle or anything, from what I read. Were they maybe chosen either for their age or for their size?"

"Likely, but we don't know which. Or it could be both. We started checking that out as soon as there seemed to be a pattern. The Task Force followed up on known pedophiles without turning up any leads. And we checked anyone with a known pattern of assaulting small women. Nothing's come up to corroborate either hypothesis.

"Somebody even came up with the idea that the Killer might have been a woman, and the victims chosen because even a medium-sized woman could overpower them. Also, that would explain why the victims would go with the Killer, even after all the warnings we've gotten out on the street. They'd think they were safe with a woman."

"But weren't they raped?"

"We can't be certain, not with prostitutes, and especially when we don't find the bodies for months. Anyway, your testimony and now the tape make it more certain it's a man."

I had exhausted my ideas. Glancing at my watch, I saw that it was almost 3:30. "Oh, Harold, I've got to start for home! It'll be dark soon."

"Yes, you probably had better go, but I'd like you to look over this transcript, make any necessary corrections, and sign it first."

He handed me a typed transcript of my statement. Whoever had transcribed it had left out all the extras that Harold had asked for. It included "just the facts," and was a pretty good job. I signed it without making any changes and handed it back to Harold.

He stood up and stretched. "I'm sorry you have to go. I've enjoyed this, and you've helped a lot. Go check out the bathroom again if you want to, and I'll put things away. Good thing that storm never did come."

The mirror showed me more alert than a couple of hours earlier. This detective work—or the dinner—or the company—was pretty satisfying!

I came out of the bathroom. "Not a chance, Sheriff," I heard Harold saying. "I know that's what we thought yesterday, but I've just spent the last three hours checking her out. Either she's not involved, or she's the world's greatest actress."

There was a pause. I stood rooted to the hall floor. I'd been looking at Harold as a possible romantic interest. He'd been checking me out as a possible murder suspect. ≠

Chapter 8

A surge of anger hit me. *I'll show Detective Harold Workman great acting*, I thought.

I went back to the bathroom, closed the door, then checked my face in the mirror again. A splash of cold water helped tone down the red. I patted my face dry, opened the door noisily, and started down the hall.

"Gotta go now, but I'll catch you later," I heard Harold say. "Uh-huh. Trust me on this one." The phone clicked down.

"Anything new?" I asked, entering the kitchen.

"No. The Sheriff wanted to know if you had thought of anything new. And he's excited about what the voice tape might mean."

"Good, I hope it helps." My voice sounded normal to my ears; I hoped it sounded normal to Harold as well.

Again, Harold helped me get in the Blazer, clasping my waist and lifting me up to the step. The contact wasn't nearly as pleasant as before.

We sat in silence while he negotiated the drive. *I've got to keep up the act 'til I get to my car*, I thought. When we reached the road I brought the conversation back to his plans.

"The Trooper said something about your buying a newspaper. Is that what you're going to do next?"

"I think so," he said. "I've always been interested in journalism, and I've been reading up on it since Judy helped me realize what I want. Newspapers can help their communities, too, so I'm back to my old desire to help people. I've been looking for a weekly to buy."

Judy again. That should be a good relationship for him; he probably wouldn't suspect a priest of murder. Does he suspect almost everyone, or just me?

"Do you have any newspaper experience?"

"I was on the paper staff in high school and college and was editor my last year at Western. Also, I've written a bunch of articles for *The Skagit River Post* and the *Concrete Herald*, and I've gotten to be good friends with the *Post*'s publishers. They're sort of advising me on the move."

"It sounds like you're going about this in a methodical way."

"That's what detectives do best," he said with an enormous grin. "Actually, there are a lot of similarities between solving a crime and chasing down a news story—or finding out how to get into the newspaper business. Of course, on a weekly, the stories are likely to be less sensational than some of what I've been working with. At least I hope they are," he finished.

"What about the technical and business side?"

"I've made contacts at the International Society of Weekly Newspaper Editors and used vacation time last year to attend the ISWNE annual conference. I can get help there, maybe get one of the editors or retired editors to come in as a consultant and make sure I'm starting off on the right foot. They know a lot about all sides of the weekly newspaper business."

"You planning on staying around here?"

"No, neither the *Post* nor the *Herald* is for sale, and I wouldn't want to try to compete with them. What I'd really like is something nearer the Sound or on the coast. I like salt water, but I've never lived much closer than now except in college. Maybe closer to a city, too, for live music and theater. And I definitely want to stay in western Washington. It's home."

What about Judy? I wanted to ask. *Can she relocate easily?* Instead, I asked, "What's your timetable for the move?"

"I'm flexible. Since I've actually quit, I'm sending out inquiries and making phone calls around the region. I'm also starting to close things up here, you know, make it easy to wrap up quickly when the time comes. I don't have a whole lot of money, but it's enough to give me time to check everything out and make the right decision."

Finally, just when I thought the topic might run out, we reached the church. My car seemed undisturbed where I'd left it.

I opened the door as Harold hurried around to help me down from the truck. He held on to my hand when I reached the ground.

"Sarah, I can't thank you enough for all you've done. I'll be in touch if we get anything else you can help with. And we'll definitely contact you if we get anyone for you to listen to. Here's my home number if you think of something I should know," he added, handing me a card with a penciled-in number. "Drive safely. I've enjoyed talking with you."

Well, that's that, I thought. "Glad I could help," I said, a tight smile on my lips. "Thanks for a great meal, and for letting me brainstorm with you. Best of luck."

"Get in touch if you come back up to see the eagles," Harold called as I drove out. He stood in the church drive and waved as I drove off. I waved back, then concentrated on remembering how to get home.

At Rockport I turned off Highway 20 and headed toward Darrington. Dead brown leaves and ferns lay in sodden heaps on the ground. Brown-green moss covered the trunks of deciduous trees, and long strands of gray moss hung over the road where the trees encroached. Both sides of the road slumped into creeks and sloughs, puddles and standing water in every depression. Dead, dripping, soggy, boggy. Lost thoughts in a wet season. Maybe the drive would have been better after dark.

Was it my mood, or had everything become monotone? Clouds nearly obscured the hills to my right. The road wound ahead, black-gray, with yellow center lines and white fog lines the only brightness. I flashed by a collection of thrown-together houses and trailers. Trashed vehicles and cast-off items were all around the yards. A bottomless red plastic laundry basket, high on a tree, was the only splash of color. Was that all the kids who lived there had to play with?

The Sauk River appeared on my right, a silvery-tan stream flowing through tan banks. The road was wet here, as though it had rained a few minutes earlier. How many of the bodies had been found along the Sauk watershed as well as that of the Skagit? How many were out there, still not found?

Huge logs were stacked on both sides of the road on the outskirts of Darrington, evidently destined for the enormous sawmills on my left. Big machines I couldn't begin to know the uses for seemed to threaten anything on the road. I felt closed in, menaced by the logs, the machines, the buildings. I'd heard Darrington was the quintessential logging town and I'd always meant to come up for the annual Bluegrass Festival. Maybe the town was more inviting in summer.

My disquiet spread to the car itself. The visors didn't seem quite right. When I reached out, the sunflower seeds weren't within easy reach on the passenger seat where I always left them when I was alone in the car. I sneezed, then reached into the pocket in the driver's door for the box of tissues that should have been close at hand. It wasn't there either.

That did it. I pulled over to the side of the road and explored the pocket; the contents were jumbled. I checked the glove compartment and the passenger pocket as well: also jumbled. The disorder looked almost the same as I had left it, but not quite. My car was always somewhat a mess, but it was *my* mess! This was someone else's mess.

A couple of tears forced their way out. *Damn it! He could have asked! I would have let them look. He didn't have to invite me to his house so the cops would have time to search my car. And I thought they had to have a search warrant!* I started the car, slammed it into gear, and drove once again toward home.

December days are short in Washington. Mercifully or not, it was dark before I hit Arlington. From there, I retraced my route most of the way home.

The car radio didn't appeal to me. Probably Christmas music and loud ads. I thought about the girl. No, not "the girl." She had a name now, Nicole Turner. I'd probably learn more about her in the paper over the next few days, then she'd drop out of sight, to be mentioned again only when the next body was found, and the next, and the next. Nicole had lived twelve years, and time would close over the space where she was, leaving hardly a trace.

I wondered why Harold thought I might have been involved in the murder. I had thought he considered me a helper, maybe at worst a middle-aged police groupie. Did cops have some sort of sixth sense, like dogs, that let them know more about you than you knew yourself? Did something about me cry out I had it in me to kill somebody, or to assist in killing somebody?

Hard thoughts on a dark winter's night. I tried to shake off the self-doubts. I knew I wasn't on the Killer's side. I'd done my bit to help catch him. Now I wouldn't be involved again unless the Task Force found a suspect. Then I might be called in. If so, maybe I could help keep some other girls from ending up the same way. What had I said to Harold about doing our best?

Ah, Harold. Too bad that couldn't work out. I had liked his broad, kind face, his brown eyes. His steadiness was a nice counterbalance to my moodiness, and I seemed to help get him back on track when he got so upset about Nicole. Even if he was overly religious and a cop, he was intelligent, feeling, had a sense of humor—and had only been checking me out as a suspect.

Gee, I thought wryly, *I fantasized about what it would be like getting him into handcuffs, while he wanted me in handcuffs for a different reason.*

I was mooning about a man who had thought I might be a murderer, a man I'd never see again. *Just write him off as one more man who might have become special under other circumstances.*

With thoughts like those, the drive was not happy. It's a wonder it was safe. I was distracted enough to overshoot the turnoff to Highway 18 and wind up in Puyallup. It wasn't much out of the way, but it added several miles and several minutes to the trip.

My spirits rose as I neared home. Back to Golda and Jesse and all my comforts. Back to the things sheltering me from anything hurtful. Back to using books to push down the kind of thoughts that had accompanied me on this drive. Maybe a call to Sharon to find out about her time with Hugh and to tell her about my weekend.

No fog tonight. The lights gleamed and shimmered on Commencement Bay. I noticed a large ship loading grain at the elevator, then the big ships moored where the old Sperry warehouse used to be. As I pulled up the 30th Street Hill I thought about what mail and phone calls might have come while I was gone. My thoughts ran ahead rather than back to Marblemount.

When I drove up the graveled drive past the house and pulled into the detached garage, the dogs barked and danced around the back yard, then tried to pretend they weren't glad to see me. That's SOP when I've been gone more than a day, but they can't hold out for long. By the time I dumped my first armload of stuff from the car on the dining room table, Jesse was ramming my stomach with his hard brown head and Golda was licking my hand. I sat on the floor to give them some loving. Golda melted into my arms, pressing as close as she could get, her tail moving in tight, anxious wags. Jesse doesn't like to be hugged, not macho enough for him. He'd rather have his chest rubbed. He rolled on his back and let his lips flop open and his long tongue fall to the rug—as though that were macho! A hind leg scratched in rhythm with my rubbing.

Everything seemed fine, except Hazel had turned off the automatic light in the back yard. I flicked it on and heard the hum of the fluorescent light start up. A note on the counter said "Sunday, 5:30. Dogs are fed and walked. Bed is made. Fresh towels out. I washed and dried the sheets and towels I used. Hope he was worth the stay. No problems here. Hazel."

I think she knows I don't pair up easily, but I'm not sure. Hazel feels "we single girls" past a certain age had better grab any man who comes along. There might not be another one.

I finished unloading the car, making several trips and dumping everything on the table to sort through later. Mail and newspapers were on the kitchen counter. Nothing important. The biggest front-page headline on Sunday's *Morning News Tribune* said "Rafters Find 34th Skagit River Victim." I skimmed the article, but the whole story was in the headline. The reporter writing for Sunday's early deadline hadn't known anything but the bare facts. Sunday's *Seattle Post-Intelligencer* had a similar sketchy story.

The answering machine light was flashing. A friend asked me to call if I got in before 5:30 on Saturday and wanted to go to the movies. Two calls from a kid pleading for help with a résumé due on Monday; his second call was a little frantic. Too bad. He should have called earlier. Another friend hoped I had a good time and wasn't worn out from the trip.

My heart leaped when I heard the voice on the last message. "This is Harold Workman. It's a few minutes after 7:00 Sunday night." I glanced at my watch; it was 7:11; he must have called while I was unloading the car.

"Don't be alarmed, but I've asked the Tacoma police to get someone to your house right away. Don't answer for anyone else. Be on your guard and make sure it's the police before you open the door. Someone will stay with you until I arrive. And don't tell anyone at all—not even the police—about helping us. I'm on my way down and I'll explain when I get there."

Harold's coming here, I thought. *I'm going to see him again!* Only after that first flush of delight did it hit me that something was seriously wrong. I didn't think Harold frightened easily. And I didn't think he'd get the police out without a damn good reason. Then another thought hit me: *Oh, God! Are the police coming to protect me or arrest me? Has he found some new reason to think it's me?*

Golda barked and ran toward the front door as I rewound the tape. Jesse followed, confused and trying to figure out what had set Golda off. I approached the door with caution. Nothing there. Spooked, I checked the deadbolt and chain, then checked the back door, slotted in the metal insert to close off the dog door, and locked the door between the kitchen and back porch.

Once the doors were secure, I made sure the blinds and curtains were closed. The dogs burst out again, running to the front door. Again, nothing there.

I got a hunk of cheddar and a Gala apple from the refrigerator and was running a glass of water when the door buzzer went off. I dropped the glass, which shattered in the sink. The dogs burst into frenzies of barking. Again, I cautiously approached the door. This time a loud male voice said, "It's the police, Ms. Tierney. The Skagit County Sheriff's Office asked us to come."

I looked through the chiffon curtain to the lighted porch. A young, clean-cut black man in uniform stood at the door, his right hand resting on his gun butt. Behind him and to the side was a smaller blonde uniformed woman, also ready to draw her gun, and in the drive was a white police car with the distinctive blue and yellow

Tacoma markings.

"Show me your I.D., please," I asked as firmly as I could over the dogs' yelping. The officer held a photo card up to the crack between the curtains. The card said he was Tacoma Police Officer Antwon Rawlings. The woman came closer and held her ID up: Tacoma Police Officer Marilyn Hawkins. The pictures matched the faces in front of me. I slid back the chain, unlocked the door, grabbed the dogs, and let the officers in.

The dogs sniffed the officers thoroughly before allowing them past the entryway. "They're friendly," I said, "just a little too friendly. They'll calm down in a minute."

"We'd like to check the house right away," Rawlings said, once he'd passed the dogs' inspection. "Skagit County seems to think you're in some kind of danger. We have to make sure no one else is in the house and see what kind of safety measures you have."

"Okay," I said, relieved that they only wanted to protect me. "I just got here, but everything seemed okay and I don't think the dogs would have let anyone in. Do you want to start here or in the basement?"

"Outside. You and the dogs stay right here," he said, motioning me to a corner, "while we check around the perimeter. Then we'll do this floor and we'll end up downstairs."

They drew guns and flashlights as they went outside through the front door. I held on to the dogs' collars and waited in the corner. Now I *was* scared! I heard them crunch on the graveled driveway as they walked on that side of the house, then click the catches on the gates as they went in one side of the fenced back yard and out the other. When they came back, they checked out the rooms on the main floor, then asked me to tell them about the basement.

I loosened the chain and unlocked the deadbolt on the door to the enclosed back porch. "The switch for the light at the top of the stairs is just inside the door to the yard. The switch at the bottom turns on all the lights on the right side of the basement. They'll give you enough light to see where the other lights are."

They returned in a few minutes. "Nobody there," Officer Hawkins said. "We checked every possible hiding place. Lucky you don't have it piled up with junk. The one thing I don't like is you don't have any curtains or shades in the basement except in that one bedroom. Anybody could see in down there."

I shook my head. "I've never especially needed it to be private. It's basically storage and work areas."

"Any second floor or attic?" Officer Rawlings asked.

"Only through the opening in the hall ceiling. Can't get through without a ladder and can't close it behind you. No one could be there."

I was relieved to see them holster their guns. "Okay, ma'am," Rawlings said. "Would you mind taking me around and explaining the premises?"

Now I knew why people had winced when I used to say "sir" and "ma'am" as I had been taught growing up in Georgia. He definitely made me feel old.

Hawkins fussed over the dogs while I led Rawlings around, pointing out the window locks, the deadbolts, and the pins in the doors with outside hinges. I also told him about the automatic lights in front and back.

"The shrubbery looks pretty good. Nothing close to the house a person could hide behind."

"Yeah, I had police volunteers come out when I first moved in. They showed me how to make the place safer. I trimmed away the shrubs and even put heavy clear rigid acrylic inside the glass in the doors. Someone could break the glass, but he'd have a heck of a time breaking the acrylic. Best I can tell, the only weak points are the dog door and the windows—and the windows would have to be broken."

"Good job, ma'am. I guess we can relax now and wait until someone gets here. Mind if we sit down?"

I gestured each of them to a comfortable chair, but Rawlings said they'd prefer to catch up on paperwork at the dining-room table instead. "Do you know what's going on?" I asked when he returned from getting materials from the car. "I don't understand why they think I'm in danger."

"No, ma'am. We don't have any idea, except we're supposed to protect you. I thought you'd know." ≠

Chapter 9

I was too hyped up to sit still for long. After a while I told the two police officers I wanted to get back to my unpacking and straightening up.

"Sure, ma'am," Officer Hawkins said. "You do that, and we'll keep working here."

They had draped their blue-black jackets over the dining-room chairs, then settled at a clear patch on the table to do their reports. I put away most of the things I had dumped on the table. Gesturing at the remaining pile, I asked, "Mind if I take these things downstairs and put on a load of laundry?"

Officer Rawlings looked up. "I guess that's okay, but better take one of the dogs with you."

I called Jesse to me and started down with a load. At the bottom of the stairs, he leaned against my leg for a moment—for his comfort or mine. I stowed the luggage, started the washer, and had just finished loading the clothes when Golda burst out barking. This time she ran from the kitchen to the back door and pushed at the closed dog door. Jesse leaped up the stairs after her, and Officer Rawlings appeared at the top of the stairs, gun in hand.

"Get on the stairs, quick," he snapped over the dogs' barking.

After I'd scrambled to the stairwell, he said, "You're visible from outside down there, and anyone could take a shot at you. We should have told you to stay upstairs 'til we know what's going on."

Just then we heard the loud repeated wailing of a cat in the back yard.

"Everything okay?" Hawkins asked from the kitchen door.

I sat on the top step and put an arm around each dog to calm them and myself. My heart was beating wildly and I didn't like this at all. Surely the officers were making too much fuss. "The dogs bark like this any time a cat or dog gets too near the house," I said as calmly as I could. "This time it happened to be a cat. And I'm sure they're picking up on our nervousness. We can't get scared just because the dogs bark."

"No, but we can't ignore them, either," Rawlings said. He edged past the dogs and me, tiptoed to the bottom of the stairs, reached in, and flicked off the lights. "Better stay out of the basement until the guy from the Skagit Sheriff's Office gets here."

The door buzzer sounded as we returned to the kitchen. "That must be him," Hawkins said with relief as the dogs raced to the door, barking.

I glanced at the clock on the stove. It was a few minutes after eight. "Hasn't had enough time."

"Are you expecting anyone else?" Rawlings asked.

"No."

I went to the door and looked through the glass pane. Sharon was pushing back the hood of her blue jacket and shaking her head to settle her glossy cap of brown hair. When she finished, it clung perfectly and smoothly to her head. I opened the door.

"Oh, Sarah," she exclaimed. "I was nearby and thought I'd stop to see if you were home. Why is the police car here? Are you okay?"

I locked the door behind her. Rawlings stood just inside the living room, eyeing Sharon. Sharon's an attorney, but doesn't look like anybody's idea of one. She's small, a slim four feet eleven, with a quick, pointed face that ought to belong to an elf and bright brown eyes. At a plump five feet six I always feel something of a moose when we're together, but she's been a good and close friend for several years. "It's okay," I told the officers. "This is my friend Sharon Cathers."

"I think I've seen you around the courthouse, haven't I?" Rawlings said. "You're with Legal Aid, if I remember correctly."

"That's right, officer," Sharon said, holding out her hand. "I've seen you, too. Glad to meet you."

I turned back to Sharon. "Officer Rawlings and Officer Hawkins are taking care of a small problem. I'll tell you about it later."

"We can keep working on the paperwork if you want to talk," Hawkins said.

"That would be wonderful," Sharon said, turning a radiant smile on both of the officers. "What's the matter? Did Sarah get robbed?"

"Let's not talk about it now," I said. "You'll hear about it soon enough." Although I usually told Sharon everything, Harold must have had a reason to ask me not to say anything to anybody.

Sharon hung her jacket on a hook near the door, then gave me a quick hug. "Okay, I won't stay but a few minutes, but I want to tell you about Hugh and me! Yesterday we spent most of the day and evening together, and he was more wonderful than ever. He's warm, he's funny, he's intelligent, he's fit, he's just everything I want! I think this one is going to last."

Hawkins and Rawlings had settled again at the dining-room table. I gestured Sharon to her favorite blue wing chair and sat nearby in the mustard-colored barrel chair. "I'd love for you to have someone who's good enough for my best friend. When do I get to meet this paragon?" I said.

"I don't know! I was hoping soon, but he's coming down with a cold now and stayed home today to nurse it. He says he's something of a bear when he's sick. Just wants to be alone and sleep a lot and get well."

Sharon's face glowed as she told me how they'd spent Saturday. It seemed a perfect low-key way to pass time with someone you love, not much to listen to, but wonderful in the doing. Maybe she'd chosen wisely in being with Hugh instead of going eagle watching with me. I listened with only half an ear and thought about my friendship with Sharon and her relationships with men.

Sharon and I were close, but many of her "wonderful" men hadn't lasted long enough for me to meet them. I wasn't sure this one would either. She had met Hugh at the State Capitol in Olympia when she took a leave to work for a State senator during the legislative session. Hugh was divorced, childless, forty-three to Sharon's thirty-six, an attorney in private practice, and a rising State legislator from Tacoma. He was already influential on the House Education Committee. They hadn't started dating until early last month, when he spoke at the November Tacoma City Club meeting and Sharon had talked with him afterwards.

The men Sharon had introduced me to in the past were among our few points of dissension. Sharon's lovers didn't even have to be a certain type, just as long as they had the basic male equipment. I remembered one who was Ashley Wilkes without the intelligence, just big soulful eyes, a peak of upswept blond hair, a job selling shoes at Nordstrom's, and—according to Sharon—the ability to go all night. Another was all muscle and motorcycle—Harley, no less—and a mechanic where she got her car fixed when he wasn't posturing on the bike. From what she said, the vibration of a bike ride turned them both into sex maniacs at the end of each trip together. At least he could have been useful with her ancient Mercedes, but she had to switch garages when they broke up after three weeks.

Hugh did sound like a much better choice, and I hoped Sharon was growing up at last. "He's not especially good looking," she had told me, "but he's intelligent, he understands my work, and he's totally involved in trying to improve the State schools. I really admire his drive and commitment. And he's so tender and wonderful in bed." At a month and a half, Hugh had already lasted as long as any of the other men she'd dated since I met her.

Since passing the bar, Sharon had shown her own strong sense of drive and commitment by working for Legal Aid, specializing in women and children. Her sense of social justice was one reason she believed in giving everyone—including every man she met—a chance. Unfortunately, her lack of selectivity left me petrified she'd catch some sexually transmitted disease. She didn't seem to understand that getting tested frequently didn't protect her; it would just tell her when it was too late to protect herself any longer.

I brought my mind back to what she was saying as she seemed to be finishing up. "We wanted to take you with us to Zoolights tonight, but then Hugh got all sniffly. You weren't here, anyway, and I didn't leave a message on your machine. Instead I arranged to meet a couple of friends at the zoo. Glad I stopped by here afterwards, though."

"It would have been fun to go with you two."

"Oh, Hugh still hasn't seen it, so we'll go later this week if he gets over his cold. I sure won't mind seeing it again. Maybe you can go with us then. It's even better than last year. More lights, animals, action. It's like being a kid again and stepping through into fairyland."

"I'd love to see it, but mainly I want to meet Hugh. Give me a call when he's up to going. Right now, though, I'd better get back to the officers."

"Sure, Sarah." Sharon petted Golda one last time and rose from the chair. I glanced over at the police. Rawlings was admiring Sharon again. She was worth admiring, even in old jeans, a bulky sweater, and boots.

"I want to hear all about the eagles soon," she said as she put on her heavy jacket. Hope you had a great time. I'm really sorry I couldn't go."

If she'd read the Sunday papers, she might have realized I was one of the rafters who found the body. Now didn't seem the time to enlighten her. "I'll tell you all about it soon, Sharon. Thanks for stopping by. Tell Hugh I hope he's lots better soon."

She hugged me again, waved and called out a goodbye to the officers, then whipped through the door and was gone.

"You didn't have to send her away on our account," Rawlings said, smiling. "We really don't have anything to do until the deputy gets here."

"I know, but Detective Workman asked me not to tell anybody anything, and she would have started asking questions. Besides, I'd like to finish putting things away. I think I'll start a fire, too. I got chilled sitting down. And would either of you like a cup of coffee, or something to eat?"

"Nothing to eat, but I would like coffee," Hawkins said. Rawlings didn't want anything.

Ignoring the broken glass in the sink, I started the coffee, put away the apple and cheese I had begun to get before the police came, and lit the fire. The smell of brewing coffee mingled with the slight scent of burning cedar. Harold likes fires, I thought, and he likes coffee. He'll be here soon. Maybe he'll be hungry. Hell, he probably wouldn't eat anything from me anyway, I remembered. This isn't a social visit, and he might think I'd poison him.

Nevertheless, I looked around the living/dining room and was pleased with what I saw. My house was old for Tacoma, built in 1910, and I had collected the eclectic furnishings piece by piece, with care, over many years, mostly from garage sales and estate sales. I had refinished most of the wood furniture myself and I liked the warm feel of the room. The house was small, but large enough for me. The overflowing bookcases made things seem a little cramped, but it was a welcoming place. The house looks okay, but how do I look? It wouldn't do to look frumpy when I get arrested. I knew I was being unfair, but I wanted to wallow in the hurt a little longer. The mirror showed me a mess. My hair had wilted, and I'd never repaired the damage caused by the morning's tears.

The phone rang as I finished mascara-ing the lashes on my right eye. Damn! I recapped the wand and ran to the phone.

"Hi, Sarah? This is Frank Randall. You know, from the rafting trip." He sounded tentative, as though he thought I wouldn't remember him, but rushed on. "I wanted to make sure you got back okay. Also, I wondered if you and Detective Workman had found out anything else. Does he think they might have any clues on the Killer?"

"Frank! I'm fine, no problems driving back. There's nothing more to tell you now, but Detective Workman seemed to think they're closer than before to having some leads. I'll keep you posted as soon as there's anything." I was glad I could put him off without actually lying; telling the truth is an important part of working the twelve-step program. "I'm glad you called, 'cause I have a big favor to ask. Would you not say anything to anybody about my talking with the girl or hearing the man's voice until Workman or I say it's okay? Workman seems to think there may be some danger, and he's supposed to get back to me on what we can say."

"Sure, if it's important. Workman asked us not to talk about it anyway, so I've only told my girl about any of it—and I didn't tell her much. Dad had to work today, though, and he probably told some of his buddies at the radio station how brave his son is. Of course he'd make it sound like I'm a big hero and I bet he didn't even mention your name."

"Good!" I said. "That is, I don't want anyone to know I'm involved in this until they catch the Killer. Did you tell your dad what I told you?"

"Not really, Sarah. Dad would rather talk than listen, anyway. I sort of clammed up on the way home yesterday. He knows you talked with the girl, 'cause you told the whole group, but he doesn't know you heard the man who was with her. And I sure won't tell him!"

Hooray for the generation gap, I thought. Maybe it's a good thing Frank and his father don't communicate well. "Thanks, Frank. I'll be in touch as soon as I can."

I put the phone down. "Couldn't help but overhear your end," Hawkins said. "Putting what I heard together with what your friend said about eagles and the fact that the Skagit County Sheriff's Office is concerned about you, I guess you're involved with the body found yesterday."

I nodded.

"If it gets out you might know something about the Skagit River Killer, you sure enough could be in trouble," Hawkins continued. "He hasn't left any evidence I know about, at least not until now. And I don't think he intends to."

The door buzzer went off again. The dogs ran to the door, barking. Rawlings and Hawkins and I looked at each other. ≠

Chapter 10

It was only 9:15. Harold couldn't have arrived if he'd stayed anywhere near the speed limit. But when I looked through the crack in the curtains, there he stood. I didn't try to analyze why I was so happy to see him.

"It's Detective Workman. Could you hold the dogs?" I asked the police officers.

Each of them grabbed a dog collar and waited in the living room. I flung open the door, then didn't know quite what to do. Harold shut the door behind him, then took my hand in both of his and smiled down at me. He looked tired. "I'm glad you're okay," he said.

He dropped my hand and identified himself to Hawkins and Rawlings. "How does the place check out?"

"Pretty well, sir," Rawlings said. "Windows and the dog door are the only weak spots for a break-in. And there aren't any curtains on the basement windows. Anyone could get a clear shot. The dogs are a big help. They go crazy at any noise."

The officers let go of the dogs' collars at that point, and Golda and Jesse ran to sniff Harold. He let them mill around for a few moments, then said "Sit!" They both sat immediately. He leaned forward to rub behind their ears as he talked with the officers.

"We'll be leaving now, ma'am," Rawlings said, gathering their papers. "Hope everything goes well."

"Thanks for your help, officers. I appreciate it."

I locked the door behind them and turned to Harold. *Keep up the act*, I reminded myself. "What's happened? You weren't alarmed when I left."

"Let me warm myself while I tell you. Or better yet, tell me where the bathroom is before I get started. I didn't stop for *anything* on the way down."

I hung his green down-filled jacket on a hook near the door, then pulled a couple of chairs close to the fire, threw on another log, and got him a cup of coffee while he was out of the room. He looked somber as he came back in and sat across from me.

"Sarah, evidently the rumor got out somebody was helping us. And it seems to be common knowledge it's a woman and she stayed at the Meeting Ground. We don't know who talked, but we think it's put you in danger."

"But how would the Killer track me down? How would he know it was me, or where to find me?"

"Someone broke into the Meeting Ground's office about 3:00 this afternoon. Maddy heard Tramp growling and went to see what was up, but all she saw was someone in a dark blue hooded jacket. The intruder was fairly small, but she's almost certain it was a man. The last thing she remembers is Tramp leaping at him. The man hit Tramp with a piece of firewood, knocked Maddy out, and stole the file box with the names and addresses of the guests."

"Is she okay?" I asked, horrified.

"Yeah. She's a little old for this kind of activity and the hospital is keeping her for observation, but they think she's going to be all right. Harry was visiting his brother and didn't find her 'til about 5:30, still unconscious and bleeding from a scalp wound. I guess there was blood all over the place, and Harry just about fell apart. By the time the ambulance got her to the Sedro-Woolley Hospital and she came to, it was 6:30. Harry called me right away, and I alerted the Task Force. Luckily there were only a few guests on Friday, and Harry remembered the names and cities of each of them."

"And luckily Maddy didn't have me fill out another card on Saturday," I said. "That would have been a dead giveaway."

"The Task Force called for police protection on a couple of older women from Panorama City. And on you, of course."

"Yeah, those women were on my raft. What about the family from Gig Harbor, the Rimbauds? They stayed at the Meeting Ground and were on my raft, too."

"It was too late," he said, staring at the fire. "We couldn't reach them on the phone. They didn't live in Gig Harbor proper, so we called the Pierce County Sheriff's Department to ask for protection 'til someone from the Task Force could get there. The deputies found the bodies of two adults, a man and a woman. They looked like the people in the wedding pictures in the hall, so we're pretty sure it's the Rimbauds. They were both strangled in separate rooms and hadn't been dead long. No sign of forced entry or struggle."

"Oh, my Lord! They're *dead*? The little girl, too?"

"No, she wasn't there. They think he might have taken her with him."

I heard the words, but couldn't really grasp what had happened to people I had talked with just yesterday. I remembered Angie's mother talking nonstop on the raft, her father saying "Not quite the trip we expected, huh?" and Angie's giving me her bag of M&Ms and bubble gum. Now her parents were dead and she was missing, maybe with the person who had killed her parents—and who liked to kill young girls. A stray thought that seemed manageable rose, and I asked, "What about Tramp? Is he okay?"

"No, he was too badly hurt and had to be put down. But Maddy might not be alive if it weren't for Tramp. He got a mouthful of cloth and skin. The Killer evidently took off instead of finishing Maddy off. The experts are analyzing what was in Tramp's teeth."

I slipped off the chair to sit on the floor. Golda snuggled against me while I hugged her and shuddered. "Tramp's dead and the Rimbauds are dead and Nicole is dead and thirty-three other people are dead—that we know about. And he probably has Angie Rimbaud. She's just a sweet innocent little girl, even younger than Nicole! She shared her M&Ms with me!" I buried my face in Golda's sweet-smelling fur. "Can he just keep going forever?" I muttered. "Is he going to get those women in Panorama City and me, too?"

Golda whimpered as I held her too tightly. Jesse lumbered to his feet to see what was wrong. Harold moved to the chair I had vacated and gripped my shoulders. "Hang in there, Sarah. It's got to be coming to a head now, and this is a strange turn of events. Serial killers almost never kill anyone who doesn't fit their pattern. We're not sure what's up, but he's evidently scared and might do something foolish and get caught. Meanwhile, we have some options on how to protect you and the others."

"I think I need some coffee," I said, extricating myself from the dogs and Harold's hands on my shoulders.

"Stay here. I'll get it."

"No, thanks. I need to move."

He sat back in the chair while I went into the kitchen and moved around, finding the cup, pouring the coffee. I gripped the edge of the sink and stared into it. Broken glass still lay in the left basin. *I should clean that up*, I thought. *Somebody might get hurt.* That seemed funny, and I realized I was starting to get hysterical.

I took a swallow of the hot coffee. The scalding liquid brought tears to my eyes, but also brought me back from the edge of hysteria. I mixed some cold water into the coffee and wrapped my hands around the cup as I started back to join Harold at the fire. I didn't even think to ask if he needed more coffee.

"Want your chair back?" he asked.

"No, I'll sit here. I'm okay now. Guess I'd better hear the options."

He settled back into the chair. Firelight highlighted the deep wrinkles in his face as he spoke. "First, we can send you away for a while under an assumed name. The Killer's already been getting away from us for at least four years, but today he seemed to feel a need to act quickly. This means he might give himself away within the next few days or weeks, while you're away."

"You mean the Witness Protection Program I've read about? Where they ship witnesses to some other part of the country and give them new identities?"

"No, that's a federal program and it's a lot more extensive than anything we can do. I was thinking more along the lines of your going to stay with a friend, or we could maybe send you to Boise for two weeks as Jane Smith." He grimaced, and I could see the strain in his face. "That's the kind of exciting protection our Task Force can offer. If you're lucky, you might get Coeur d'Alene instead of Boise.

We can't send you far, and we can't send you for long, but it may be enough."

"And the other options?"

"We can give you 'round-the-clock police protection for a few weeks. Again, it may not be long enough, but we just don't have the resources to offer indefinite protection."

"Anything else?"

"Not officially. You can arm yourself and live in a state of siege. That gets real old fast, and it wears you out. It usually isn't effective either. And you're more likely to shoot the paper carrier than the person who's stalking you."

"I don't like those options, Harold." I bent over my almost-empty coffee cup. "They may or may not protect me, but they aren't likely to help much in catching the Killer."

"We're doing all we can," he interrupted.

I looked up at him. "Wait a minute, please. I'm not criticizing you and the Task Force. I'm just trying to figure out another option. What would happen if I stayed here as bait? I don't mean without protection, but maybe with hidden protection? Maybe it would draw him out so you could catch him?"

"We can't ask you to do that."

"You didn't ask me. I offered. Or at least I may be offering it if we can work out the details. I'm not being brave. It just seems more practical. Because with the other options, if you don't catch him within a couple of weeks, I'm out there all alone." ≠

Chapter 11

Harold sat silent for a few minutes, mulling over what I'd just said. He turned his empty coffee mug around and around in his big hands, all the while staring at the mug. Then he looked up at me.

"We'd thought of that. You're right, you would be out there all alone. And I'd thought of what you're suggesting, but decided it was too risky. You could get killed, or seriously hurt."

"It sounds as though I could get killed or seriously hurt anyway. This might be a way to get it over with and let me get on with my life without being afraid he's coming after me. And of course, it might keep him from killing anyone else."

Jesse came over, alert to the agitation in my voice. I fondled his ears while Harold pondered what I had just said.

"It could work," he said. "If it were me, I'd take that option. I'd rather spend a short time being cautious and frightened than risk going indefinitely without a resolution. But I'm trained to take these kinds of risks. And I'm paid to take them. You aren't."

"I don't really think I have a choice, do I?"

"You'd have to carry on your life as normally as possible so he'd think he could get to you," he said, planning as he talked. "We could have somebody secretly here with you, and work something out for surveillance from a neighbor's house. We could also give you an alarm you could wear to alert the police instantly. What about work?"

"I work from my home. There's a computer in the other room.

Basically, I sit at the computer and write and edit, or I make phone calls. But sometimes I go out for assignments or to do research, and sometimes people come here."

"That simplifies things. If you have to go out, we could arrange undercover protection. Dozens of cops are working on this, and every one of them would work 'round the clock to close in on the Killer. How about personal commitments in the next few days?"

As we planned how to handle the situation, my answers came more easily. "Twelve-step reunion group here tomorrow night. There's a Christmas party on Friday, and dinner and a video on Saturday. Both of those are at friends' homes. I try to keep week nights free so I can put in extra work hours, but I have a tentative date for Zoolights one night this week."

"What's that?"

"The Point Defiance Zoo puts it on in December as a fundraiser. They string up lights all over the zoo in the shapes of animals. You don't see the real animals, but you stroll around and look at the lights. Last year was the first time they did it, and I've heard it's even better this year,"

"Anything else this week?"

"No, but if you need me to go any further, like get into Christmas, I'll have to get my calendar."

"I don't think so. It only took him a couple of hours to come after the Rimbauds. In fact, my main worry right now is getting things in place for tonight. May I use your phone?"

"Sure. The one in the office is the best. Pencils and paper are on the desk, and the phone book is on the shelf."

"You'd better come with me. I might need to ask you questions as I go."

He dialed the first number from memory. "Chuck? This is Harold. Is Sheriff Potter in? Well, can I get him at home? Okay, you page him and have him call me immediately at 876-5432 in Tacoma. I'm at Ms. Tierney's house and we have a plan. Hold just a second, will you?" He covered the mouthpiece and asked "Do you have Call Waiting?"

I nodded.

"He'll be able to get through when he calls. Thanks." He hung up and dialed another number. "This is Harold Workman from the Skagit County Sheriff's Office. Who's on tonight? Good. Let me speak with Fred, then."

He had been pacing as he talked, but now he pulled out the desk chair and sat. I sat at the computer and swiveled to watch him. His broad forehead furrowed in concentration as he wrote notes to himself. It smoothed out when he started talking again.

"Fred, I'm at Ms. Tierney's house. Yeah, in Tacoma. She's the witness I'm working with. What?" he said, then waited a few moments. "Thank God! Hold on while I tell Ms. Tierney." He covered the mouthpiece and said, "The little girl, Angie Rimbaud? She's okay. She was spending the day with neighbors and now she's at her grandparents."

I sighed with relief as Harold turned back to the phone. Angie's parents were dead, but at least she wouldn't wind up as Nicole had. I had not wanted to think about what might happen to her.

"What did the two women at Panorama City decide?" Harold asked. "Doesn't surprise me," he said after a pause. "I'd probably leave town, too, if I were them." I had the feeling he was echoing everything so he wouldn't have to repeat it all for me later. I liked the technique; it let me feel included in the conversation.

"Look, Fred, Ms. Tierney volunteered to be bait. Uh-huh, it was her idea and she realizes the danger. Yeah, she saw the problems with the other options. Yeah, yeah. Uh-huh. I went over all that with her," he said. "Let's get on with making arrangements. I have a call in to work things out with Sheriff Potter. I'll stay here. I can probably get the Tacoma Police Department to take my truck away and store it. You'll arrange for surveillance ASAP? Yeah, you line up the officers and I'll talk with Ms. Tierney about the neighbors. I'll call you back soon. Meanwhile, will you get someone to coordinate everything with the different departments involved? Good. Thanks."

He hung up and swiveled around to face me. "What can you tell me about the best lookout spots and about the neighbors?"

"We have a Neighborhood Block Watch, so I've met everyone on this block. Don't know any of them well. The corner house across the street would have the best view of the front and left side of my place and of both streets. The guy who lives there is about forty to forty-five, Vietnam vet, has his own yard maintenance business. I think he was in the Green Berets."

"Single?"

"Yeah, but he's had a couple of long-term live-ins since I've been here. I think he's alone now. Keeps pretty much to himself. He's been a good neighbor and participates in the Block Watch. I think the upstairs front room is his bedroom, but the view ought to be great from there."

"Sounds pretty likely, if he'll cooperate. Who else? How about the house to your right?"

"No. That's the neighborhood grouch. She won't participate in the Block Watch and she always worries about infringements on her rights. Complains about parties or kids walking across her grass or people parking in the street in front of her house. I just don't think she'd help us."

"Okay. Who would you suggest for that side?"

"I don't know their names, but the young couple cattycornered across the alley from me might do it. We've talked a few times. No kids. They could see along the back fence and maybe see the back door from their house. And they can cover the whole alley. None of the neighbors are going to be able to see into the trees between my house and the one to the right, but that couple can see as much as anyone."

"Do you know their address? We can use that to find the name."

"The numbers are pretty logical. It's got to be 9832."

"Anybody else?"

"No. Others might be willing, but their locations aren't as good. Can we start with those two and I'll think of something else if they don't work out?"

The phone rang just as Harold started to pick it up. He handed it to me.

"Yes, he's right here. Just a minute." I handed it back. "Sheriff Potter."

Harold explained the situation to the Sheriff, expanding on what he had told Fred, the officer he'd talked with earlier. "I think this is our only chance," he finished. "Fred's setting up the net and

I'll stay here." He was quiet for what seemed a long time, then said, "Look, Sheriff. I didn't ask you to pay me overtime for this. In fact, I didn't ask you to pull me away from vacation, which I'll lose anyway if I don't use it up. If you don't like the way we want to do it, then I'll just go back on vacation—as of now!"

He was silent again, and I watched him. "I don't like unfinished business. And I feel responsible for getting Ms. Tierney into this because word got out some woman who stayed at the Meeting Ground knew something. She volunteered to be bait, and I'm volunteering to protect her—on my vacation." His voice relaxed and he slumped in the chair. "Yeah, Carl. Sorry I got stiff with you, but I thought you were trying to pull me off the case. Yeah, I know. It could get sticky, so maybe it's better like this. Okay, then."

He was quiet again, listening. "Thanks. I'd appreciate your giving Connie a call to tell her I'm off on a job and not to worry. She's due in a couple of weeks. Tell her she can reach me through you if she needs to."

I started into the living room. Harold put a restraining hand on my arm and continued speaking into the phone. "Okay. Okay. Good. Yeah. Then I'm back on vacation and on the case as a friend of Ms. Tierney's. Uh-huh, I'll remember."

"You're volunteering?" I demanded as soon as he got off the phone.

"Sure. You heard."

"But just a few minutes ago you were justifying your taking these kinds of risks because you were paid. And I wasn't. Now you're not being paid, either, and you aren't forced to do it like I am. He's not going to be stalking you."

"I don't have to do this, but I want to. I don't like loose ends—or leaving a job undone. I let you volunteer, so why don't you let me do the same? I might as well do something worthwhile for vacation and I'd just as soon end my law enforcement career with a bang."

I wanted to protest further. Then his last words registered. "Is that really the best way to say how you want to end your career?"

He checked his memory for the exact words he had used, then smiled. "No, I guess not. But as far as we know, the Killer never uses a gun."

We looked at each other and laughed. Nothing like a little gallows humor, I thought.

"I'd better call the Tacoma PD," he said, turning back to the phone. "Could I have some more coffee? It's likely to be a long night." ≠

Chapter 12

I brought Harold the coffee, then went to the bedroom to get a sweater. Glancing into the mirror I realized I had never finished putting on my mascara; the lashes were dark on one side, bare on the other. I whipped into the bathroom to finish the job. The mascara wand lay on the counter where he couldn't have missed it. I treated my left eye and put the wand away, then ran a comb through my hair in a vain attempt to make it look less wilted.

I sauntered back into the office just as Harold hung up the phone. He looked at my face. "Well, you look a little less unbalanced," he said, grinning.

"I hoped you hadn't noticed," I said with as much dignity as I could.

"No more than you'd notice if I shaved only half my face. You were decidedly lopsided, but I figured you had enough to worry about without my telling you you looked a little strange."

Without waiting for a response, he switched gears and said, "The Tacoma PD is sending some people over to take my truck away and rig you up with an alarm. I told them I'm basically here to protect you, and I have no special standing except that I have a lot of friends on the Task Force. And I just happen to know these friends want to catch the Killer almost as badly as I do."

"Okay. What do I do now?"

He flashed a quick look of approval at me. "You and I have to contact the neighbors to set them up for the Task Force contact.

It's about 10:20, so we might wake them up. Can you start by calling the vet across the way? Explain as little as possible, then let me talk with him."

I found the list of Block Watch members and dialed the number.

"Yeah," Jim answered. I knew he liked beer, and he sounded like he'd been drinking. I hoped he hadn't drunk a lot—or been smoking something he shouldn't.

"Hi, this is Sarah Tierney across the street. Sorry to call so late, but I need to ask you a big favor, and I need you to keep it quiet."

"Sure, Sarah. What's up?"

"I can't explain in detail, but the police think I may be in some danger. There's a detective here with me who wants to talk with you. If you don't mind, I'd like to put you on the speakerphone."

"No problem."

I hit the speakerphone button. Harold introduced himself, then told my neighbor I was helping with an investigation and might be in danger. "We need to set up some surveillance points in the neighborhood, and Sarah thought your house would be the best. We've got to get some people in fast and secretly. Our suspect may already be in the neighborhood. Are you willing to talk further?"

"Yes, sir!" Jim spoke with a briskness I'd never heard in him before. "I did some intelligence work in 'Nam. Had top secret security clearance, and I know how to keep quiet. I'm willing to let cops in to watch Sarah's house." He paused, then added, "At least if they're willing to ignore any smells they don't like."

"We're worried about something more important than weed, if that's what you mean. I'm making an advance contact for the Skagit River Task Force and I'll have somebody else call you in a few minutes. They're rounding up people now for the stakeout. How can we get them in without raising suspicion if somebody's watching?"

Jim paused a few moments before speaking. "I party from time to time with some rambunctious friends. Could you maybe have a couple carloads of rowdy undercover guys drop by? If they seem high already, they can sort of barge in and try to haul me out. You know, act like old friends and all. I'll resist and push them out, but nobody will notice if a few stay behind. That ought to seem normal enough, even to someone who knows the neighborhood."

"That's great," I put in, grinning. "That would be realistic, all right. I remember some of your parties."

"Good thinking," Harold added. "I'll relay this to the Task Force and somebody will contact you for further arrangements. Thanks."

He dialed the Task Force, hit the speakerphone button, and asked Fred to check on my neighbor's security clearance immediately. "At the same time you're checking, have someone talking with him about getting into his house." Harold explained the plan. "He seems sharp, and more than willing to cooperate, but the guys might have to overlook some funny smoke smells. If he checks out, I'd be inclined to involve him as much as feasible. Ms. Tierney and I will work on the other arrangements and I'll get back to you."

"Sounds good, Harold."

"And Fred, I'd better tell you that after talking with you earlier I put myself back on vacation, with Sheriff Potter's blessing. I'm not here officially. I'm just helping out my friend, Sarah Tierney. So you can ignore everything I say if you want to."

Fred's voice sharpened. "Is Ms. Tierney there?"

"Yeah, she's right here, listening on the speakerphone."

"Ms. Tierney, this conversation is being taped. Are you comfortable with what you just heard Detective Workman tell me?"

"About as comfortable as I can be, knowing somebody might be trying to kill me," I said. "If you mean am I upset because Detective Workman's not here officially, that doesn't bother me. I agree with what he's working out."

"I've known this guy for a while, and I think you've made a pretty good choice, Ms. Tierney. Since he's a friend of mine as well, I guess I won't ignore his suggestions. And I don't think anyone else on the Task Force will, either," Fred finished. "We'll keep in touch, Harold. Enjoy your vacation." Both men hung up.

"Thanks, Sarah," Harold said, touching my shoulder. He stood and stretched. "I'd better get some stuff from the truck before the cops get here." The green and black wool check shirt he wore as a light jacket pulled up as he stretched, and I saw a holstered gun on his right hip. "Lock the door after me, will you?" he asked as he put on his down jacket.

I waited for him with my hand on the key. He was back in a few minutes, carrying a soft-sided suitcase that he put on the sofa and unzipped.

"You knew it would turn out like this!" I said, looking at the suitcase.

"No," he said, peeling off his down jacket and putting it on the sofa. "I knew we'd have to give you protection one way or another and I knew I wasn't going to make it back home tonight, whether I was staying here or at a motel. Of course I came prepared."

He lifted a smaller bag out of the suitcase and placed it on the floor, then gestured at the empty suitcase. "Do you have something we can stuff in here to give it bulk and weight? Books and crumpled newspapers would do fine."

I stood looking at him instead of getting what he asked for. He sat on the sofa next to the empty suitcase. "I didn't try to scare you into making this decision, you know," he said. "And it's not too late to change your mind. You can always take one of those other options."

"No I can't," I said. "This really is the only option. I may have chosen it, but I'm feeling railroaded. Even though I know it's the situation, instead of you, doing the railroading." I pulled some large books out of the shelves at random and put them in the suitcase. "I'm sorry I said that. This is the second time I went on attack today, and you've been in the way each time."

He put his hand on mine. "That's okay, Sarah. You're under tremendous strain. If this is as bad as you get, I'm not real worried."

We both jumped as the door buzzer went off.

I looked through the crack in the curtains. "It's a couple of men," I said, under the dogs' barking.

"May be the plainclothes officers, but be careful. I'll cover you."

He drew his gun and stood around the corner, back to the wall. I left the chain on and opened the door a crack.

"Ms. Tierney? We're from the Tacoma Police Department. Is Detective Workman here?" one of them said.

He was about Harold's size and looked a lot like him. I asked, "May I see your identification?"

He slipped in two photo IDs. "We were told someone may be

watching," he said. "Treat us like buddies."

I flung open the door. "Uncle John!" I called to the man who looked like Harold. "I didn't recognize you without your beard! Come on in, and bring your friend!"

I dragged both men in and closed the door behind them. Harold came around the corner, gun still in hand.

"May I see the commission cards?" Turning his body sideways to protect his gun hand, he reached out the other hand, took the photo cards and examined them, then holstered the gun. "Glad you got here so quickly. Nice job on matching me. You know what's at stake?"

"The Skagit River Killer?"

"Yes. What do you have to get help here right away for Ms. Tierney?" he asked the man who looked like him.

"Couple of things. First, 911. If she has a programmable phone, we'll code it in and alert the dispatchers that any call from this address is top priority." He turned to me. "We'll also give you an alarm you can wear that operates independently of your phone system. You hit that and the surveillance teams in the area will be over here like flies on a corpse."

I winced.

"Not a good simile, pal," Harold said.

"Oh, hey, I'm sorry, Ms. Tierney. Wasn't thinking. Anyway, they'll be here quick if you hit the alarm, and the dispatchers will automatically be notified through those phones in case yours is out." He looked back at Harold. "I understand you're staying here?"

"Yeah, that's why we needed a lookalike to drive my truck away. You'll wear my jacket and take my suitcase out to the truck, then leave. 'Uncle John' will stay here—and that was a good touch, Sarah—while the friend who brought him leaves. If anyone's watching, we hope it looks like a civilian relative is the only one here with Sarah. If he's not watching, then we went to a lot of extra trouble."

"Too bad 'Uncle John' didn't think to bring luggage," Harold's lookalike said, "but at least I have this; it might pass as an overnighter." He held up a small case. "Makeup. I'll fix you so you look more like me, and me so I look more like you. The officer who set this up and faxed us your photo and description said I should wear khaki. I hate switching clothes with anybody. Always binds or sags. You sit here," he directed, gesturing Harold toward a dining room chair.

The other man stood near the door as Harold's twin opened the makeup case, fitted a magnifying mirror contraption around his own neck, and positioned it so he could see his face. His glance flitted between Harold and the mirror as he deftly sketched wrinkles into his own face, then brushed a touch of gray into his hair. He seemed to be painting a portrait of Harold on himself. Harold sat, looking bemused at seeing his face appear on the man in front of him.

Next the man who looked like Harold worked on Harold's face, covering lines, darkening the gray in his hair, and subtly altering the set of his eyes. He spoke over his shoulder to the other police officer. "You call the Department and set up 911 as I told Ms. Tierney. I'll be done soon and we'll get out of here."

I sat watching and holding the dogs out of the way. In a couple of minutes I felt as though I had just watched the police officer and Harold exchange faces.

"I'm in charge of makeup at Tacoma Little Theatre," the lookalike explained, seeing the expression on my face. "Helps a lot in undercover work."

The other officer came back into the room after several minutes in my office. "Okay, 911's all set. Detective Workman, they had the name and number you wanted for the neighbors across the alley."

I was feeling like a spectator in my own home, and I didn't like it. These men all knew their roles, but I didn't know what I was supposed to be doing.

Harold—with a new face—rose and fitted the makeup case into the suitcase I had started filling with books. "This will work nicely," he said to the man with his face. "Here's my jacket. Understand you have a safe place for my truck and gear and someone will take me to it when this is all over."

The lookalike nodded.

"Okay, then you two had better go. Thanks. Sarah, can you see 'Harold' and 'Uncle John's friend' off convincingly and fairly loudly? 'Uncle John's' spending the night here."

"Sure." I leaped up and we all went to the door together. I shook "Harold's" hand and said I was sorry he couldn't stay after all. He took the suitcase and started toward the truck. Then I thanked the other man for bringing "Uncle John" to the house. "Uncle John" thanked him as well and we stood together in the doorway as the second man left.

I was feeling giddy as I slipped my arm around Harold's waist to keep in character as the loving niece. Good ol' Unc draped his arm over my shoulders and we waited until the two vehicles started up before going back in. It was cold in the doorway, but I felt warm as we closed the door.

My family weren't touchers, and I don't touch others easily. I'd come to like the hugging at twelve-step meetings, but I still think of most other physical contact—especially with someone I'm attracted to—as sexual. Harold didn't feel like any of my uncles. And my feelings weren't those of a niece. I was aware of the warmth and firmness of his waist under the khaki shirt and of the warmth and weight of his arm on my shoulders. And I was aware he no longer suspected me of murder.

"Good acting, Sarah," Harold said, moving away. "The masquerade wouldn't fool anyone close up, but we did pretty well on short notice. Now we'd better call the couple across the alley."

I went to my office and dialed the number Harold gave me. A sleepy male voice answered. "This is Sarah Tierney, your neighbor across the alley. I have an emergency and need your help."

"Oh, hey, yeah. What time is it? What's the matter?"

I could hear a woman's voice in the background saying, "Who is it? What do they want?"

"It's about 11:30. I'm sorry I woke you." I explained pretty much as I had to my neighbor across the street, but had to repeat myself while the couple woke up enough to understand what I was saying. At last the woman took the phone and asked, "You're the woman with the two dogs, aren't you?"

"Yes."

"Okay, what can we do to help?"

"I'd like to turn on the speakerphone and have you talk with the detective who's here with me. Do you mind?"

"Sure. Put him on." Her voice was muffled as she said to her husband, "You pick up the kitchen phone, Hon. This is weird."

Harold's explanation was as succinct as before, but the couple seemed much less inclined to believe him. "How do we know you're who you say you are?" the man asked.

"You don't. I can give you a number you can call and ask about me."

"How do we know you don't have an accomplice at that number?" This time the woman asked.

"Again, you don't. Look, call 911 and tell the operator you got a call from Detective Workman at Sarah Tierney's house. Ask them to patch you through *immediately* to whoever can vouch for me. Then call me back at this number. Once you know I'm okay, I'll tell you what we want."

He slammed down the phone and looked up at me, still wearing the other man's face. "Dammit! Somebody uses all the precautions we tell people to use and it just makes me angry. How come I want them to be suspicious of everybody but me?"

"Because you're the only one that you know has a pure heart," I answered.

"Oh, if only . . . ," he started to say.

"What in the world?" I interrupted, as a couple of loud cars and motorcycles roared up the street. We both ran to the front door and peered through the curtains.

"Looks like the vet's rowdy friends are here!" Harold said with a grin. He put a hand on my shoulder. "They better be quick or everybody in the neighborhood will call the cops."

The cars unloaded and a mob milled around the front door. Some called for him to come out. Others shushed those who called. My neighbor appeared in the doorway, shaking his head and telling them to go away. After a couple of minutes everyone swarmed inside and the door slammed.

Harold and I kept looking through the curtains and waiting for the next scene to play out.

A few minutes later, Jim pushed the mob out again. From our vantage point, it looked as though everyone left.

"You ain't no fun tonight," a biker called before revving up his bike.

"Get out of here, man. I got to live here. You want the neighbors to call the cops? All you guys clear out!"

The cars and bikes roared off, making sure everyone around knew they were gone.

"Are all cops actors?" I wondered aloud.

"All the undercover ones are. At least all the good ones are. They handled that well, didn't they?"

"Yeah. And now we're covered in front."

"You have any ideas if the neighbors across the alley don't play?"

We moved away from the door, Harold's arm still on my shoulder. Again, I was aware of his touch and wondered what it meant to him. He probably came from a long line of touchers: he was so casual about the way he held on to my hand, helped me into his truck, or put an arm on my shoulder. It probably didn't mean anything to him. Maybe I could think of it in the same light as the hugs at twelve-step meetings. Once I got used to them, I had come to enjoy that loving human contact. Undoubtedly I could get used to this easily. And I already liked it.

"Maybe the people directly behind me across the alley, but I don't know them at all. We could . . . ." I broke off as the phone rang.

"You'd better get that," Harold said, dropping his arm.

"Sarah? Is Detective Workman there?" I recognized the woman's voice.

"Yes. You'll help?"

"Whatever we can do."

I punched the speakerphone button. Harold overrode her apologies. "It's okay. You did exactly what we tell everyone to do, and now you know we're legitimate. We'd like to put a surveillance team in your house. Sarah may be in danger and we want the place staked out from a couple of angles. I understand you can see the whole alley and maybe Sarah's back door from your place?"

The husband answered. "We can see the alley and part of the back yard, but not the door and not right inside the fence. But look, if you're worried, you should know there was someone in the alley earlier. Sarah's dogs went crazy about 6:30, maybe 6:45, and I looked out to see what was bothering them. I thought I saw a man, but I'm not sure. If someone was there, he didn't stay long."

"Thanks. The surveillance people will question you for details. For now, let's figure how to get someone in your house. We just had a noisy insertion across the street, so we'd better keep yours quiet. Do you have a garage? Is it full?"

"Two-car garage, but my car's in the shop," the wife responded. "The garage is attached, so we could open the door and they could drive right in."

Harold worked out a code with them, then called the Task Force to pass on the information. I barely registered what he was saying.

It struck me that it was after midnight and I was beat. The day had been long and trying, especially after the previous day's demands. In the last sixteen hours I'd probably felt more emotions than I'd experienced in the last sixteen months. Now the only thing I felt was exhaustion.

"Harold, I'm sorry," I said when he got off the phone. "I feel like I'm about to pass out. I'd better let the dogs out, rig up some place for you to sleep, and get to bed."

"The dogs sleep outside?" he said in a surprised voice.

"No, they sleep in the bedroom with me. But they haven't been walked since I got home. Besides, I always let them out in the back yard last thing before going to bed."

"How do you do that?"

"Usually I make them go out through the dog door. Sometimes I go out with them."

"Can you put them on a rope or something, so they can't go too far?"

"The yard's fenced."

"Yeah, but I don't like what your neighbor said about the person in the alley."

"That would have been before I got home."

"And the dogs have been inside with you since you got home?"

"Yes."

"An intruder might have come back and left something for the dogs. I'd just feel better if they couldn't explore the yard too much."

I was too tired to argue further. I got the retractable leashes from the front hall, clipped Jesse's on his collar, and let him out through the dog door. He pulled toward the back fence. *Is something out there*, I wondered, *or is it just that he always goes there to poop?* Golda cuddled against my left side as I sat on the step inside the door and held Jesse's leash in my other hand. As Jesse whined and pulled, I was aware of Harold's rummaging in the kitchen. It sounded like he was cleaning up the broken glass, then running water in the sink.

"Here," he said, coming down the steps behind me and placing a small plate of cheese and apple slices on my lap. "I'll bet you haven't eaten anything since you left my place. You're not only worn out, but your blood sugar's probably down to nothing."

"Thanks. What about you?"

"I fixed some for me, too." He sat a couple of steps higher and bit into an apple slice.

Golda wagged, hoping some was for her, but was too polite to stick her nose into the plate. I managed to eat a couple of slices before the pull on the leash slacked off, then I thrust the plate toward Harold. "Keep this away from Jesse." Jesse pushed through the door, slowing down when the leash caught on the doorframe. As soon as I unhooked him, he headed toward Harold and the plates of food.

"No," Harold said, motioning Jesse up the stairs. "Sit." Jesse sat, then lay down at Harold's further command. I hooked the leash on Golda so she couldn't travel far and pushed her out the door, then ate everything but one apple slice before she came back.

I felt less tired than I had a few minutes earlier. I handed the plate back to Harold and unhooked Golda. "Would you give half of that slice to each dog?" I asked, locking in the dog door insert for the night.

Jesse was alert but still lying on the kitchen floor as Harold had commanded. Golda sat, then lay, as Harold directed her. He gave each of them a piece of apple, then something else.

"What else did you give them?" I asked, curious.

"I didn't know they liked apples, so I saved each of them a piece of cheese," he said.

"You're a pushover for dogs, Detective Workman."

"And pretty women. Just can't resist feeding them every chance I get," he said. ≠

Chapter 13

I knew I'd crash again when the boost from the food wore off, so I decided to work out sleeping arrangements while I was still functioning. Leaning against the kitchen counter, I turned to face Harold. "Look, I just realized there's no good place for you to sleep. I moved the guest bed to the basement when I started working at home, and you can't stay down there if it's dangerous. The sofa's too short and isn't a sofa bed. Maybe that thing that looks like a psychiatrist's couch would be best. I can make it up with blankets, sheets, and pillows."

"I'm sleeping in there, with you," Harold said, gesturing toward the bedroom.

I was dumfounded for a moment. "I really don't think we know each other that well," I stammered.

"Damn! That didn't come out quite like I meant it."

I was alert enough to see Harold was flustered and—yes—blushing.

"I'm not trying to be sticky, Sarah, but with the Rimbauds there were no signs of struggle, no signs of alarm. The likelihood is he somehow caught them in separate rooms and managed to kill each one quickly and quietly. We don't have any idea how he pulled it off."

"But the dogs will be in there with me," I protested. "Nobody's going to get in the room."

"I can't risk it. We can put blankets on the floor, or use a sleeping bag or whatever else is handy, but I'm going to be in there with you."

From the determination in his voice, I thought I understood why the dogs obeyed him so readily. He seemed gentle, but was immovable when he decided something. I was used to making my own decisions, having my own way, but he was the expert in this situation. And I was so tired!

"Okay, Harold. I just remembered I have one of those foam chair/bed things. It's downstairs, but I'm sure I can get it in the dark. It unfolds and makes up like a bed."

"That'd be great! You can put it on the floor next to your bed and I'll be fine."

I closed the dogs in the kitchen while Harold and I went to the bottom of the stairs, then waited while our eyes accustomed themselves to the dark. I was surprised at how much light came through the uncurtained windows.

"I'm here with my gun, just in case," Harold said. I felt the heat of his legs at my back as he stood behind me one step higher. "Go as quickly as you can."

I walked toward the guest room, banging my hip against the dehumidifier as I moved through the dark basement. *Damn! I knew I should have put that away for the winter.* Mostly by feel I found the foam chair right where I expected it, on top of the guest bed. *Was that a noise in the closet? Under the bed? Something moving in the closet?* I grabbed the chair and started through the doorway, then bounced back as the chair hit the doorframe. My breath seemed ragged to me. *Is someone behind me?* I turned the chair to fit through the door and scuttled back to the stairs.

"It's okay. I got it," I said, pushing past Harold. "Let's get upstairs." The dogs danced around me as I opened the kitchen door, and Jesse lunged at the chair. Harold put a hand on my shoulder and I dropped the chair, then flopped on it, panting.

"What in God's name is the matter? Was somebody down there?"

"No, nothing. It's all right."

"Sarah! Don't hold out on me. What's the matter?"

"It's silly. It's just my imagination."

"I'm going down there."

I had caught my breath by now. I grabbed his arm. "No, Harold. It truly is nothing but my imagination," I admitted.

He looked at me and I stumbled on with my explanation. "When I was a kid I read a vivid horror story about some creature. Back then I was convinced it lived in our attic. Marilu believed in it too. I think it was easier to worry about the creature than about our parents. Sometimes when I'm really tired and don't seem to have things in control I start feeling it's in the basement here." I mustered a shaky laugh. "I just went a little crazy. There was absolutely nothing objective to scare me. Nothing!"

"Sarah, it's okay. You're under a lot of stress and you're worn out. And you're not crazy." He slid his gun back in the holster.

I was relieved he took my panic attack calmly. "I'm sorry, but I'm so tired," I babbled. "And I've never gone in the basement in the dark before."

"It's okay," he repeated, reaching a hand down to pull me up from the chair. He wrapped his arms around me and patted my back as though I were a child. "It's okay. You just need some sleep."

This time I leaned into the embrace. I had it figured out. He was a father, and this was how he treated his kids. Worked well, too; the kids must have loved it. Probably didn't mean anything special to him, but it was comforting to me. The phone rang. *Damn phone. Every time Harold touches me, the phone rings. Worse than a chaperone.* I picked up the kitchen phone and answered, "Yes?"

"Ms. Tierney? This is the FBI. May I speak to Detective Workman?"

"It's the whole FBI," I said, covering the mouthpiece as I handed the phone to Harold. "At least that's what he said."

"This is Harold Workman. What's up? Uh-huh, I should have known you'd want to be in on the stakeout. Vantage point pretty good from across the alley? Great. We're going to turn in. Yeah, I'll be in the same room, and so will the dogs. I'll be sleeping, but not too soundly. I think we're about as well protected as we can be for tonight. We'll see tomorrow if we need to do anything else. Thanks for letting us know you're in."

"FBI?" I asked as soon as he hung up.

"Yeah, the FBI works on serial killer cases. This guy has been involved with the Task Force, but it's unusual for an FBI agent to do this kind of stakeout. I think he's got a lot of emotional investment in the case."

"I didn't know FBI agents were allowed to have emotions."

"There you go with the stereotypes again. Actually, they've all been allowed *some* emotions since Hoover died. A few of the younger agents I've known even seem to have the normal complement."

I grinned and moved toward the bedroom. "I'm fading fast," I said. "You need anything?"

"Maybe some towels and a glass. And you'll have to excuse me for sleeping in my skivvies."

"Won't bother me. I think I have a robe you can borrow if you'll wait a minute."

I rummaged through the back of the closet and found an extra-large rust-colored man's bathrobe. I hung it on the back of the bathroom door, then set out towels. Harold took a glass and his toilet kit into the bathroom as I unfolded the chair/bed next to my double bed and made it up. There was room for only a narrow path between the beds.

The decision on what I was going to wear seemed monumental. Somehow neither of my usual choices seemed right: a paint-smeared 'Last ERA Walk' T-shirt or nothing at all. Nor did the lacy sheer peach-colored gown and matching peignoir I was surprised to find at the back of the bureau drawer. Looking at my other choices, I decided a flowered flannel nightgown was my best bet.

Just as I gathered up my nightwear, Harold came out, wearing his own face and hair. He looked good. Nicely shaped calves, well covered with dark hair, showed under the knee-length robe. I was relieved he wore a pair of cloth slippers; I've always disliked short socks on men's bare legs. I wished I hadn't offered the robe. Now I'd never know if he wore wild shorts under his plain khaki exterior.

"These okay on the chair?" he asked, gesturing with his folded shirt and pants.

I nodded and started into the bathroom.

Harold put out a hand. "Say, Sarah, I don't want to mess up anything between you and your friend."

"My friend?" I echoed, wondering if my tiredness had made me miss whatever would make sense of what he was saying.

"Well, I mean, do you need to call him and explain why you have some other guy staying here tonight? Is he likely to show up?"

"But I'm not going with anybody," I said, bewildered.

"Back at the station," Harold forged ahead, "it must have been yesterday, you said something about a friend who had a key and *he* could come over if necessary to take care of the dogs. And then this robe and your dinner date this weekend. I just thought . . . ."

Again he was blushing. I burst out laughing. "Well, yes, I do have a male friend with a key. He's seventy-two years old, and I met him and his wife at ACOA. Bert comes over sometimes when I'm not here and uses the computer. He's in my twelve-step group now, but he's certainly not my boyfriend. His wife isn't even worried about the key."

"I guess I jumped to conclusions," he said. "Not an example of good detective work."

"You certainly did! The robe isn't his, either. I got it for myself at a rummage sale, but it's too big around and too short. It leaves my legs cold. I was thinking of giving it to the King Center. Never thought I'd need it to keep a detective warm! And the dinner date's with a woman friend."

I went in the bathroom, still grinning. Harold had hung his towels on an empty rack and placed his toilet kit on the back of the toilet. The bathroom was tidy, the counter dry, and the seat down. *A true prince,* I mused, brushing my teeth. *A paragon. More to be treasured than . . . than what? I'm too groggy to think. Anyway, unusual. Hope Judy's grateful for what she's got.*

He was in his small bed when I came back, looking tired against the white pillow. The robe was laid over his feet, and his belt and holstered gun lay next to the bed, with the holster's snap undone. A pair of handcuffs were on the belt as well.

The dogs looked up from their fuzzy bean-bag beds. *It's my house; I can do as I want,* I thought, but I felt self-conscious as I went through my usual nightly ritual. "G'night, Golda," I murmured, stroking her head. "You're a good girl and I'm glad you're here." She licked my hand, then settled down with a sigh. Going to Jesse I petted him. "Night, Jesse. I'm glad you're here. You're a good boy." His sigh was more of a grunt, but he settled back and closed his eyes.

"What about me?" Harold asked as I climbed into bed.

"Good night, Harold. I'm glad you're here, too." I realized as I said it how true it was.

"I never could figure whether my 'good nights' to Alex were for his benefit or mine," Harold offered as I settled in and turned off the light. "I just know it never seemed right to go to sleep without saying it when I was away. And after he died, at first I had trouble sleeping if I didn't say good night to the empty room. Night, Sarah. Sleep tight."

"Don't let the bedbugs bite!" I finished up.

"That's the kid's version. The dog's version is 'Don't let the fleas bite.' At least that's what my kids and I worked out for Alex."

"Makes sense."

We were silent for a few minutes. Sleep seemed far away. I wasn't used to having anyone other than the dogs in the room with me, but I didn't think that was the whole problem. I wiggled around, trying to get comfortable.

"Do you have the feeling we're in one of those fifties movies?" Harold asked.

I grinned. "You mean Doris Day and Rock Hudson? There *are* some similarities. Night."

"Night."

I was getting more wakeful every minute. It wasn't an alert wakefulness, but the hateful feeling that I wasn't going to be able to sleep all night. I arranged the pillows, then adjusted them once again.

"What's the matter, Sarah?" Harold asked. "Are you worried? Or scared?"

"Not really. I've pushed all that to the back of my mind, and it seems so impossible anyway. I think it's because I *always* read before I go to sleep. I've done it ever since I can remember."

"What's stopping you now? It won't bother me."

"Shield your eyes, then," I said, flipping on the light and reaching for the *Lear's* magazine on the bedside table. "Thanks."

"S'nothing. Night."

"Night," I said again, finding my place. I read a couple of pages, then sleepiness hit me—hard. I put down the magazine and glanced at Harold. He was asleep. His upflung hand covered his lined forehead and the gray streak in his hair. His wide mouth was relaxed, and the wrinkles around his eyes had smoothed out in the dim light. Despite the outline of what looked like a greasepaint beard, I could see what he must have looked like as a little boy. I turned off the light and sank into forgetfulness.

At some point during the night, I roused to a slurping sound and Harold's quiet, "Aww, Jesse. Cut it out!"

Later, my own muffled shout woke me from a nightmare. My heart was pounding and I was drenched in sweat, but I couldn't remember what the dream was about. "It's okay, Sarah," Harold said from the darkness beside me. I thrust my hand toward his voice and felt it gripped between two larger hands. "Just relax, now. You're all right. Jesse and Golda and I are all here to protect you. Go back to sleep. Just relax, now. You're safe."

His voice was hypnotic and reassuring in its repetition. My heart rate slowed and the terror that had waked me receded. I drifted back to sleep, my hand safe in his.

When I woke again, I was alone in the bedroom. A dim winter light filtered around the blinds. The clock radio showed 10:18; I must have forgotten to set the alarm. I threw on my robe and staggered into the living room, where Harold sat, dressed for the day, with a cup of coffee. He looked fresh, well groomed, and awake. The dogs lay on either side of his chair, tails thumping to greet my entrance.

"Your office calendar didn't show any appointments, so I let you sleep," he told me. "I fed the dogs and let them out like you did last night. Also, I made coffee, but held off on breakfast."

"Um. Coffee?" I pushed into the kitchen and poured myself a cup. "Thanks. Back in a few minutes," I said, heading for the bathroom. It smelled of Irish Spring soap and some other scent I didn't recognize.

The mirror showed the worst. I ran a brush through my hair, then decided an immediate shower was essential. By the time I turned off the water, I was starting to come around. The coffee helped. I looked and felt pretty good by the time my hair was dry and my mascara on (*both* sides, this time). I brushed my teeth, put my robe back on, and went out to face Harold and the world.

"Sorry. I'm not much of a morning person, even at the best of times. Thanks for letting me sleep. More coffee?"

He nodded.

I filled both our cups and took the other chair flanking the cold fireplace. "Look, I appreciate your being so supportive last night. I'm not usually such an idiot about the basement—or anything else. I just don't cope well when I'm exhausted."

He grinned. "Actually, I was beginning to think you were being a bit *too* strong until you fell apart about the monster in the basement."

"It's not a monster," I said with some dignity. "It's a *creature*. Monsters are huge and fierce, while creatures are small and sneaky. I wouldn't have a monster in the basement. It'd have too much trouble getting in and out."

"I should have known that," he said. "Monsters are almost always outside, aren't they? Deep in the woods or something? You're right; undoubtedly this was a creature."

I'll bet his kids thought he was a great father, I thought. *He lets me act like a child without making me feel like a weakling or an idiot.*

He spoke more seriously. "I'm relieved you're finally reacting visibly to all this. You're responding more or less normally, you know. Judy says it's not good to be too controlled when something like this is going on. She and Jung—maybe for different reasons—would probably think the creature and the nightmare were healthy."

So he even reads Jung. And quotes Judy, I thought.

"Guess I was trying to hold myself together 'cause I thought I might fall to pieces. And no telling what would happen then!"

"You can cope with whatever comes along, Sarah. But it's okay to be scared, too."

"I probably *am* scared, but even today the creature seems a lot more likely than some killer stalking me. And it sure helps to have enough sleep. Right this minute, neither of them seems likely. Is there anything new?"

He leaned forward in the chair. "I've checked in with the Task

Force. Nothing to report from either surveillance team. Since the teams got in, nobody's tried to get near your house except the paper carrier. The garbage collectors went by out front, but you hadn't put any garbage out."

"Damn," I muttered. "Forgot that in all the excitement."

"It's doubtful the Killer's around during the day on a weekday. He probably has a job, and there's too much chance he'd be seen, anyway. We should still act as though you're the only one here. If he saw our charade, we'll hope he thinks 'Uncle John' left while he wasn't watching. That's why I haven't opened the curtains or brought in the paper, and I'll stay away from the windows once the curtains are open. The dogs wanted out, so I put them on the leash like you did last night and let them out one at a time. Also, I looked at the back yard through the dog door. Jesse's particularly interested in something near the back fence. I think you ought to check it out after you get dressed."

"What kind of something?'

"It looks like a dead cat." ≠

Chapter 14

Our playful mood dissolved. "I'd better get dressed, then," I said, turning back to the bedroom, where I put on a fresh pair of jeans and a sweatshirt. While there, I made up my bed. After debating whether Harold was likely to stay another night, I made his as well.

All business, I strode into the living room. Harold's head was bent over a book.

"I'll open the curtains now," I announced, proceeding to let the gray winter light into each window before I checked out the yard. Harold flicked off the table lamp and watched. His forehead seemed more wrinkled than ever. I wondered if he, too, regretted our abrupt return to reality.

Jesse tried to push outside as I went out the back door, but I shoved him back. Harold was right. Just inside the back fence lay a large gray cat I had seen around the neighborhood without knowing who owned it. It lay on its side, its back arched, limbs stretched and stiffened into tortured shapes. Its fur was damp in the cold gray morning, its mouth open in a final grimace of bared teeth, bright red gums, and remnants of froth on its lips. Bending closer, I saw more froth on the insides of its forelegs.

Several pieces of raw pink fish were strewn along the inside of the fence. I walked around the perimeter but saw no other signs of intrusion.

"Pieces of fish and a dead cat," I told Harold, who was waiting for me inside the back door. "No wonder Jesse kept pulling at the leash."

"Can you put everything in plastic bags? Then we'll see if the poison can be identified and traced."

"How did you know he might do something like this?" I asked, looking up at Harold in anguish. "If I had let them out as usual, Jesse and Golda might both be dead."

"I didn't *know*, Sarah, but I had a strong hunch he might try to get the dogs out of the way. He'd just been bitten by Tramp and might not want to face your two, but he had to move fast. Also, a strangler is more likely to use poison than a gun or other messy or noisy means. If he hadn't done anything, you would have taken another unneeded precaution. If he *had* tried something, you and the dogs would have had a better chance because you took the precaution."

I rummaged in the bottom kitchen drawer for plastic bags, then straightened. "I guess now we know for sure he's after me."

"I'd say we're 99% sure. It'd be some coincidence for someone else to try to poison your dogs the same night we think the Killer might come after you. He didn't come back, though. Maybe he saw through our charades—or got sidetracked."

"Could we have scared him off for good?" I had a surge of hope that I might be safe, followed by the realization that I couldn't be as long as the Killer was free.

"I doubt it. And we may have lost our best chance to catch him—if we ever had one. He's probably going to be very cagey now."

Feeling sick to my stomach, I collected the rigid cold body of the cat and the pieces of fish, careful to get every morsel. Jesse leaped for the bags when I entered the house.

"Down, Jesse," Harold said. Jesse dropped down but looked at the bags with interest.

"How do we get these to the Task Force?" I demanded, lashing out at Harold just because he was there.

"They can send someone to get them, probably disguised." Harold took the cat from me and looked at its contorted face through the clear plastic. "Poor thing. Almost certainly cyanide.

Look at the gums. The fish smell would have drawn the dogs to gobble it up, and the cyanide would have worked before you could do anything. The cat probably cried out. Did you hear it squalling last night?"

I shuddered in response. "That could have been what Golda heard when the officers were here. I thought it was neighborhood cats fighting or mating. They do that around here all the time."

"Do you have a box to put these in?" he continued.

"Yeah, I have a box. He wasn't wearing a collar," I said. "Should I call around the neighborhood to find out whose it was? 'Hi, Merry Christmas, is the gray cat yours? He's dead.' Oh, Harold! That poor cat! And the poor owner! Right now I'm more mad than scared! And this is affecting the whole neighborhood!"

"The neighbors are going to have to stay in the dark for now. It would be hard to explain that the cat's part of a major criminal investigation without revealing anything."

I put the dead animal and pieces of fish in a cool spot in the basement, well out of the dogs' reach, before rejoining Harold. "We better eat. Fruit and cereal okay? Or do you want lunch?"

"Fruit and cereal's fine. Let me know how I can help, as long as I can stay out of sight."

"You go ahead and call the Task Force. I'll fix breakfast."

Preparing our simple meal helped me calm down, and I had everything on the table when Harold returned from the office. Conversation was general as we dug into our cereal and bananas. We could almost have been two old friends or a long-married couple at breakfast. Over a final cup of coffee, I asked, "What were you reading this morning?"

"Just doing morning devotions. It helps keep me anchored, especially during a homicide investigation."

I was surprised. "Anything especially good today?"

I was being flip, but I thought Harold was serious as he went to get the *Book of Common Prayer*. "Yeah, Psalm 44 had some great lines. I was reading along and came to this." He turned to the psalm he wanted and started reading: "'Surely, you gave us victory over our adversaries and put those who hate us to shame.'"

He put down the book and grinned. "I thought that was

pretty encouraging in our present situation." He paused. "At least it would have been if I'd stopped there. The next part gets into God rejecting and humiliating his people and ends with a plea for him to wake up and help them."

We both laughed.

"If that's the best you got today," I asked, "how did it help keep you anchored?"

"Beats me. Actually, I had finished the daily readings and was looking at some favorite passages when you woke up. All I know is I feel calmer afterwards. Part of the effect might just be talismanic, like my nightly ritual with Alex and like what you do with Golda and Jesse."

Both dogs pricked up their ears when they heard their names, and Golda moved under the table to lie on Harold's feet. I didn't say anything.

"I might be praying to an empty place, just like I'd say good night to the empty room after Alex died, but I don't think so. I just proceed on the assumption there is a God, he cares about me, and somehow he intervenes in our lives. I think it helps me stay on some sort of ethical course in the middle of a lot of unethical situations. And it's helped me through personally difficult times."

"I remember how badly I was doing before I more or less 'came to believe' in a higher power, and how much progress I've made since," I said. "But for me that doesn't have much to do with the Bible or church. Most of the time I use Sundays to catch up on my sleep."

"Yeah, you do seem to need your sleep." Harold laughed and started to clear away the breakfast things.

"I can do that," I said.

"No, you have to get to work," Harold objected. "I think you told me something about having to earn a living—and how hard it is to keep your nose to the grindstone when you're working for yourself and doing it from your home."

"Well, yes, but I can't just leave you on your own."

"I'm not a guest, you know, and I can take care of myself. I'll do KP and follow through on some leads about newspapers for sale if I can use the kitchen phone to make some calls. I'll pay for the calls, of course."

"Newspapers! I forgot to bring in the paper." I jumped up and retrieved the morning daily from the front porch. "Here's the Tacoma *Morning News Tribune*, I said holding the front section out to him. I get the *Seattle Post-Intelligencer*, too; it generally comes about 4:00 each afternoon."

He skimmed the *Tribune*'s front-page story on the murders of the couple in Gig Harbor while I looked over his shoulder. "It doesn't say a word about the raft trip and the connection with the Skagit River Killer," he said. "And thank goodness, it says nothing about you! I wonder how long the Task Force can keep it quiet. At some point, a reporter probably is going to break it rather than let anyone else get a scoop. If we're lucky, we might have another day or so to let the Killer stew about what we know."

"You mean the media have the story?"

"Surely they do, but they must have agreed to hold off—although maybe the *P-I* will decide they can't wait any longer. I can imagine the pressure they're getting. They can't risk being blamed for giving the Killer too much information when we finally have a chance at him. And they can't risk putting anyone else in danger. Let's see if there's anything about Nicole."

We both bent over the paper again. "Here, page B-1," I exclaimed, skimming and reporting the gist of the article. "'Skagit River Victim Identified.' It gives her name, age, she was identified by her uncle. Her mother says, 'I just couldn't handle her anymore. She wasn't a bad girl, but she kept running away after I remarried. She and her stepdad didn't get along too good.' Then it rehashes all the Skagit River Killer stuff the papers have been reporting for years. It also covers the same ground as yesterday's article about her being found by the eagle watchers. Doesn't give any new information about that."

"I'm sure the reporter made the connection. It's the same byline as on the Rimbaud story. He's showing real restraint. There's a picture, too, the most recent Nicole's mother had, taken two years ago."

Marilu looked out at me from the paper. She wore no makeup and was still a little girl in this photo. I thought she had the face of an often-punished child waiting for Christmas. Her smile was hopeful, but her eyes betrayed a fear there would be only lumps of coal or no presents at all.

I plopped back down in my chair, reminded of one Christmas Eve I read *A Christmas Carol* to Marilu. When the story was finished, the sounds of our parents fighting came through the closed door. Marilu had looked like this when she asked if the noise would scare Santa away. I closed my eyes.

"Your sister?" Harold asked.

"Yes, partly," I said, opening my eyes and brushing away the tears. "And Nicole herself. Ten years old in this picture and already she knows better than to expect too much of life! She'd aged a lot more by the time I spoke with her."

"Her last two years must have been especially hard ones," Harold commented.

We sat for a moment without saying anything, paying tribute again to Nicole. There didn't seem to be anything else to say.

Finally I stirred myself. "Guess I'd better get to work." Then I remembered we'd never cleared the air on why he had suspected me. I settled back into my chair.

"Harold," I said, "I heard you on the phone at your house, telling the Sheriff you *no longer* suspected me."

"I thought you might have. You didn't seem the same on the ride back to your car."

"And I'd hoped I was doing the great acting job you seemed to think I was capable of," I said.

"Good, but not great. I knew something was different, but I no longer felt I had to force you to talk."

"Anyway," I said, pushing the words through a constricted throat, "I was wondering why you suspected me in the first place. Was it something I did or said, or do I seem a likely killer?"

"No, Sarah," he said. "You don't seem a likely killer. But this one's been getting away for so long that it must be someone who's *un*likely. You do know we no longer think you had anything to do with it?"

"Yes, now I know, but it upset me a lot that I was under suspicion in the first place. Why was I?"

He leaned back in his chair and picked up his coffee mug. As he had the previous evening, he turned the mug around and around in his big hands. This time, however, he looked at me as he spoke. "First, because you insisted you wanted to stay with the body. That was unusual, probably a decent and compassionate impulse, but possibly a warped one. Then when we talked at the police station, you said you were glad you hadn't seen any street people in Tacoma on the drive up. Since most of the victims have been street people, that set off alarms. And then your *next* statement was about seasonal depression."

I snorted. "So in the throes of some cosmic pre-Christmas PMS-type attack I offed the first street person I saw? Then I was overcome with guilt and wanted to stay with her body in penance?"

He shrugged. "Something like that. We've seen stranger motivations. And *then* you suddenly told me you couldn't go on like that."

I couldn't help it; I laughed. "You must have thought I was about to confess!" He looked sheepish. "Admit it! You did, didn't you?"

"Well at least that sure piqued my attention—and made me wonder if I had a Miranda card on me. Imagine my feelings when I realized you just meant you wanted to treat your narrative seriously. Then I wasn't sure how to factor in your parents being alcoholics and your being involved in ACOA."

"Oh, you mean my 'unstable background might have predisposed me to violence'?"

"Well, yes. All these things could have come together to unhinge you. Besides, I could tell you were hiding something about the encounter at the Meeting House. When I forced you to explain, what you said about Marilu took you in deeper just as much as it helped exonerate you."

"It all hangs together when you look at it like that," I admitted. "And the ACOA involvement *is* relevant, but not in the way you thought. One of our more fatiguing characteristics is an overdeveloped sense of responsibility. I'm sure that's a big part of why I wanted to stay with Nicole."

"Most of these things didn't point to your being the Skagit

River Killer or even necessarily an accomplice, but they could have meant you did *this* murder or were involved in it. We weren't yet sure it was part of the series. And of course there was no corroboration for your account of what happened in the Meeting House. It could all have been false or been only partly true. You might have been with her there, but you could just as well have killed her there and dumped her off the bridge yourself. She was small enough for you to manage it easily."

"No corroboration until the tape," I interjected.

"That didn't come out until the next day, and even then, you could have been an accomplice. I believed you by that time, but the Sheriff argued that maybe you weren't guessing; maybe you *knew* that someone called the State Patrol because you were with him. Besides, we had no other leads at all."

"Couldn't you tell I was trying to help?"

"I felt you were, but you might have been playing a cat-and-mouse game with me. You know, bamboozle the dumb cop. If you had been an accomplice to the other murders, maybe you and the Killer were bored because we hadn't come close enough to make the chase interesting. I *had* to check out all the possibilities."

"Okay, all of this makes some kind of weird sense. But why didn't you ask or get a warrant or something before you had my car searched?"

Harold looked across the table at me. "What do you mean? We didn't have your car searched." ≠

Chapter 15

"*Somebody* searched it while it was at the church," I insisted. "I didn't notice 'til I was driving home, but everything was subtly rearranged. And since it wasn't broken into, I figured it had to be somebody from the Sheriff's Office. Wasn't that why you invited me to your place? So they'd have a chance to search the car?"

Harold looked disgusted. "No," he said. "That wasn't why. I had to continue checking you out, but I could have done that at the Meeting Ground or the police station or anywhere. I saw you at church and invited you to my house on impulse. Besides, I thought we'd both enjoy the meeting more if it was informal. And I didn't order a search."

Some of the pain I had felt over his suspicions burned away. "So who *did* search the car, then?" I persisted. "Couldn't one of your people have gotten overzealous?"

"Not like that. Even the newest deputy knows that illegally obtained evidence could cause a case to be thrown out. Are you sure it was searched?"

"Yes. The contents of the glove compartment had been shifted, the stuff in the pockets was all moved around, the visors were in a different position. You know, all that kind of thing. And the deputy who drove my car to the station wasn't the one who did it. The car was fine yesterday morning when I drove to church."

"Had the car been vacuumed?"

"No," I said, puzzled. "There was mud and sunflower seeds on the floor, as usual."

"If we'd done it, we would have vacuumed it for traces of the girl. Where do you keep your registration?"

"In my billfold, with my license and insurance card."

"I'll bet that's what he wanted," Harold said. "He could have been trying to get your address from the registration. Might he have seen your car at the motel?"

"Sure, he *might* have. My cabin wasn't far from the Meeting House, and I parked out front both nights. But it was dark and rainy. You mean he stole the motel registration cards because he couldn't get my address from the car?"

"Maybe. Did you write down the make and license number when you registered?"

"No. No, I didn't, because Harry just said to fill out the top three lines."

"And Harry probably told everybody the same thing. So even after the Killer got the registration cards, he couldn't have been sure who to go after."

"The way the car looked should have told him it wasn't a family of three. Why would he have gone after the Rimbauds?"

"I don't know, Sarah. Whoever searched the car isn't necessarily the Killer. It could have been a run-of-the-mill break-in, even though we haven't had one for years. And maybe somebody saw a prowler and can give a description. But I think the Task Force should go over your car for prints and anything else they can find." He forced a grin. "Do you want to sign a permission form, or should they get a warrant?"

"I'll sign, of course. And maybe we could have a triple A tow truck take it away; I'm a member."

"This is getting spooky," Harold said, rising from the table.

"What?"

"You. You're starting to think like a cop."

I stirred myself again. "I'd better get to work. Is there anything else I should do here, first?"

"No, we're about done. I'll tell the Task Force about the car and I'll clean up here." I gave him a grateful look. "But, Sarah, before you get started, it might be a good idea for me to know your normal routine. Then I'll tell the surveillance teams what to expect."

I had to think about it for a minute. "I generally get up around 7:00, walk the dogs, shower, eat breakfast, and start work by 9:00. Keep at it pretty straight until 5:00 or 6:00, except for lunch and maybe to take an extra walk with the dogs or do something around the house. And then I often work evenings. Since I'm just getting the business going, I tend to overdo."

"Does anybody come here during the day?"

"Rarely, and then usually by appointment. A couple of clients occasionally drop off assignments or stop in to chat about them."

"And you sometimes have appointments outside, or have to do research?"

"Yeah, maybe two days a week I leave the house for several hours."

"While you're gone the dogs can go between the back yard and the back porch through the dog door?"

"Uh-huh. Harold, I don't suppose I could take them for a walk now, could I? They get obnoxious when I don't walk them, and I need the exercise, too."

"We couldn't protect you on residential streets without being obvious. If you have to drive anywhere, we can get undercover cops following you, but walking's hard to cover. It'd be safer for you and easier for us if you can stay home for a couple of days."

I didn't like what he was saying, but it made sense. "Okay. I'll play with the dogs in the yard whenever I need a break. That'll help burn off some energy."

Someone in a Thrift Village van showed up for the cat then, just as though they were collecting used clothes or furniture. After I handed over the box with the fish and the cold body, I spent several minutes throwing a stick for Jesse and chasing Golda around the back yard to give us all some exercise. It was almost 1:00 by the time triple A had towed away my car, I'd moved the load of laundry I'd done the night before to the dryer, and I'd settled at the computer.

I've always been able to immerse myself in work. Despite everything, I was deep into a containerized shipping report for the Port of Tacoma when the phone rang. I glanced at the on-screen clock: 2:30. "Tierney and Associates," I answered with my business name.

"Sarah? This is Jane Carmody. I hate to bother you during working hours, but do you have a couple of minutes?"

"Sure, Jane, I always have time for you and Kate. What's on your mind?"

Jane and Kate are friends who share a house. They're both in their late sixties and about as different as any two people can be. Jane is tall, Kate is short. Jane is mechanical and physical, Kate is into books and movies. Jane leads marches in support of people with AIDS, Kate runs the Altar Guild at their church. If Jane says it's day, Kate says it's night. I love each of them, but prefer visiting with them separately. When they're feuding like the Bickersons, it's hard to keep conversation going in a straight line. Even so, I envy them the family they've forged with each other over the past eighteen years.

"We just got around to reading the papers for yesterday and today," Jane said. "Kate said you must have been one of the people who found the girl in the river, but I said no. Then we got into an argument about it and finally I said I'd call and ask you, just to put an end to the dispute."

I didn't know what I should say. This whole situation was so far outside my normal life I'd thought of it as walled off. Harold and the Task Force and I had contained it, and nothing should intrude until the Killer made his move and we caught him. It especially wasn't supposed to connect with friends from my "real life."

I was trying to come up with an acceptable answer when Kate picked up an extension. "I didn't say you were one of the ones who found the body," she protested, "just it was probably one of the rafts in your group. I'll bet there isn't more than one group each day. I don't know why Jane thinks it wasn't yours."

"There could be loads of raft trips each weekend during eagle season," Jane interrupted. "The paper would have given a local tie-in if it were Sarah's group."

I cut into the quarrel, irritated yet grateful for the time it had given me to think. "Yeah," I said, then stopped to clear my throat. "It was the people on my trip who found the girl, but we've been asked not to say anything. I'll tell you all about it later when we're cleared to talk, but not now."

"Was it awful?" Kate asked. I thought I detected a slight ring of triumph and wondered how long she'd be telling Jane she'd been right.

"I really can't say anything now, not even to you two. And please don't tell anyone else."

I'm sure they were disappointed, but they agreed, especially after I assured them again that I would tell them everything as soon as I could. When I got off the phone, I went to talk with Harold.

He was sitting at the dining room table, a yellow pad and a map of the Puget Sound region in front of him and several different newspapers spread around. It surprised and delighted me that while I worked I had forgotten he was in the house. Now I realized he had settled into his own work without doing anything to distract me from mine. The only sign he was here had been the dogs' uncharacteristic wanderings between the office and the dining room, where he was.

"You seem to like working without distractions, too," he said, as if reading my thoughts. "Was that call anything I need to know?"

"Mm, yeah, I can think better when it's quiet." I sat down across the table from him. "That was a couple of friends wanting to know if I was involved in finding Nicole. How should I handle such questions?"

"How *did* you handle it?"

I repeated what I'd told Jane and Kate.

"You did fine. Told the truth as far as you could, didn't give anything away, and asked them to keep quiet. I don't see how you could have improved your response, short of an outright lie. Why are you asking me?"

"Well, you're the expert in stuff like this," I said, surprised. "I don't want to lie, but I don't know what I can and can't say, and I don't want to jeopardize anything."

"I'm the crime expert, but you're the expert in running your life. And that includes how you interact with your friends."

I felt miffed. "You mean I shouldn't rely on you?"

"I'll make suggestions whenever my experience might have taught me something you don't think of, like about letting the dogs out last night. And I'll protect you as best I can. But you can't turn over all decisions to me. I've seen too many people lose their sense of self-reliance when they go through something like this. Then it's hard to get it back."

"What do you mean?"

"People who're victimized often feel helpless. They want somebody else to give them better advice than they think they can give themselves. It can be even worse when they're being stalked, because the waiting wears them down. But, you know, except for a couple of areas, you'd do fine without me."

"What if my decisions weren't that good? I've never had this kind of life-and-death situation before."

"You're intelligent, you've kept a series of good jobs for many years, and you're making it in business for yourself. You've adjusted to each new situation as it came along. That's prepared you to adjust to this one as well."

I'm sure I looked doubtful, and Harold interpreted my expression correctly. "Come on, Sarah! Think of the ideas you had at my place yesterday! You applied yourself effectively to a new challenge then. In fact, you seemed to get a kick out of working the puzzle out."

"Yesterday I didn't feel personally threatened."

"Yeah, you *are* a lot more vulnerable now, but you'll be even more vulnerable if you let him short-circuit your thinking."

"I thought part of why you were here was to tell me what to do!" I said.

"Come on," he said again. "You can't stop thinking for yourself just because I'm here. I *am* here, as much as I can be, for you. But in the final analysis, you're still you, and you're still in charge here. Besides, you'd probably have a fit if I did try to tell you what to do. I hate to stereotype, but I've sure noticed a temper under that red hair."

Again, I realized he was right, and even that insight gave me a flash of anger. Then I burst out laughing.

"What's so funny?"

"This whole exchange! It could almost have come from a book about ACOA. Victimization! Self-reliance!"

Before Harold could respond, the doorbell buzzed. As always, the dogs burst into frenzied barking. This gave Harold a chance to say, "I'll slip into the bedroom, but I'll be listening and covering you."

The owner of a small firm for which I'd written several pieces stood at my door with a marked-up copy of his current project in his hand. As soon as I grabbed the dogs and opened the door, he pushed in. He smelled far too strongly of some designer men's cologne I'd encountered once as a scratch 'n sniff while leafing through an *Esquire* in a doctor's office.

"Hi, Sarah. Thought I'd drop these off if you weren't here, and stop in and talk about them if you were. Have a few minutes?"

"Just about that much time," I said. "Come on back to the office."

A friend of mine says people have the faces they deserve by the time they're forty. Generally I feel uncomfortable with that idea, thinking of several nice people with not-so-nice faces. However, this guy's weasely looks seemed to prove the saying. He had always been flirtatious, and lately he'd taken to dropping in much more than I thought necessary. I always made a point of being businesslike with him and keeping everything focused on work. Even if he weren't married, he was mistaken in his conviction that he was charming. And to cap it off, he made fun of my dogs! The only things in his favor were that his projects were somewhat interesting and he always paid his bills on time.

The makeshift bed wasn't visible from the doorway as we passed the bedroom. Neither, I saw with relief, was Harold. The closed closet door, usually open in western Washington's damp climate, told me where he'd gone.

I put the marked draft on the desk and went over it, making sure I understood the changes and corrections. My client stood just a little too close behind me. When I straightened up and turned around, he moved even closer, forcing me to lean against the desk. I held the draft between us.

"You're looking real good, Sarah," he said without any preamble. He was inside my comfort zone, and I didn't like the invasion. I pushed with the hand holding the draft, but he didn't take the hint. "Except today you look a little tired," he continued. "Why don't you take a break and visit with me?"

"Can't. This Port study's urgent, and I've got to keep flat out on it 'til it's done."

"You'd work even better if you took a short break. Tell you what! How about running down to the Antique Sandwich Company for a quick cup of coffee? I could have you back here in twenty minutes."

"Thanks, but I really can't. I've got too much to do."

"Sarah, I've been giving you a lot of business lately. I guess you know that's because I like you."

The old letch! I didn't know anyone still came on quite this badly! "I thought it was because I do good work," I interrupted.

"Yeah, well, that too," he said, backing off a few inches. "But you're a single girl and nice looking. Wouldn't you kind of like a little afternoon delight now and then? No strings?"

I stifled a snort over his hackneyed offer and phrasing. "Not interested. That offer doesn't show much respect for me, for your wife, or even for yourself. And if that's why you bring me work, you might as well take it elsewhere. If you brought it because I do the best work at the best rates, then you'd better stick to business if you want me to keep working for you."

He turned red and puffed up for a moment, then deflated. "Can't blame a guy for trying," he said. "For all I knew, you might want it as much as I did. I'll stick with you for now. I like your work."

I started edging him toward the front door. The dogs usually avoid this client, and Golda had retreated under the dining-room table as soon as she saw who it was. Jesse, however, had gone into the bedroom and was making loud snuffling noises at the louvered closet door.

"Look at old Bozo" the client exclaimed as I ushered him past the bedroom. "You must be hiding someone in the closet. No wonder you don't have time for me."

I looked at him sharply to see if he was serious. He wasn't; he'd just found another way to be annoying. "No such luck," I said. "One of Jesse's toys is in there, not one of mine."

After I pushed him out the door, I locked it behind him and

watched as he started away in his car. Then I burst out laughing. The phone rang just as I called, "Oh, Harold! You can come out of the closet now!" ≠

Chapter 16

I stifled a chuckle about Harold in the closet and picked up the phone. "Ms. Tierney, this is the surveillance team across the street," a peremptory voice said. "Who was that and why didn't we know about him?"

"Now wait a minute!" I said, letting my anger at my obnoxious client and at this pushy person combine and explode. "That was a client, and you didn't know about him because *I* didn't know he was coming. Besides, I would have pressed the alarm for you if I'd needed you." I patted my belt where the alarm was supposed to be and discovered it wasn't there. *Oh, damn! It's still on the dresser*, I thought. Harold watched me from the doorway, and I was sure he hadn't missed that motion or the look on my face.

"I've told Detective Workman what I expect for the day, and I'll tell him about the people who are coming over tonight," I continued with a little less assurance. "To the best of my ability there won't be any surprises, but I can't help it if clients or salespeople drop in."

"Look, ma'am, I'm sorry. We were almost ready to send someone in, just in case . . . ."

"I'm putting you on the speakerphone so Detective Workman can be part of this conversation," I told him, punching the phone button while I continued talking. "I thought Workman was supposed to cover the inside of the house while you people watched the outside. Besides, the Killer isn't likely to walk up to the door and ring the bell. And even if he did, I'm not likely to invite him in."

"What's the problem?" Harold asked.

"I'm watching from across the street, Harold. I got a little worried about that unexpected visitor."

"Sarah's right. We'll tell you what to expect as far as Sarah knows what's coming. For the rest, we're taking care of the inside, and we'll ask for help if we need it."

"Sorry, Harold. There's so much at stake."

"Don't blow your cool. We might have a long wait."

When we hung up, I looked at Harold and grinned. "Well, at least I could handle that client."

"You handled the officer across the street, too. And you didn't even lose that creep's business. Do you have to put up with much of that?"

"Nobody else quite that blatant, at least not for a long time. It can be an unwelcome part of the territory for younger women."

"At least he took no for an answer, but it must be demoralizing."

"Not the way it used to be when I thought I was doing something to provoke it, but it's not my favorite thing. Anyway, I guess you're right. I can pretty much handle what I have to—at least short of physical violence."

Harold gave me a hearty clap on the back. "Good job! Say, while you're already interrupted, let me ask about dinner. I'd be happy to cook, so you can catch up on some of your work."

"Thanks. I'd like that."

"Want anything special?"

"No. I don't even know what food's in the house; I'd meant to go shopping today. Feel free to look for anything you might need in the kitchen or pantry. Or in the bathroom, for that matter."

"You keep food in the *bathroom*?" he asked.

"Of course not. I just meant feel free to look anywhere for anything you might need while you're here."

"Okay, thanks. I'll rummage around and come up with something for dinner. I wouldn't want to cook for a living, but I enjoy it and it'll give me a chance to feel useful while we're waiting."

I realized the vigil was getting to him, too, and he couldn't lose himself in work as I could, or even get exercise playing in the yard with the dogs. Camping out in someone else's home during a stakeout couldn't be invigorating or relaxing. At least he could telephone about leads on newspapers to buy, but how many leads did he have? How was he going to keep himself occupied after he'd finished that? And tonight during the twelve-step reunion group I'd have to cut him off altogether.

"I might as well tell you about the group members now," I offered, while I was thinking about it. "Then you can relay the information so the guys across the street don't have a fit. We start at 6:30 and if everybody comes, we have eight. There's Bert, the seventy-two-year-old man who has the key, and his wife, Anna. He's balding, and what hair he does have is white. Anna has tightly curled gray hair."

"What do they drive?" Harold interrupted.

"Generally a small gold car, a Honda, I think. They might be in a red pickup with a camper on it."

"Okay, go on," Harold said, taking notes.

"Paul is thirty or thirty-one, black, and pudgy. He drives a yellow Rabbit. He doesn't like dogs, so I put up the movable gate and they have to stay in the kitchen while he's here. That's probably good tonight, since it'll keep Jesse from sniffing at the door where you are. Paul's relatively new to the group, so I don't know him as well as the others."

Harold nodded, still writing.

"Then there's Jonathan and Marianne. Jonathan is Chinese-American. Marianne's white, and they're both short and dark-haired. He drives a beat-up blue Volkswagen beetle and she drives a new blue van—some American make, but I don't know which. They might come together in either car or they might come separately.

"Rosalie is a nurse and may be in uniform; she often comes straight from work. She's almost six feet tall, thin, with short brown hair. She has a big old white Chevrolet—late fifties or early sixties. Then there's Sharon. She's small, dark brown hair, and . . . ."

"Is she the one in the picture on the refrigerator?" Harold interrupted again.

"Yeah, the pic with Mt. Rainier behind us. How'd you know it was Sharon?"

"Great detective work," he said. "You expect me to tell you all the secrets I learned in twenty-three years of work and study?"

I looked at him.

"Well, it *is* labeled. It says 'Sharon and Sarah, July 9,' and you're the other person in it. What was the occasion?"

"Hey, a great detective should be able to figure that out!"

Harold grinned at my comeback.

"Okay, I'll tell you. We'd just hiked from Mowich Lake to Knapsack Pass. It's only six thousand feet high, but it was a thousand-foot gain in elevation in two miles and we were pretty proud of ourselves."

"You both look proud—glowing, in fact!"

"That was sweat, not glow! We asked another climber to take the picture as our proof, to show we'd made the climb. Then we both liked the photo so much we had blown up copies made to stick on our refrigerators as incentive for a climb up Rainier next summer."

"It's a great shot of you, and if Sharon's half as pretty as in that picture, she's really something!"

"She is," I said with a twinge of jealousy. "She's a super person, too, and she may finally have found the guy she deserves. Anyway, she drives an ancient midnight-blue Mercedes, polished to within an inch of its life."

I counted mentally. "That's seven. Let me figure out who I left out." I ticked everyone off on my fingers, but couldn't think who I'd forgotten.

"Great Detective say, 'Maybe eighth person is Sarah,'" Harold suggested with a deadpan expression.

"You're absolutely right," I said, laughing. "I'm glad your detecting skills are good for something besides reading captions!"

"We detectives always come through. And now you get back to work while I tell the surveillance teams what to expect. Want to eat about 5:00, so we're all done and cleaned up before the meeting?"

"Sounds good!"

I stopped in the bedroom to clip the alarm onto my belt

before taking the dogs out for another play session, glad Harold hadn't said anything about the alarm. At least I was handling *most* things fairly well.

Work went better than I could have expected, and I was feeling good as I reread the nearly completed first section of the report. I rolled to the desk and picked up the phone to call the library's quick information number for a figure I wasn't sure of.

Harold's voice filled my ear, saying, "Okay, Judy. I won't see you tomorrow, then." My good feelings were frayed around the edges as I hung up. *Too bad this is messing up his love life*, I thought. *Hope he doesn't mind too much.*

By the time Harold called me for dinner, the house smelled wonderful. In rummaging through the freezer, the refrigerator, and the canned goods in the pantry, he'd managed to pull together a feast of baked salmon with lots of onions and lemon, baked squash, and a superb mixture of green beans, onions, and tomatoes.

"The great detective's also a great cook," I said after I'd eaten enough to cut the worst of my hunger. "The salmon's been in the freezer for months. How'd you get it to taste so good?"

"Heloise says 'Thaw frozen fish in milk for fresh taste,' and I read lots of Heloise after Alice and I split. If I was going to take care of myself, I was going to do it as well as I could—and as easily as I could."

"You sure did this well. I'd be ashamed to cook for you after this and yesterday's ratatouille. My mom was a great cook before she started drinking, but somehow I never learned. I'm more into takeout Chinese. Or eating out. Or delivered pizza."

He started to answer, but began coughing instead. By the time I'd pounded on his back and he'd drunk some water and wiped his tears away, the light moment was gone again.

"What startled you?" I asked, moving back to my side of the table.

"The idea of the wrong person getting in here with a pizza!" He tried to lighten up. "Let's wait and go out for pizza when this is all over. Meanwhile, if you're really that bad a cook, I guess I'm elected for the duration."

"I can make do in a pinch," I said, "but as long as we're back to business, what did you hear from the Task Force?"

"Not much. Tramp got a good chunk out of the guy's leg, and we'll be able to match tissues if we ever get a suspect. Also, anybody who tries to get medical treatment for a dog bite is going to have a hard time in western Washington."

"Too bad Tramp didn't have rabies!" I commented.

"Yeah," he said with a short laugh. "That'd be what the Killer deserves."

"What else?"

"They haven't found any leads about the Rimbaud murders. There's nothing at the scene and their house is isolated, so nobody saw anything. The little girl didn't know anything either."

"They had to question Angie?"

"I'm sure they were as gentle as possible. She's doing as well as can be expected with her grandparents, but that's a hell of a thing for a kid that age to have to face. At least he didn't get her." He paused, then continued the report, "Also, there's been no activity concerning the two older women from Panorama City."

"I thought they went away!"

"They did, but we've staked out their home and tapped their phone—which is being answered with call forwarding by a cop who sounds just like a little old lady."

"That's funny, 'cause those two don't sound at all like little old ladies," I protested. "They're vigorous types who were as agile as any of us."

"Stereotyping again! Let's hope the Killer doesn't know that."

"Anyway, it sounds like the Task Force is still trying to get the Killer on a lot of different fronts, not just here."

"We are," he said. "You may be our best bet, but I'd like it a lot better if we took him down someplace else."

"So would I! Did I hear you right about dozens of people working on this?"

"Yeah, more than fifty from various law enforcement agencies. We've been criticized for not trying harder because the victims were 'just prostitutes,' but we're doing everything we can to get this guy. And the Tacoma police involvement you saw is extra, adjusting to the situation until we could get enough Task Force people down here."

"Seems to me you're trying pretty hard," I said, glancing at my watch. I stood and took the empty salmon platter. "I keep asking everybody not to come early, but sometimes they do, anyway. I'd better get things cleared away. I should have just enough time to do the dishes before they get here."

"You wash, I'll dry," Harold said, starting to clear.

"But you cooked!" I protested.

"Doesn't matter. We'll finish more quickly if we work together. And Sarah, I've been thinking about your group. I know enough about twelve-step programs to know everything's supposed to be confidential. As long as you're wearing the alarm and don't let anybody in except long-time group members, it's probably safe for me to be where I can't hear the conversation unless you call me. What do you suggest?"

I was relieved that Harold thought of the need for privacy without my having to tell him.

"How about in the bedroom with the door closed?" I suggested. "It'll be cool, since I've sealed off the heat duct, but it's the only place on this floor where you wouldn't hear everything. And you'd have to leave the lights off. I'm notorious for turning out the lights when I leave a room."

"Sure, fine way to treat a friend! Just throw me into the cold and dark! I'll probably take a nap, in that case."

"You don't snore, do you?" I asked in mock alarm.

"I don't think so. Nobody's ever complained, and you didn't hear me snoring last night, did you?"

"I wouldn't have heard the last trump last night! And how many people have had a chance to complain anyway?"

"I'll take the fifth on that question," he said. "Just wake me when it's all over—or earlier, if you need to! I sleep lightly."

I stopped washing and turned to look at him. "Harold, I appreciate your understanding about staying out of earshot. I'm not going to ACOA anymore, but this twelve-step group is a logical progression for me. It's one of the most important things in my life."

"I figured that from the way you talk about it. What makes it so important?"

"The honesty and openness. We're all recovering from one problem or another and most of us share freely. We can do that only because we respect each other's confidentiality. And then when we make a promise to one another, we take it seriously."

"That's good. We all need people with whom we can be totally honest." He started to say something else, but stopped himself.

"You don't need to caution me. Even with them, I won't tell the *whole* truth tonight."

He grinned; I had interpreted him correctly.

I let the water out of the drain and rinsed the sink while he dried and put away the last pan, then hung the towel to dry. "Great timing!" I said. "It's 6:15 and you should have time to get settled before everybody gets here." ≠

Chapter 17

I was glad we finished when we did. Harold waited with the bedroom door ajar—and his gun ready, I was sure—until Rosalie arrived at 6:20, with Bert right on her heels. I was aware of the bedroom door closing just before I got caught up in welcoming them.

"Anna's a little under the weather tonight, so she stayed home," Bert explained, "but she told me what to say about her. Here, I'll do that," he said, taking the matches from me and bending over with great effort to get the fire started. I knew he was bothered by arthritis, and he seemed to move even more stiffly than usual tonight.

I let Marianne and Jonathan in, while Rosalie moved the folding gate and set it up to keep the dogs in the kitchen so Paul wouldn't be upset; he always complained if Jesse and Golda were still loose when he arrived. Uncharacteristically, Paul was a few minutes early. He looked as handsome and bland as ever as he sat next to Rosalie on the sofa, but he winced when he crossed his legs. "Fell down jogging in the rain last night," he said. "I've talked so much about losing weight I thought it was time I did something about it."

We all chatted as we waited for Sharon. After several minutes, I looked at my watch and said, "It's 6:40. We'd better get started. As far as I know, Sharon's coming. At least, she didn't say otherwise when she dropped by last night, and she didn't call."

Just as we finished the Serenity Prayer, the doorbell buzzed. "Sorry I'm late," Sharon said as I let her in. "Hugh and I were on the phone and didn't notice the time. How come the door's locked?"

"Oh, force of habit," I answered, locking it again before giving her a hug. "Hang up your coat and have a seat."

Our meeting followed its usual format of each of us sharing what had been happening and telling how we felt about it, without any "crosstalk." I found it soothing each week to talk without interruption or advice. As I listened to the others, I felt more "normal" and relaxed than at any other time since finding Nicole's body.

I hadn't thought of what I was going to say when my turn came, so I had to stumble through it. "There's some pretty heavy stuff going on in my life, but I can't talk about it yet," I said. "And I'll have to ask you not to say anything at all about this to anyone outside the group. You know I went on an eagle watching trip, but you probably don't know my group found the girl who was murdered." Sharon jerked her head up at that, and I thought she seemed a bit flushed.

"We've all been asked not to talk about it, so I'll just say I'm feeling sad, especially because the girl, Nicole Turner, looked a lot like Marilu." This group had heard about Marilu before, so I could speak a kind of shorthand, without having to explain everything. "I guess I still have to deal with some things I thought I'd taken care of. I'll tell you more when I can."

I'd only recently learned to share everything with these friends, so I didn't feel right about condensing my account. I hoped my instincts were correct in telling me to say as little as possible to everyone.

Sharon, settled at Bert's left, spoke about her concerns after everyone else had finished. "I know all I ever talk about any more is Hugh," she said. "He's been down with a bad cold yesterday and today. He's grouchy and discouraged. He doesn't want me to get sick, so he won't let me see him, not even to bring him chicken soup," she said with a grimace. "We've just talked on the phone, and I miss him."

Knowing Sharon, we waited for her to continue. "I'm feeling more and more this relationship is good for both of us, but I wish I could get him to go to twelve-step meetings with me. I think he'd understand me better and it might help him work on some issues too. He's just hinted at his background, but I know his parents were really poor and didn't want him to get an education. He had to work his way through high school and college and his family are still upset with him. And then he taught high school before going to law school, which is why he's so interested in education. Oh, and I want him to get well quick so I can see him," she finished up in a rush.

Clasping hands, we stood in a circle and finished the full group session.

"Mid-month. Time to change partners," Paul reminded us as the circle broke up.

"I want Sarah!" Sharon called, embarrassing and pleasing me at the same time. Sometimes Sharon seemed more like six than thirty-six!

"Bummer!" Paul said. "It's my turn for Sarah. I have a book I want to discuss with her."

Sharon stuck out her tongue at him, still acting like a six-year old. "Too bad! You can have her next time. I've got stuff I need her for now."

Everyone paired up for the next month to discuss concerns in more depth and to arrange for frequent telephone contact.

"Can I talk with you after group?" Sharon asked.

"Sure. Just stick around after the others leave."

"Nobody's going anywhere until I get hugged!" Rosalie demanded. I knew how she felt! We traded hugs all around, then everyone but Sharon put on their coats and left. I noticed Paul was limping as he went and I called out, "Paul! Sure hope your leg's better soon and you're back to jogging."

"Okay if I let the dogs in here?" Sharon asked as soon as Paul was out the door and I had locked it behind him.

"Of course."

I poked the fire as Jesse came bounding out of the kitchen. He greeted Sharon, then ran to the bedroom door and sniffed. Golda walked straight to Sharon, then settled down for Sharon to pet.

"What's with Jesse?" Sharon asked.

"Oh, he got so obnoxious with one of his toys that I shut it in there."

"I don't mind playing with him," Sharon offered, getting up.

"No!" I said. "Thanks, but he's going to have to learn to do without it."

Sharon settled back and called Jesse, who left off sniffing at the door and came to lie in front of the fire. I relaxed in my chair.

"I'm so sorry I babbled on about Hugh and me yesterday and didn't even ask about the float trip," Sharon apologized. "I never dreamed the police were here for anything that serious. I should have paid more attention to you. I feel awful!"

"It's okay, Sharon. I couldn't talk about it anyway, and I enjoyed hearing about Hugh. Your Saturday was a whole lot nicer than mine! I still can't talk about it, so don't feel bad."

"Well, I hope those officers stayed here with you last night," she said. "You shouldn't be alone after something like that. In fact, I could stay over tonight if you'd like me to," she offered.

"That's sweet, but Shadow and Moondance would probably boycott—or boycat—their litter box if you didn't come home."

Sharon groaned. "You must be okay if you can say things like that! Your puns are always awful, but that's the worst yet. Bad, really bad."

I grinned. "Actually, I am all right, now. It was a shock, but it's over. The officers stayed for a while, then my Uncle John showed up unexpectedly and spent the night."

"I didn't know you had an uncle around here!"

"Well, he's not from around here, but he had a layover at SeaTac Airport and stopped to see me. We stayed up late talking, and that helped." I thought I was getting over lying so easily. And to my best friend and group partner! Well at least I'm lying for a good reason! "I'd just as soon talk about something else, but I appreciate your offer."

"Okay, Sarah. You call me if you need anything at all."

"I will. But what did you want to talk with me about?"

Her pretty face crumpled a bit and she kneaded Golda's ears so vigorously Golda whimpered. "Oh, it's worse than I told the group! Hugh was absolutely wonderful on Saturday, like I told you. But then he told me not to call him yesterday so he could sleep all day. He called me last night, but he spoke for only a few minutes and was in a foul mood. I told you he had a temper and he gets real moody, but not like this."

She looked into the dying fire as she continued. "I didn't sleep well, and had a lousy day at work. Don't think I was as helpful as I should have been to a new client, a woman who'd been beaten up again by her boyfriend and finally decided to press charges. Then I was on the phone with Hugh from the time I got home until I came here tonight, and he was downright weird! He apologized, but then he started saying he was no good for me and we should break up!"

"Hey, Sharon," I said, getting up to hug her again and pat her on the back, "he's sick and probably just feeling rotten. What did you say?"

"I sort of tried to laugh and said he couldn't get rid of me that easily, and we should talk about it in person when he was well. Of course all kinds of things were running through my head, like maybe he was bored with me."

"You don't really believe that, do you?"

"Well, maybe not, but who's rational with that kind of stuff? Anyway, he apologized again and said he loved me. And then he asked about this group and whether he could come when he got well! He especially wanted to know about group partners. I told him how it works with you and me and how much you've helped me. Then I said the group had to vote before we took any new people."

"Did he take that okay?"

"No, he got mad again and said maybe he should set up a meeting separate from the group; maybe that would be better for him. I saw I was going to be late and told him I had to go. He did another flip-flop and said he was sorry he yelled at me. Then he said again he loved me. I'm supposed to call when I get home, but I don't know what to say."

"That is tough! No wonder you don't want to go home yet."

Sharon had been stroking Golda throughout the conversation, and now she leaned forward to give her a quick hug. Jesse couldn't take being ignored any longer, and came to me for some affection. I rubbed behind his ears as I thought out what to say.

"If I understand you right," I said, "he's never acted this way before. That could mean it's just the cold talking. For now maybe you should assume he's just sick. If he's still this way after he's well, you can worry."

"That makes a lot of sense, Sarah, but maybe it's more than a cold and he needs to get to a doctor. Or maybe he really does want to break up."

"You can suggest the doctor in another day or so if it seems warranted. Right now he doesn't seem to want mothering."

The phone rang, and I excused myself to take it in the kitchen.

"Hi, Sarah? This is Frank Randall. I got kind of worried when you didn't call to tell me what Detective Workman said. And Dad's being really obnoxious, wanting to know what's up, but I don't want to tell him anything. Also, there's something I should maybe tell Detective Workman. I don't know if it's important, and I want to talk with you first. Is everything okay?"

I'd forgotten all about Frank, and I hadn't even told Harold about his call! Poor kid. I owed him. "Yeah, Frank, I'm doing fine. Can't talk right now because a friend's here. Can I call you back in a little bit?"

"Sure, Sarah. Any time before 11:00."

"Who's Frank?" Sharon asked as soon as I put down the phone.

"Just a friend."

"A new male friend?"

"A very young male friend."

"What's wrong with younger men?" she said with a grin.

"Sharon, he's sixteen years old!"

"That is a little too young. I just wish you had somebody as wonderful as Hugh usually is. Maybe he has a friend he can fix you up with."

"I'd enjoy that, but first let's see how soon this mood of his is going to straighten out. You go on home and call him. I'll be fine."

She got her coat, then turned at the door. "Oh, Sarah, I forgot! Even if he gets over the cold soon, I don't think Hugh's going to be up for Zoolights before this weekend. I'll give you a call after I talk with him tomorrow. Maybe we can plan for later this week, but you might want to think about going with someone else."

"I might even skip it this year. I've got lots of work."

"Oh, no you don't! It's even better than last year, and you've got to go. And go early so you'll have plenty of time to see everything and won't be too crowded. You have to! Promise?"

"I will if I can," I promised.

Sharon gave me a tight hug, then went out the door.

As soon as she left, I thought about waking Harold but decided to let him sleep if he could. I looked up Frank's number. Walt answered on the first ring. I identified myself and asked for Frank, but Walt chattered at me.

"I want to know what in hell is going on! Frank says you and that detective still don't want us to say anything, but I don't even know what we're not supposed to talk about—and who we're not supposed to talk to! And why didn't the detective contact us directly?"

Oh, God help me! Now I have to explain to Walt! "There isn't anything specific, Walt. Workman just told me it was better if nobody said anything at all. Then whoever did it won't know whether anybody does or doesn't know something. The only reason I said anything to Frank is because he called last night. It probably isn't important enough for the detectives to contact everybody."

I could hear Frank's voice in the background, "Dad, that's for me. How about letting me have the phone!"

"I think it's damned inconsiderate to expect us not to talk about this even now," Walt bulled on. "Haven't they heard about freedom of speech?"

"Oh, for Pete's sake, Walt! We're talking about someone who killed this girl. I think we can keep quiet for a few days if it'll help catch him."

"Dad, give me the phone," Frank insisted, louder this time.

"I'd like to speak to Frank," I also insisted.

"Oh, all right. Here!"

"And how about some privacy, too?" I heard Frank say.

A door slammed, and Frank spoke into the phone. "Sarah, I'm sorry. Dad's flipping out about this. He makes such a big deal of things! He's driving me crazy, but don't let it bother you."

"It's okay, Frank. I should have called back when I heard from Detective Workman, but it was pretty late, and then I was just busy and forgot about it today. There isn't really anything else to report, anyway."

"But Sarah, there is! You know that family that was with us

on the raft . . . ."

Frank's made the connection, I thought. I wonder if anyone else has. I thought I heard someone pick up an extension. Harold? Walt? Someone else? I broke in, "Frank! Don't say anything at all, please. Not to anybody. And don't talk about it on the phone, either, not even to me."

"Then I need to see you! I tried to reach Detective Workman, but he wasn't there and I didn't want to talk with anyone else. I'm not going to tell anybody but you or him!"

"Can it wait 'til tomorrow? I really can't see you now, but I might be able to reach Workman tonight if I have to."

"Oh, it can wait. I read the paper after I came home from work and thought of something. It's probably not real important anyway." He sounded discouraged, and young.

"Maybe we could meet tomorrow. Then you can tell me your idea and we can figure out whether to tell Workman."

"Not 'til after work. I have a job after school and don't get off until 5:00. Tell you what," he said. "Why don't we go to Zoolights? It's really neat, and we can talk then."

"That's funny! The friend who was just here was telling me I had to see Zoolights this year. She's supposed to call tomorrow to tell me if her boyfriend's well enough to go later this week."

"You can go more than once! And my girlfriend and I have both been volunteering at the zoo, so I have a lot of free tickets and can tell you some of the behind-the-scenes stuff. My girl and I went last night, and we loved it. I'll pick you up about 6:00 and we'll have time to talk and see everything too."

"I can't promise right now, Frank. Can you call me back tomorrow, after 3:00, and I'll let you know?"

"Okay, Sarah. But if you can't go, we still have to meet. I need your opinion."

It was almost 9:00 when I got off the phone. I let the dogs out, wondering for a moment if I should put them on the leashes. I've got to trust the surveillance teams not to let anybody close, I thought. I can't always be suspicious.

I checked the doors, made sure the fire was out, and closed the damper. Could I get my nightgown without waking Harold? I opened the door. In the dim light from the door, I saw Harold sit up, fully dressed, gun in hand.

"I hoped I wouldn't wake you," I said. "Everyone's gone, but there's no need to get up. We could both use an early night."

"I'll get back to sleep. Thanks, though. Didn't I hear the phone ring?"

I sat on the bed and told him about my conversations with Walt and Frank—and about someone coming on the line. "You didn't pick up the extension in here, did you?"

"No. I wouldn't do that unless we'd agreed to it ahead of time. Walt sure sounds like a winner, though, and it might have been him. How'd such a nice kid come from that father?"

"Don't know, but evidently Frank's made the connection between the Rimbaud murders and the Killer. I'm pretty sure that's what he wants to tell you. Walt hasn't figured it out or he would have bragged about it to me. I hated to put Frank off, but I figured that would give us time to figure out what to do and what to tell him about going to Zoolights."

"As far as we know, the Killer hasn't been back since he tried to poison the dogs," Harold mused. "If he hasn't tried something by tomorrow night, we might try to force his hand by having you go out. Maybe he'll try to break in while you're gone. Or he might even try to follow you to the zoo."

"There are too many ways out of here for him to follow me," I objected.

"There aren't as many ways as you think. The Team found two vantage points covering all possible ways to get away from here by car. They haven't seen anyone else watching those points, but it's possible."

"Even so, he wouldn't know what I'd be in. I mean, he might know my car, but he wouldn't know Frank's car."

"You're right, he wouldn't know the car and it would be dark so he wouldn't see you. Let's keep Zoolights with Frank as an option, and you can decide tomorrow. It might be a good way to smoke the Killer out." ≠

Chapter 18

When the radio came on at 6:30, I had no trouble getting up. I said good morning to Harold—who lay tangled in the blankets on his chair/bed—grabbed underwear and a sweatsuit, and dressed in the bathroom.

I let the dogs out, went to the bottom of the basement stairs, and switched the light on to locate the exercise bike. As soon as I saw it, I turned the light back off. Going straight to the bike in the dark, oblivious to any creatures possibly lurking in the basement, I wrestled it up the stairs. I was breathing hard as I hauled it through the kitchen. Harold stood at the sink in his robe, measuring out coffee.

"What's going on?" he asked.

"Exercise. You can ride the bike while I do my exercise tape, or you can do the tape with me, or you can wait in another room, but you can't just watch, 'cause I'd get embarrassed. And I've got to do something more physical than just playing with the dogs."

Harold grinned, his teeth showing white in his unshaven face. "I'll ride."

"What's so funny?" I asked.

"Looks like you're back in charge of yourself. No asking what you can or can't do, just figuring how to make the best of the situation. Are we exercising right now?"

"Yep. Before showers and before breakfast. Maybe some fruit and a glass of water, or hot water with lemon, if you want."

"No, I'll just get the coffee going so it'll be ready when we're done."

By the time I'd fed the dogs, positioned the bike, and had the exercise tape ready to go, Harold had started the coffee and changed to khaki pants and a V-neck tee shirt. Hairy chest, too, I noticed. Incipient love handles. Big, but solid.

He looked at the bike and laughed. "I should have known you'd have a bookstand on this. Wait a minute while I adjust the seat and get something to read while I ride. Can't watch the kiddie cartoons if you're using the VCR."

We exercised in companionable silence—at least, no noise other than the music and instructions of the woman on the tape and the whir of the bicycle. My body felt good as I moved with the music; I was graceful enough, didn't jiggle too much, and managed not to twist anything I shouldn't twist. I'd worked up a good sweat by the end of the thirty-minute intermediate tape, and Harold, who had pedaled the whole time, almost fell off the bike.

"Would you believe twenty miles?" he gasped. "And I zipped through fifty pages of Moby-Dick."

I just looked at him while the tape rewound.

"Didn't think you'd buy that. How about eight and one-half miles and three pages of Beloved?"

"That I might believe!"

"Hey, it's not easy riding when you haven't been on a bike for a while—and I'm not used to reading while I ride!"

"You don't have to make excuses to me, tough guy. If you'll notice, there's less than a hundred miles on the thing, and I've had it a couple of years. You want the shower first?"

"You go ahead. Want to do devotions together afterwards?"

"Yeah, I guess. Right before breakfast?"

"Sure."

My thoughts weren't exactly reverent as I watched Harold's thick black lashes move while he read Morning Prayer. His religiosity didn't seem to get in the way of his brain, but it wasn't anything I was used to. Nonetheless, this was a good, centering way to start the day. We had fruit and cereal again, and coffee, of course, for breakfast. Nothing new was in the paper about either the Killer or the Rimbauds.

Even after playing with the dogs outside in the crisp, cold, clear morning, I was at work by 8:45. The morning went well. I was refreshed from the sleep, the exercise, the devotions. A sense of safety and solidity seemed to radiate from Harold's quiet presence in the other room. The Port study hummed along, calls came in verifying I had gotten two jobs I'd bid, and a check came in the mail to offset some of the bills that also came.

The door buzzer shattered my peace just before noon. The dogs burst into frenzies of barking. I moved from the computer to the front door as Harold rose from his seat at the dining room table.

My caller wore a skirt and was bundled into a dirty orange jacket. At first I didn't recognize the squat figure with her face shadowed by a hood of wispy fake brown fur. I unlocked the door, glad Harold was around the corner with his gun ready.

"Have you seen my cat?" a rusty voice squawked as soon as the door was open.

"What did you say?" I stammered, recognizing the woman I had characterized as the neighborhood grouch.

"I live next door. My gray cat's been gone since Sunday. Have you seen him?"

"No, I'm sorry," I lied, with a pang. "I've seen a gray cat around the neighborhood, but not recently. Have you checked the other neighbors?"

"You're the only one home during the day. Besides, I got to tell you about something funny going on."

Oh, boy, I thought. The eyes and ears of the neighborhood at work. "Why don't you come in? It's cold out there."

"I've got to look for Gremlin. But there was someone in my little grove of trees this morning, watching your place through binoculars."

My heart jumped; I hoped Harold was hearing everything. "I think I need to hear this," I said. "Please come in, so I'm not heating the whole outdoors." I held onto the dogs' collars and she came in as far as the living room. Harold wasn't in sight.

"I won't sit down," she protested. "It's just when I got to thinking, I figured I'd better tell you."

I looked at her but didn't say anything. She pulled her hood down. Her face was gray with innumerable layers of dead skin cells and her short gray hair unkempt, but I saw the intelligence I'd noticed before behind the suspicious look in her eyes.

"Look, you're not a bad neighbor," she said. "You keep those dogs fenced in and they don't bark much, but they went wild Sunday evening. Then you had a police car here on Sunday night for a long time and you had other people here real late—and it looks like you had a new boyfriend stay overnight."

Obviously she kept tabs on everything in the neighborhood. I wondered if we'd fooled her with the surveillance teams. "A minor problem, no big deal," I said, "but it was my uncle, not a boyfriend, who stayed."

She didn't look as though she believed me, but she continued. "Anyway, I was out for a while yesterday and there was no problem with your usual Monday night group, so I forgot about it 'til this morning. It wasn't really light yet when I opened the back door about 7:45 to see if Gremlin was back. He never stays away this long. I saw something in the middle of the grove. Can't be too careful, living alone, so I got my pistol and went out. When I got close I said, 'get out of my yard,' and he took off like a bat out of hell. He went through my yard and jumped the fence into the yard next door. I think he ran through that yard and the next one and hit the cross street."

"What did he look like?"

"I couldn't tell. Kind of runty, and he was wearing a blue jacket with a hood. He ran awkwardly, so I thought he might have been standing there a long time."

"I think I know who it might be," I said. "If I get the police to investigate, will you show them where he was?"

She gave a short, surprising laugh. "Yeah, sure, I'll show the police. And look, if an old boyfriend's jealous of the new one, get a restraining order. I had to do that with my ex-husband once."

She brushed off my thanks and left to look for her cat. Harold came out of my office, looking sober.

"Maybe it's working," he said. "I'll call the Task Force."

"Yeah," I said, shuddering. "Maybe it is."

He relayed the information to the Task Force, telling them that the yards evidently hid a way of getting in we hadn't known was there. He also told them that my neighbor thought the intruder was an old boyfriend, and asked them to send someone to look for evidence. "While you're out there, let us know what he's likely to have seen. Would he know I'm here, or know the surveillance teams are there?"

"Does that bother you?" I asked when he got off the phone.

"What?"

"Asking someone else to look for evidence instead of walking out there and doing it?"

"Yeah, it bothers me. I like to look at the scene myself. And I'm used to a lot more active role in investigations, but this has to look like your neighbor called in the Tacoma police, just in case the Killer is watching."

"Doing pretty well on not complaining," I commented.

He grinned. "It's like my grandmother used to say, 'No use to moan and groan about it. Doesn't do a whit of good and only makes an awful noise around the house.'"

"I'll try to remember that."

"You ready for me to fix lunch?" he asked.

"Sure. How about my helping?"

Harold put me to work on a tossed green salad while he made sandwiches. I wondered how we were doing for food, and whether I'd have to go shopping soon. I had visions of me pushing a cart through Albertson's at the head of a small parade of undercover cops.

The sandwiches—an odd combination of tuna, onions, and vinegar Harold mixed up—shouldn't have tasted good, but they did. We finished up with fruit and coffee, then I brought our conversation away from Harold's search for a newspaper he could buy and back to the search for the Killer.

"I've been feeling as though we can't do anything but wait, but that's not really so, is it?" I asked him.

"How do you mean?"

"Well, we talked out everything we knew on Sunday, but now we have some information we didn't have then and maybe things fit together in a new way. You told me you don't look for clues, but for evidence, and this isn't exactly evidence. But it's more than nothing, too. I think you called the bits and pieces leads?"

"Sure, maybe they can lead us somewhere. I'd like to hear what you think we've learned since Sunday and where it takes us."

I looked to see if he was patronizing me. If so, he didn't show it; his face was serious and he seemed focused on what I was trying to puzzle out.

"Okay, but I'm talking as I think to maybe speed up the process. You and the rest of the Task Force may have already thought of everything I bring up, but at least I'll feel like I'm doing something."

"You talk, I'll take notes, and I'll speak up if I can add anything or have any questions." He got a tablet and pencil from the papers he had cleared off the table for lunch.

I felt as though I were giving a formal statement, as when I first talked with Harold in the police station. Although I had some of the same nervousness, I decided that was all right. At least this time Harold knew I was on the same side he was.

"Okay," I said. "We now know from two witnesses he's small, 'runty.' That is, if we assume the person who hit Maddy at the motel and this morning's watcher are the same person and he's the Killer. We don't know just how small, though. Anyway, his size could have a lot to do with how and why he chooses his victims."

Harold wrote a heading of "New Info" and jotted "small size confirmed" under it.

"This next idea isn't new since Sunday, but nobody knew it until I met Nicole Friday night and we didn't really do anything with it." He nodded at me to continue. "She said 'He told me to stay in the car.' Although she could have meant that loosely, I'm sure he was driving a car, or at most a small pickup or small van. That is, he wasn't driving a big truck."

Harold made more notes on his pad.

"I was trying to figure who might go between here and Highway 20 fairly regularly, and thought of a long-distance hauler, a logging trucker, or a delivery truck driver."

"Yeah," Harold interjected. "One of the theories we've been checking out is the guy's a trucker who could pick up a prostitute at a truck stop or a strip mall without anyone thinking anything of it. And a trucker could drive all over, day or night."

I shook my head. "But that doesn't fit any more. Most truckers aren't particularly little, especially if they have to do any loading or unloading. And from the sound of it, the man who was with Nicole on Friday wasn't driving a big truck. Also, his voice isn't a street voice, or even lower middle-class. He's educated, and most truckers I've heard don't have educated voices. So I thought about who else might travel between here and that area."

Harold looked up. "And?"

"And I thought maybe a salesman or repair man. More likely a salesman than a repair man, for two reasons. First, you want immediate service if you call repair, so you wouldn't call anyone who would take several hours to get there. And second, the educated voice would be more important in sales than in repair. Maybe someone working with computers or office machines. I see him as probably wearing a suit. It fits with the voice and the car, and might seem less threatening to street prostitutes who're uneasy about the Killer."

"That might also fit with the neckties," Harold added.

"What neckties?"

"Most or all of the victims were strangled with ties. We haven't let that out. It's one way we could tell if we had the real Killer or a confessor."

"You didn't tell me that!"

"I wasn't deliberately keeping it from you. I think I've just disciplined myself not to discuss some things with anybody."

"Well, who'd be most likely to have neckties, anyway?" I asked.

"Fathers," Harold responded.

I looked at him a moment before I burst out laughing.

"Okay, but even if he's a father, he's still most likely to be a father who wears a suit," I said, bringing us back to the business at hand. "I couldn't think of what other kinds of businessmen would travel this circuit regularly. I mean, I considered attorneys or accountants, but it didn't seem as likely they'd travel much around several counties. Most government officials would either be statewide and come from Olympia or cover just one county. And even for computers or office machines, it seems more likely someone would come from Seattle or Redmond than Tacoma; Tacoma's just too far. On the other hand, there must be hundreds of occupations I've never even heard of."

"I think you're on to something," Harold said, "but you don't have to have all the details worked out. We can pass the ideas on to the Task Force and let them work on what kind of person it might be and how to track him."

I noticed my finger was circling my left thumb, so I put both hands on the table and clasped them. "My last idea is someone who has family up there, maybe elderly parents he visits frequently. Most people would dress casually when visiting family, but not if the family is super-formal—or if he's trying to impress them with reaching a higher status than they did. I'm thinking about some of the stories I heard in ACOA about children trying to earn their parents' approval. It can't be done, but they keep trying."

"That might be a really perceptive idea."

"I'm afraid that's all," I said. "We don't have any hard evidence to support these suggestions, but maybe they're worth checking out—if they can be checked out. And I thought maybe nobody else had thought of them."

"Some are new, to me at least, and they make sense. Let's see what happens when the Task Force chews on them awhile," he added.

I cleaned up from lunch as he phoned the Task Force, then I cleaned up the poop in the back yard and played again with the dogs. Even with throwing the ball for the dogs, I was starting to feel claustrophobic. I wondered how Harold was dealing with being cooped up. Before I got back to work I noticed activity in my next-door neighbor's yard, indicating the search for hard evidence continued apace.

Sharon called about 2:15. "Hi, Sarah, you were right. I think it was just the cold that made Hugh so grouchy. He was a dear when I called him last night, and today he's feeling a lot better. He's not up to promising anything for Zoolights, though. It'll depend on how he feels later in the week and on the weather."

"In that case, why don't I go with another friend tonight? I can meet Hugh some other time. And my friend and I will go early, as you suggested. How does 6:00 sound?" I asked with mock formality.

"That's great," she said. "I'm glad you've finally learned to take my advice. You have fun."

"I will. Thanks for calling."

I stretched and wandered into the living room. Harold was drowsing in the recliner, a dog on either side and Toni Morrison's Beloved in his lap. He looked up at me.

"That was Sharon. Her boyfriend's better, but may not be up to Zoolights this week. I told her I might go tonight."

"And?" he questioned when I paused too long.

"And I want to go, unless it would be too much of a problem for the Task Force." I started giving him reasons why I should go. "Last night you said my going out might help smoke out the Killer. I can talk with Frank here if I have to, but I'm getting a little stir crazy knowing I can't go out. It's probably even worse for you, but I can't do anything about that."

"You don't need my permission," he said. "We can arrange coverage. Just tell Frank to come to the door when he picks you up. I'll talk with him before you go."

"Yes, Dad."

He grinned. "Sounds like that, doesn't it? I just mean you're right about not telling him anything on the phone. He's a good, solid, kid and I trust his discretion, but I don't trust his father. You can't even tell Frank I'm here until he gets here. Then I'd better explain what's up."

"I wish you could go, too. Will you be okay?"

"I'm quite comfortable here except for the tension and a touch of cabin fever. I'd like to get out, but that can't be helped."

"Frank won't be in any danger, will he?"

"You should both be safe away from here. We'll have undercover agents following you, though, just in case. To tell the truth, I'm glad you want to go out."

"Bored with me already, huh?"

"No. But I'd sure like to catch the Killer and get this whole thing over with!"

"And you think my going out might speed things up?"

"Maybe. We don't know what he was watching for this morning, or what he saw. He might try to get in the house so he could be waiting for you, or he might make another attempt on the dogs . . . ." He broke off at the look on my face. "Come on, Sarah. You know I'll keep them in and not let anything happen to them."

"I know, but that seemed like such a real possibility, while the threat to me still doesn't seem real at all."

"It is real, Sarah. Believe it. But I don't think he'd try something away from here. His whole method has been secretive and non-bloody, except for the attack at the motel. And that probably was just because Maddy startled him. He's strangled every victim we know about, including the Rimbauds. He's not likely to try to run you down with a car or attack you in a crowd. And while he probably searched your car, the guys said there was no sabotage. If he used a gun, he could get you here as easily as anywhere else."

"That's a comforting thought!"

"Thought you'd like it. Actually, I think a gun's pretty unlikely—here or anywhere else. But I'd love it if he tried to get in here while you're gone. I'll be waiting, and the surveillance teams are ready for him."

In a small voice I said, "Somehow the threat to you seems real, too. I don't like the idea of leaving you here alone to face the Killer."

"I'm trained for it, I have my gun, and I'll have your alarm, since it wouldn't help you away from here. To tell the truth, I'm not worried about my safety, although I'll be careful. How about a light dinner around 5:00?" he said, changing the topic. "And we can have something else when you get home if we're hungry then."

He was telling me he knew his business and I should let him do it, just as he had when I first protested about his volunteering to stay with me. Again, I knew better than to argue. He had to make his own decisions, just as I had to make mine. ≠

Chapter 19

The buzzer sounded promptly at 6:00. I went to the door with the dogs while Harold waited around the corner, ready in case it wasn't Frank. Since I've always hated guns and swore I'd never let one in my house, it seemed odd I could accept his gun so easily.

Frank was more neatly dressed than he'd been on Sunday and seemed about to explode with energy. As soon as I locked the door behind him, he dropped to one knee and started fussing over the dogs. "Oh, cool," he said as Golda licked his face and Jesse beat his big wagging tail against Frank's back. Frank looked up, eyes shining, just as Harold walked around the corner. The boy's eyes widened and he stood up. "Detective Workman! What are you doing here?"

"I'm about to explain, Frank."

"I've got something for you, first," Frank said, stumbling over the words in his excitement. "Two people were killed in Gig Harbor on Sunday, and I think it might be connected. They were on our raft!"

"That's a good deduction, and you're right. But we already know about it." Frank's face fell. "That's part of why I'm here," Harold continued. "Take off your coat and have a seat. Then I'll tell you the rest."

I could see Frank taking in the situation as Harold filled him in.

"So Sarah's in danger because she stayed at the Meeting Ground, but because we stayed someplace else Dad and I aren't?"

"That's right, and because the leak evidently specified a woman was helping."

"So why hasn't he done anything since he tried to kill the dogs?"

"We just wish we knew. Of course he might have planned to do something this morning, but the neighbor stopped him. There's no way we can second-guess him. We don't know anything about him, and this is the closest we've come to a break on the case. It's a slim lead, but it is a lead."

"So you two just sit here and wait? Aren't you supposed to do something to catch him?" Frank asked.

Harold seemed stung by the implied criticism. "Yeah, we think, and we pass on whatever ideas we come up with, and then we just wait, but the rest of the Task Force is continuing to check out every lead we've ever gotten. Nothing else has worked yet, and this is one more way to try to catch him."

"'They also serve who only sit and wait,'" I put in, eager to defend Harold.

"That's 'who only stand and wait,'" Harold corrected me.

"Comfort ought to be worth something," I told him. It was dumb, but both of us laughed.

Frank switched his gaze between Harold and me as we talked, like a tennis spectator. I thought I saw a flash of awareness in Frank's face, and he said, "Hey, cut the comedy act and I'll back off. I guess somebody's got to watch the trap once it's baited."

"You got it, pal," Harold said. "And the best way you can help right now is to get Sarah out of here for a while before she goes stir crazy. Several undercover cops will follow you to the zoo and stick close all evening, but you keep a close eye on her, too."

"Sure, Detective Workman. Tell me how to recognize them and I'll be careful not to lose the cops tailing us."

Harold stifled a grin. "Don't worry too much about losing them. They're experts at following. It's better if you don't know them and don't keep looking for them. They'll find you. Your assignment is to act natural and don't let on anything's unusual."

"I'm sure we can do that," I said. "Let's go."

"Frank, there's something else," Harold said. "You showed

good judgment about the Rimbaud murders and you've proved you can be trusted, so we've told you everything. I probably don't need to add you can't repeat this to anyone until I say you can, but I'll say it anyway."

"I won't even tell my girl."

"Or your dad," I added.

"Especially not my dad."

"Okay, then, you'd better get going," Harold said. "It's almost 6:30, and we want to give the Killer enough time—if he wants it—to try to get in here while Sarah's gone. Can you stay out until 9:00 or so?"

"Sure, no problem. We can do Zoolights real slow. The South Pacific Aquarium's open too, and we can listen to the singers and get some hot chocolate. Then if it's still too early, we can go somewhere else for coffee." Frank paused for a moment, then continued with an exaggerated air of puzzlement, "But you know, it sure is different taking out an older woman!"

"How's that?" Harold asked, the perfect straight man.

"Well, my girl's father tells me how early I have to have her back. And you tell me how late you want me to keep Sarah out."

"Who's doing a comedy act now?" I complained as we all laughed. "C'mon, let's go!"

Frank looked at me. "You'll need to wear more than that. It's clear and really cold out there. You'll freeze your buns off. Oh, sorry," he broke off in confusion.

"That's okay," I said. "Even older women have buns. I'm wearing long johns, top and bottom, and a Woolrich jacket. Won't that be enough?"

"I dunno, Sarah. I'd put on a couple more layers. They taught us about layering in Boy Scouts. You can always take some off if you need to."

I went to the bedroom and added another pair of wool socks, a heavy turtleneck shirt, and a zippered sweat jacket with a hood. Then I got my heavy hooded jacket from the front hall. "Maybe a scarf and a hat, too, and gloves, of course," Frank suggested.

"This is Tacoma, not Alaska. It can't be that cold!" I protested, but grabbed all the things he recommended and stuffed them in the jacket pockets.

"Let's go," I said once more, and led the way to the door. I unlocked it and let Frank out. Harold stood to the side of the door and I had a sudden pang of wishing I were going to Zoolights with him. I took his hand for a moment. "Be careful."

He nodded. "You, too, Sarah. See you later."

It's only a mile or so from my house to the Point Defiance Zoo, and I wasn't aware of anyone following Frank's car down Pearl Street. No visible undercover cops. No visible Killer lurking in a sinister car that roared to life as we passed. I decided not to worry about the mechanics of how the Task Force would protect me. They knew what they were doing, and I didn't. I would just trust it would work.

"You and Detective Workman sure did surprise me!" Frank said as we pulled into the upper parking lot and started searching for a space.

"You can see why I didn't think to call you and why we didn't want to talk on the phone. Harold and I were busy, and then when you called we didn't know who might be listening."

"Well, yeah, that too. But you two have something going, don't you?"

I had a flash of annoyance. I wouldn't have asked an adult that kind of question when I was his age. But then so few adults had treated me as an adult at that time. "No," I said. "I don't think so."

"Why not? He's staying there with you and you like each other. I could tell by the way you both acted."

"It's not quite that easy, Frank. He's staying there because he has a job to do. That doesn't mean we 'have something going.'"

"I guess that would distract him from his work, huh?"

"For sure. But I think he might be involved with someone, anyway, a priest up in Marblemount."

"A priest! Priests aren't supposed to fool around! And Detective Workman sure doesn't look gay!"

I laughed. "Oh, Frank, the priest is a woman, an Episcopal priest, and I doubt they're 'fooling around.' Harold's active in his church. Besides, you can't tell if people are gay by the way they look or act."

"Huh!" he snorted. "I never thought about a detective being religious, either."

"Well, Harold keeps telling me not to go by stereotypes. That's good advice. I guess detectives can be gay, or religious, or both, or anything else, for that matter. And priests can be female and can marry—at least in the Episcopal Church. And teenagers can be reliable in a crisis," I added with a grin, as he found a parking place.

"And older women can be interesting to talk with," Frank finished up, getting out of the beat-up Toyota and coming around to open my door.

"Hey, no more cracks about 'older women,' kid," I said with mock ferocity. "Show some respect for your betters."

"That's elders, not betters."

"Again with the comedy," I lamented. "In this case, it's both. Hey, one more thing about this whole business, and then I just want to enjoy Zoolights. Do you think Walt's figured out about the Rimbauds?"

"I don't think so. Dad never remembers anybody's name. It's like he wants everybody to remember him, so he's on stage all the time. He couldn't be expected to learn the names of his audience, and he probably didn't get their names. Besides, he'd tell me if he did know."

"What does your dad do?" I asked, curious.

"He used to be a deejay full time, but now he mostly does radio ads and fills in as a deejay on different stations around Western Washington. He's the potato chip salesman on the ad for Bamford's chips. And he does the Furniture Factory Funhouse Fair ads. You've probably heard him a million times with a million different voices."

There was a sense of pride in Frank's voice. Maybe he loved his father despite his complaints.

"What's your mom like? Does she work outside the home?"

"I dunno. She and my sister left when I was nine."

"Oh, Frank! Do you ever see her?"

"Hardly ever. They moved to Houston and she married again. My sister comes up sometimes during vacation, but I've seen Mom only twice since she left. You sort of remind me of her—or like I wish she was," he added.

"Thank you. You mean I look like her?"

"No, you don't look alike. You're about my height, while she's real short and dark-haired. I mean you act like you're interested in me and that's what I always hoped she'd do. I got the passes," he said, changing the topic as we arrived at the head of the stairs to the zoo.

Right away I was glad we had come. Directly in front of us three moving figures made of lights—an elephant, a llama, and a dolphin—pulled Santa's sleigh, while other lights shone in trees and bushes all around. From where we stood the multicolored lights spread out below in a gorgeous panorama, backed by the lights of Brown's Point shimmering on the other side of Commencement Bay and those of the bedroom community of Des Moines in the distance.

An arch of thousands of tiny white lights led us to an open area where the wind caught us. I put on my wool hat, pulled the sweatshirt hood over it, and covered that with the hood on my heavy jacket. The wind still came through. I zipped the jacket and snapped all the snaps, then wrapped the scarf around my neck before I pulled on my wool gloves and closed the Velcro wrist tabs. Even with the long johns, I could feel the wind cutting through my heavy jeans.

"Told you," Frank said, watching me pile on the layers. He flashed the passes and we were waved through the left gate, bypassing the line of people waiting to pay admission. Several workers greeted him by name, and I could see how proud he was.

We followed the upper path to the right, taking our time and looking at all the lights. Subdued Christmas music played in the clear night. Below us, Mount Rainier in lights filled the outdoor stage and a giant octopus had captured the old aquarium. The paths were outlined in white bulbs set about a foot high, letting us see where we were going while leaving everything else dark except for the lighted outlines of animals and the multicolored lights in the trees.

The zoo was comfortably crowded, even in the bitter cold. Everyone seemed to be having a wonderful time. Several children riding on their parents' shoulders shouted "Look at the monkey" in unison as a blue monkey swinging from a tree flashed on and faded out. Two small boys ran toward us, laughing in a high, delighted burble. One called, "Lions, lions, lions," while the other yelled "El'fants, el'fants." As we rounded the corner, we saw the two families of lights that had pleased them so much.

Farther along the path an eagle perched high in a tree, bent to look down, swooped and plucked a fish from a stream, then took it up to two eaglets nestled in another tree. We stood and watched the sequence several times.

"You know, I'm sorry we didn't get to finish the eagle float," Frank said as we moved on. "I bet we could work something out with the raft company if we wanted to go back next month. The birds were cool."

"I'm not sure I want to go back. I'd probably expect a body around every bend."

"Oh, think about it. A good trip would help erase that idea. And finding a body's got to be a once-in-a-lifetime kind of thing."

"That's what Harold said, too, but I'm not sure. I'll give it some thought, anyway."

Behind the old aquarium, a red-and-green spider waited in a gigantic web of white lights, and a chameleon's flickering tongue chased and finally caught an elusive fly.

Frank told me about his work as a zoo volunteer as we walked slowly along the paths and watched the moving displays. "My girl volunteers here, too," he said. "I'd like you to meet her." He stopped and asked, "Do you want to go in the aquarium and get warm?"

"Not yet. Let's wait. But I would like to meet your girl one of these days."

"I'll tell you about her sometime and make sure you meet. Right now let's take the path down to the penguins," he suggested. The lights along the path let us see the real penguins swimming in their pond. "I've never seen them this active," Frank commented as all the penguins dove underwater at once. "They must like the cold weather."

Two beluga whales in lights caught my eye, then Frank said, "Now turn around and look back." To my delight, a series of penguin outlines in lights showed us a running penguin taking a bellyflop, sliding down the hill, righting itself, and running off again.

Sharon was right; this was even better than the previous year. And it was good to be outside, walking and seeing other people. I wondered if Harold would have liked the lights as much as I did. They didn't have much to do with Christmas, but they had a lot to do with wonder and magic and beauty. It bothered me I had so little idea what Harold would like.

Up the hill to our left was perhaps the loveliest sight of the exhibition, a tree straight from fairyland. Hundreds of tiny green lights made its trunk, and thousands of fuchsia lights made it burst into riotous bloom. Tonight its branches swayed in the stiff wind.

We headed toward the path to Rocky Shores. The hoarse barking of the real seals and sea lions and the loud grunts of real walruses sounded above the Christmas music. "How about some hot chocolate?" Frank asked. I nodded. "Okay, back in a minute," he promised as he went to join the line outside a kiosk a short way up the hill.

I moved down the path and perched on a solid metal handrail near an Aurora Borealis tunnel above the path. From my seat I watched lights flicker on and off in the trees and studied the faces of those passing in front of me. In a crowd like this, the people-watching was nearly as good as the lights. I still hadn't figured out who was watching us; evidently the Task Force people were real experts. I hoped they were enjoying Zoolights.

The taped music shut off. A few moments later, a small brass band next to the kiosk struck up God Rest Ye Merry, Gentlemen, and a large chorus of people of all ages clad in Victorian attire appeared and started singing. Everybody pushed toward the kiosk. Frank was near the head of the line and I started to move toward him so I could see and hear better and help him carry the hot chocolate.

I felt a powerful jerk on the ends of my scarf and opened my mouth to call out. Before I could make a sound, I was over the railing and flat on my back on the ground, with all the breath knocked out of me. In another instant I was hauled into the bushes and flipped over. Someone knelt on my back and yanked at my hoods. I couldn't get my breath! The cold hit my head as my hoods were jerked down and my hat snatched off. I strained to pull in some air, tried to kick at the person on my back, tried to make a noise, roll over, do anything! I couldn't!

My head was yanked back and something passed in front of my face, then choked me through the triple roll of my turtleneck collar. I could feel someone breathing at the back of my head and jerked back as hard as I could. I banged my head against whatever was behind me. Hard. Someone grunted and the pressure lessened for a moment. I managed to gasp a breath of air, then the pressure started again. It hurt. My lungs and the front of my throat hurt, then whatever was choking me slipped upwards and dug into my neck just above my collar. That felt like a cut. Oh, God, I thought. Not now. Help me! I tried once more to kick. Then the pressure was gone and a deep rasping breath grated as it went in and out of my throat.

I heard shouts and running feet and the scuffling of leaves. I also heard voices singing "Oh, tidings of comfort and joy, comfort and joy."

I turned over and kicked when somebody reached for me. "Sarah!" a high, frightened voice said, "It's Frank."

Someone below us yelled, "We've got him. There's a fence down there," and I heard more running feet. Then metal screeched on metal, four times in all.

Frank pulled something off my neck and held it up. In the dim light I saw it was a man's necktie. He felt my neck. "You're bleeding. Don't move. Somebody will be here soon. I'm sorry. I'm so sorry." He was almost crying.

I tried to say something to comfort him, but could only manage a croak. My throat throbbed, but at least I was breathing! I patted his arm.

Someone pushed through the bushes and shone a flashlight on me, blinding me for a moment. "I'm with the FBI," he said, kneeling and examining my neck. "It doesn't look too bad, but don't move! Did you see anything? Would you recognize him again? How did he get you?"

I shook my head and pointed to my throat.

"She can't talk," Frank protested. "Get her to a hospital and ask questions later. Right now she needs help!"

A large older man with a Zoolights jacket and a walkie-talkie pushed into our small clearing. I wondered why it had taken him so long, but then I heard the brass band playing the final notes of the same carol they had started while I sat on the handrail.

"What's going on here?" the large man demanded.

The Task Force man held up his ID and shone the flashlight on it. "I'm FBI. This has nothing to do with the zoo. We're on a case and we need your help."

"What can I do?" the large man asked. My eyes turned to each speaker in turn.

"Somebody grabbed our friend here and tried to strangle her," the FBI man said. "Three plainclothes cops chased him, and they ran through a turnstile at the bottom of the fence. Get the police down below the turnstile—and keep it as quiet as possible. Then get an ambulance."

"It won't be quiet if we call the police," the older man objected, pulling out his walkie-talkie. "The media'll get it."

"We'll keep them off," the FBI man promised.

The older man spoke into his walkie-talkie. "Attention all staff with radios. Stop all radio contact immediately. We have a Code Two near the Northern Lights. Park Police, get to the turnstile by the old bear cages ASAP. Dangerous possible assailant and three good guys in plainclothes. Front gate, call 911. Get the Rescue Unit here and get the TPD to help the Park Police below the turnstile. Phone contact, not radio. No sirens closer than 50th!"

He turned away from the instrument and asked, "Okay, so far?"

"Uh-huh. Keep it up—and keep it as quiet as you can."

The man turned back to his walkie-talkie. "Station someone at Gate Seven to let the Rescue Unit in. Get the musicians to move toward the petting zoo. They can take the people with them, like pied pipers. Get some staff here to encourage everyone to follow, then clear the path between here and Gate Seven. And keep it quiet! No panic!"

I was still lying on my back and breathing hard. I saw other faces peering into our space and just wanted to get home, back to Harold. But I still couldn't say anything. I tried to sit up and realized

I was much shakier than I could have imagined.

"You stay quiet," the man with the walkie-talkie said, helping me lie back down. "We'll cover you up and keep you warm. Someone will be here in a minute."

Frank found my hat and started to fit it on my head. "Don't do that!" the man ordered. "She may have a neck injury."

Frank opened his jacket and lay on the ground next to me, pressing close and covering me with the jacket. In an unsure, somewhat squeaky voice, he tried to joke, "Hey, I'm not trying to get fresh, but body heat, you know."

I felt tears slipping down my face. They were cold by the time they ran into my ears. The liquid on my throat felt cold, too, and sticky.

The older man spoke again into his walkie-talkie. "We need some blankets over here right away." When he finished, he shooed the other faces away and stood guard in the small gap leading to the path. The singers were into Oh, Come, All Ye Faithful, and the words grew less distinct as the group moved away.

The FBI man had been searching the area with his flashlight, without finding anything. Now he knelt beside me again. "I'm sorry, ma'am. We all seem to have looked away at the same moment, and you disappeared. Then Frank yelled. I don't think the cut's deep or wide, but we'll have you thoroughly checked. Are you injured anywhere besides your throat?"

I had to think. Everything hurt, but I didn't think the pains were serious. Everything had happened so fast! I tried to answer, but again couldn't get the sound out. I rolled my head from side to side.

Tears continued down my face, and the man handed Frank a handkerchief. That's FBI, I thought, he can't cope with tears. Frank reached up and wiped my face. Someone spread a blanket over Frank and me and put another one so it covered the top of my head. I closed my eyes. I might have been killed! I could be dead now! Then they'd be pulling the blanket over my face!

I heard running feet on the path, then the rustle of parting bushes. I opened my eyes again and squinted against the bright lights shining on me. Frank scrambled up, and two men in yellow slickers knelt beside me. "We're with the Tacoma Fire Department," one of them said. "Where do you hurt?"

The FBI man answered, "She's been choked and there's a cut on her neck. She can't talk."

At that the two firefighters pulled off the blankets and set to work. One wiped blood away and placed a light bandage on my neck. The other fitted a mask over my nose and mouth. "Now breathe deep. Concentrate on your breathing." I did, and felt myself becoming calmer as my breathing slowed.

Two more slicker-clad figures arrived. The men who had been working on me stood back and reported to the new arrivals. One of the new men knelt next to me and said, "We're paramedics. The technicians tell us you don't seem to be badly hurt, but we're going to make sure. We're going to put a cervical collar on you and strap you to a backboard. And we're going to put a foam brace around your head so you can't turn your head. This is all standard stuff to keep the Emergency Room people happy. Just lie back and relax as much as you can."

I closed my eyes again as the paramedics spiraled a collar around my neck, fastening it with Velcro. They tipped me on one side, slipped a board where I had been, and laid me back down. The board was cold, and I felt frozen right through to the bone. Then they fitted something soft and slick against either side of my head and pressed the pieces down until I heard more Velcro fasten. A strap tightened across my forehead.

"Okay, let's strap her in," one of the paramedics said. I felt them securing me to the board at shoulders, hips, and legs. "Cross your arms over your chest," the other one ordered. I did.

Four firefighters lifted the board and hauled me through the bushes, put me on a gurney, and buckled more straps around me. Someone threw a blanket over me. It didn't help. The cold seemed to radiate from the inside out.

The firefighters elevated the gurney and wheeled me through the arch of the Aurora Borealis, up a steep hill, and over a short unpaved stretch. Then they loaded me into the back of the rescue unit.

"I'm riding with you," the FBI man told a paramedic.

"Okay, but sit next to the door, out of the way."

"I'll meet you at the hospital," Frank said as the doors closed. I tried to smile at him.

I don't remember all the details on how they got me to Tacoma General Hospital's Emergency Room, but do remember being grateful for a big heater that was turned on as soon as the ambulance started. One paramedic drove and the other checked me as well as he could, given the jackets, the backboard, all the straps, and the jolting ambulance. I didn't feel good, but minute by minute I became more convinced I wasn't seriously injured.

The paramedic's young, earnest face hovered over me as he removed the oxygen mask and substituted a tube with a prong running to each nostril. The hissing oxygen covered some of the other sounds, but I thought he was talking on a phone, rather than a radio, and reporting my condition to someone. "I'm going to start an IV," he said, unfastening the Velcro wrist tabs on my jacket and pushing all my layers of sleeves up. I concentrated on his blue eyes as he stuck a needle in the vein running down my arm and started a liquid flowing through it. Now I knew the cold was coming from the inside out.

At some point, after we were well away from the zoo, they turned on the siren. I wondered if Harold and the dogs heard it when we passed near my house.

By the time we pulled up to the emergency entrance, I felt less shaky. I didn't think I was hurt badly, and the bracing seemed unnecessary, but I still couldn't tell them so. The paramedics rolled the gurney out with me on it and hustled me up to the Emergency Patient Evaluation Desk.

"Room Four," the woman at the desk directed. The paramedics wheeled me into the room and transferred me—backboard and all—to a gurney-bed. The FBI man hovered near the door.

A nurse came in right away. "She can't communicate orally," the paramedic said.

"Thanks," the nurse said, then turned to me. "I'm here to take care of you. We'll get some x-rays in a few minutes to see what's going on inside your throat. Until then, you just concentrate on your breathing and relax."

Someone put a heated blanket over me. Nothing had ever

felt better.

I heard a slight commotion outside the door. The FBI man stuck his head out and said, "I want the kid with us," and Frank came in the room. He stood over me and was so miserable I could hardly bear to look at him. Worse, he kept apologizing. I was calm now, but I didn't know what I'd do if Frank started crying! I closed my eyes.

Another commotion occurred, and somebody wheeled me down to the x-ray unit. The technician shooed everyone out while he took pictures. Not being able to speak or move somehow left me feeling mentally deficient, even though the technician spoke directly to me. Someone wheeled me back to the room, where Frank and the FBI man came back in and waited with me for the results. The clock said 8:30. I hoped someone had called Harold. I hoped he was okay. I hoped he was worried about me.

The nurse came back in. "Doctor says the x-rays are fine. Just to see how much you're roughed up, the doctor will give you a thorough exam. We'll want you to get into this," she said, holding up a hospital gown. She turned to Frank and the FBI man, "You two will have to wait outside." After helping me ease my clothes off and put on an examination gown, she brought a new warmed blanket. "It'll only be a few minutes, now," she told me.

Another woman bustled in. "I'm from Admitting. Can you fill out this medical history while you wait? I'll stay here and help." I nodded, glad to be free of the restraints. She held the clipboard for me, and the form didn't take long. I didn't mind the mundane task; it helped me feel like I was part of my normal world.

The nurse came back. "Doctor's delayed. Those two men want to wait with you until the doctor comes. Is that okay?" I nodded, and she let Frank and the FBI man back in.

"I'd like that pen and clipboard and some paper," the FBI man told the woman from Admitting, not noticing the effect his demand had on her. He turned to me. "I want you to write down everything, every little detail you can remember."

It wasn't much help, but I wrote what I could while Frank held the clipboard for me. The FBI man took it as soon as I had finished, and tried to decipher my writing.

"I forgot," Frank blurted out. "This was around her neck." I glanced up and saw he was holding a necktie. He looked a little more composed.

The FBI man lost all his composure and grabbed the tie. "Oh, shit! It was him!" Then he clammed up and wouldn't explain anything.

The doctor came in, short, athletic-looking, and pretty. The nurse gestured the men out the door, while the doctor checked my throat with practiced fingers. "The cut on your neck is superficial, just enough to bleed and hurt a lot. I'll have the nurse bandage it in a moment. Your neck's bruised, your throat's swollen, and your larynx got a bit damaged, but everything should be okay after a few days," she told me. "The x-rays don't show a fracture of the larynx or any real damage to your soft tissues or spine."

She looked at and felt the rest of my body, then continued her report. "Also, you're going to be pretty sore the next week or so, and I hope you don't want to wear anything revealing to holiday parties—unless it's color-coordinated with your all-over bruises. It's a good thing you had on as many layers as you did or you'd be a lot worse off.

"We're going to send you home, but have your own doctor follow up if the pain worsens or if you have any real problems." She turned and spoke to the nurse, "You can help her get dressed, and I'll finish with her privately afterwards."

The doctor wrote up her notes as the nurse helped me into my jeans, the long-john top, and hooded jacket, then found a bag for the rest and left the room.

I sat on the edge of the gurney-bed until the doctor finished. She put down her notes and spoke. "You were brought in by the paramedics, weren't you?" I nodded. "Domestic violence?" I shook my head. "Were you mugged?" This time I nodded. "Look, whoever did this was really trying to get you. Without that turtleneck you might be dead. I don't want to scare you unnecessarily, but we have people in the hospital who can help you find a safe place if you want." I shook my head, but regretted the action. "Do you have protection?" I nodded once again.

"Okay. Then all I can do is give you something for the pain, without knocking you out. Here's a prescription for Tylenol #3. You can get it filled upstairs at the pharmacy. Your voice will start coming back soon, but you won't feel much like talking and you'll be hoarse for a week or so. In fact, you could probably talk now if you had to, but I don't want you talking any more than necessary. When it is necessary, whisper—sort of a breathy whisper from your mouth, like this, rather than from your throat," she said, demonstrating for me.

I mouthed, "Thank you" to her. She helped me down from the examining table and took me to the door. "Be careful," she said in parting. ≠

Chapter 20

The FBI man and Frank walked me upstairs to get the prescription filled, and out to Frank's car for the drive home. This time I was aware of the two cars following us. My muscles were already starting to stiffen as Frank helped me to my front door and I unlocked it. Harold stood just inside the door, his hand on his gun. Frank remained silent until the door was closed and locked, then started explaining to Harold, stumbling over the words in his haste. The dogs milled around, confused, but for once not leaping and barking.

I headed for Harold's arms. He wrapped them around me and rocked me. "It's okay, Frank," he said, over my head. "The FBI agent called from the hospital and explained. He took full responsibility. He said you did everything right and it wasn't your fault. I made a mistake in thinking you and Sarah would be safe. And the watchers didn't watch closely enough. Don't blame yourself. It was our fault."

Frank responded, but I didn't listen. I just relaxed and felt myself grow really warm for the first time since Frank and I had arrived at the zoo. *The hell with what Frank thinks about Harold and me!* I heard Frank preparing to leave. I pushed away from Harold and took Frank's hand and squeezed it in thanks. It was so strange not to be talking; how does a verbal person cope without words? Then I let him out the door and locked it.

Harold helped me off with my jacket, then folded his arms around me again. "Sarah, I'm sorry. The FBI agent says you'll be okay, but I was so fearful for you."

I felt the tears sliding down my face again, and then I was sobbing. The spasms hurt my throat and I tried to stop, but couldn't. Harold pulled me to the sofa, handed me a handkerchief, and held me as I cried. Finally my sobs died, my breathing got more controlled, the tears dried up, and I rested against Harold's chest, worn out. His heart beat in my ear. I could feel Golda leaning against my leg, and Jesse grunted and settled down nearby.

Harold talked to me, and I responded to the sound rather than the meaning. I was relaxed when I thought I felt a kiss on the top of my head. That roused me a little, and I heard him say, "I called Judy after the FBI agent phoned, and she alerted the prayer network at church."

I tensed and tried to get up. A new torrent of tears seemed on the way. Harold wouldn't let go.

"Why did you pull away?" he asked.

I pulled harder, but he wouldn't let go.

"Sarah, why are you pulling away?" he asked again.

I *could* talk! Words came pouring out. "I don't understand you! I don't know what you're doing, and I can't cope with this."

He held my arms and looked at me. He looked more than ever like Claude Akins, big brown eyes all caring and concerned, his mouth turned down at the corners in dismay. "What do you mean?"

I knew my words were childish, but I couldn't stop. Having to whisper didn't help me feel any more adult, either. "I don't think hugging means the same thing to you and me. You even kiss me—or I think you just did—and then you talk about Judy! It's probably all my fault, but your signals seem all mixed up to me!"

"What does Judy have to do with anything?" His face was a picture of total confusion, about like I felt.

"You talk about her all the time. You act like you like me, and then you talk about Judy again! I tell myself you're just acting fatherly, but it doesn't seem fatherly to me! But then you don't exactly act like it *isn't* fatherly, either. And then you bring up Judy!" This last was almost a wail, and I knew I must look as idiotic as I sounded. He still wouldn't let go. I buried my face against his chest again so he couldn't see me.

"Sarah, Judy is my spiritual advisor and she's my best friend," he said. "She's important in my life. She started out as a career counselor before she became a psychologist and then a priest. She still works full time as a psychologist, 'cause we don't pay her for being a priest."

His arms went around me again, and he patted my back as he talked. "We met when my marriage was breaking up. She was my therapist. When she was ordained, I had a lot to do with getting her at our church. Now the relationship is more friendly than therapeutic, but she's been helping with my career plans. And she helps me on my spiritual journey. She and her husband and I sometimes do things together." He paused. "Yeah, I guess I talk about her a lot, but we're not involved like you mean."

I didn't say anything. What could I say when I'd just made a fool of myself? Again I tried to pull away, but he held on as he continued, in a tone as though he were talking to himself.

"And I guess I *am* sending mixed signals. That's because I'm having a hard time living up to my own standards, but I figured I could hold out until this is over. Right now you're vulnerable, and I'm the authority figure. It would be as wrong to take advantage of that as if I were a teacher and you a student, or I a counselor and you a client."

He stroked my hair back from my forehead and tilted my head so he could look at my face. "Sarah, I'm interested in you, but I'm trying not to be, not now. I don't think I have the right to do anything about it until you're through with this situation and we can get to know each other as equals. I hope you'll still be interested in me after that. But you might just want to forget anything and anybody that reminds you of this time."

He not only let me go, but also helped me stand and pushed me away. "Tonight I thanked God you weren't dead. Sarah, I want to see if something might work between you and me. For now I'll just tell you I don't feel the least bit fatherly toward you."

He walked me a couple of steps toward the bedroom before continuing. "Night before last I realized maybe I was touching you a bit too much. I was trying to be comforting without coming on, but I wasn't clear about my own motives and had to try hard not to take advantage of you. So I pulled back until tonight, when we both seemed to need it."

"I did need it," I whispered, "I do need it." My throat ached, but inside I was fairly shouting for joy.

I put my arm around his waist. He detached it. "I'm sorry, Sarah. But now that how I feel is out in the open, I still can't do anything about it until we finish up with the Killer. I just won't, now; I've *got* to wait. *Then* we'll see how we both feel! Right now, let's go to bed. You're asleep on your feet!"

I knew he wasn't suggesting going to bed together. I knew I had to respect what he had just told me. But now I also knew the feelings weren't all on my side. "I think I'll still be interested when this is over," I said.

He searched my face, as if to make sure of my meaning, then smiled. "We'll see, Sarah. I hope so." ≠

Chapter 21

If it hadn't come so close to being true, I'd say I slept like the dead. I woke to the sound of the phone. More accurately, I came to when the phone rang. Although I heard it ringing, it wasn't enough to make me want to get up. The machine answered it. I heard a voice, but couldn't hear what it said. It would wait.

I didn't move. I didn't quite go back to sleep, but I didn't quite wake up, either. Something deep inside seemed happy, and I couldn't get my mind focused on what it was. Not Christmas; I haven't felt like this about Christmas for decades. What, then? I came a little more awake. Harold. Harold Workman's here! The thought was delicious. I smiled, then stretched.

Another awareness hit me as my body moved from the position it seemed to have held all night. Somebody tried to kill me last night! I could have died! That's why I hurt so bad. I tried moving one part at a time, stretching my legs, my arms, wiggling my buttocks, twisting my shoulders, then turning my head. They all hurt, but everything worked. I stretched again; this time was easier.

The clock showed 9:35. The door opened and Harold said "Good morning. Ready for coffee?" Golda and Jesse crowded in, wanting their morning petting.

I pushed up to a sitting position against the headboard, an enormous smile on my face. "Good morning," I tried to say, but it came out in a croak and it hurt. I tried again, this time whispering. It came out better.

"Stay there, I'll bring coffee," Harold said, disappearing. I reached my hands out to pet the dogs. Golda licked my hand, while Jesse moved his head from side to side so each ear got equal attention.

"How do you feel?" Harold asked, coming back with a big mug of coffee. Our hands touched as he handed me the mug; I held the contact longer than necessary.

He looked beautiful! Big and clean and solid! His warm eyes were just the color of the coffee in my mug. I wanted to tell him about the joy, but remembered we weren't supposed to talk about that. "Not too bad. Achy," I whispered.

He pulled the oak rocker next to the bed and sat down. "Are you awake?"

"I don't think so."

Harold laughed. "I think the Tylenol knocked you out. You look sort of loopy to me. And you even snored last night!"

"I did not!" I whispered.

"How would you know? You were asleep."

I sipped at the coffee and eased myself into wakefulness. Harold rocked and watched me. "Who was on the phone?" I asked.

"Frank's dad, Walt."

An idea hit at the edge of my brain. I jerked more upright, almost spilling the coffee. "What did he want?"

"I listened to the message. He called to apologize," Harold said. "Evidently Frank told him you got mugged last night and he wanted to tell you how awful he and Frank feel. He'll stop by about 2:00 with some fruit. Don't look so upset; we're about out of fresh food. We can use the fruit."

The idea took form. "Walt! I've got to tell you about Walt. He has lots of voices! And he knew when I'd be at Zoolights."

Harold leaned forward in concentration. "What do you mean?"

"Frank says Walt's a deejay and he does radio ads. He does a lot of different voices. Maybe that's who I heard." My thoughts seemed thick and slow, and my throat hurt, even though I whispered.

"He was up there—at the river—last weekend, but Frank was with him," Harold said, following my thought. "You can't think Frank's involved!"

"No, but maybe he left Frank and said he was going out for a drink or something. I don't know how he would have gotten Nicole up there, but he's at least a possibility. He travels around to different radio stations, too, when he substitutes, so maybe he gets up that way often. And he knew when I'd be at Zoolights because he listened on the phone."

I paused and tried to remember what else Frank had said about his father. "His wife! She was small. And she left him about seven or eight years ago. Moved away, doesn't even see Frank. Probably hate each other!" I paused again, then continued. "I don't really think it's him, just that it's a possibility. He did try to rearrange Nicole's skirt when we found the body. And he's short and thin."

"He could have been trying to help—or to confuse the evidence."

"And he could have gotten in to see the Rimbauds without any trouble, since they'd met him on the trip."

Harold's expression showed he was now considering Walt as a suspect. "Yeah, but he knew it was you who talked with Nicole the night before, not the Rimbauds. Walt probably would have come straight here if he was the Killer. Unless he wanted to get all possible witnesses out of the way. Did Frank say anything about his limping or getting hurt Sunday?"

"No, but he could have had all kinds of cover stories if he were hurt. I do know he was away on Sunday, 'cause when Frank called that night he told me Walt had gone to work that day. All I'm saying is we should look at him, not that I have all the evidence to pin it on him."

"You're right, Sarah. Look, I'd better tell the Task Force to start checking Walt out. And alert them he's coming at 2:00."

"He wouldn't make an appointment, would he, if he's the Killer? 'Hi, I'll be over at 2:00 for a spot of murder—bringing fruits for the funeral feast! Black tie not optional.'"

"The Killer uses regular ties, not formal wear. At least you wouldn't have to dress for the occasion," Harold said, standing and making a poor attempt at humor.

The humor didn't work and he looked haggard as he continued, "Sarah, I have no idea what the Killer would do! I could have sworn you'd be safe at Zoolights, but I was wrong. Let's just get the Task Force to find out everything they can about Walt between now and 2:00. And we'll be super alert when he comes. If he makes a move on you, we've got him!"

Maybe this would all be over before the day ended. But if it is Walt, what about Frank? I decided to cross that bridge if and when I came to it.

Harold headed for the phone. I inched out of bed and into the bathroom. A box of bubble bath sat on the counter. "A long soak will ease the aches," Harold called through the door, "then follow up with a hot shower and as much movement as you can."

Some women have bath salts, I thought. I have bubble bath left over from my cousin's kids. Oh, well. It'll do.

My tub's straight back isn't meant for soaking—at least not by anyone who's taller than four feet five and whose neck doesn't bend to a 90-degree angle. Nevertheless, I wiggled around in the hot water to loosen up the muscles, and the bath did ease my achiness. I looked at my feet, propped on the wall over the faucets, and studied my calves. Harold's never even seen my legs, I thought. I wonder how he feels about all-over freckles. Had he been checking me out the same way I'd been looking at him?

The hot water was about to run out when I cut off the shower. I was able to move more freely—and was more awake—as I stepped out of the tub. I examined my body in the mirror, something I don't often do. The shape and tone weren't too bad. It wasn't what it was at twenty, but then what is? At least I wouldn't be ashamed for Harold to see it when the time came.

Bruises showed up in places I couldn't imagine would be affected by what I remembered of last night's action. A thin zipper line looking like a briar scratch ran horizontally across my neck for about three inches. There probably wouldn't be a scar, and meanwhile a turtleneck would cover the cut.

I blew my hair dry and put on lipstick and mascara. I'm alive, and I'm going to make the best of it! Wrapping my robe around me, I went into the bedroom. No jeans today! I pawed through the hangers in my closet and came up with some forest-green wool slacks, a tan turtleneck, and a tan-and-green sweater tying everything together. Not dressy, but a couple of steps up from jeans.

"You look nice," Harold said as I went into the kitchen. He looked at the collection of food on the counter. "Milk and eggs are almost gone, and the bread's getting stale. How about French toast? If this goes on much longer, we'll have to get some supplies in."

"French toast is fine, but I'm getting spoiled with your cooking. What can I do?"

"How about bringing me three or four small branches from the evergreens in the back yard, some that look good."

"Whatever for?"

"You'll see." He grinned at me, but it seemed forced. I felt my high spirits recede.

I broke several small branches from the Douglas firs hanging over the back fence and took them to Harold. "What now?" I asked.

"I'll call you when breakfast is ready," he said. "You can play with the dogs in the yard 'til then. That'll loosen you up and work off some of Jesse's energy."

By the time Harold called through the back door, I had worked more of the stiffness out of my muscles, but Golda's blond hairs were all over my slacks and Jesse had managed to smear my jacket and slacks with dirt and slobber. Yeah, this is why I always wear jeans around the house, I thought. So much for celebrating life through my clothes!

I washed up and went to the table. In its center was a wreath of evergreens, with four candles set around it. "An Advent wreath!" I said with pleasure.

"You don't have any decorations up at all, and it's less than a week 'til Christmas. I couldn't find the right kind of candles, though."

Again, Harold seemed stilted. What had happened to the easy camaraderie of the past few days?

"I've kind of stopped decorating for Christmas unless I'm entertaining. Are we going to light them now?" I asked.

"Three of them. We can't light the last one 'til next Sunday and after. But we can use the wreath every mealtime from now 'til Christmas." He handed me a box of big fireplace matches. "Here, you light them, and I'll pray."

I lit the candles, cognizant of the pronoun he'd used in talking about the wreath, then took Harold's hand as he started to pray. It seemed to me he stiffened, but I held on and watched his big, dear face over the flickering candles as he said grace. He gave my hand a quick squeeze with the "amen," then dropped it and headed for the kitchen.

He brought in the French toast he'd kept warm in the oven. Conversation was stiff, and we ate quickly, then blew out the candles. "I'll do that," he said when I started to clear the table. "You get the paper, and we'll see if last night's attack made the news."

Poor Harold, I thought as I brought Wednesday's morning paper in, he hasn't set foot outside since Sunday night! As before, we checked the Tribune together. There was a note in the "Police Beat" section that a woman was mugged at Point Defiance, then treated at Tacoma General and released.

"That's good," he said with satisfaction. "Enough so it's not obvious we're hiding anything, but not enough to reveal anything we don't want known, either." He rose from the table and headed toward the kitchen. "I'll do the dishes. You probably want to get to work. But get up and move around every half hour or so, so you won't stiffen."

I wondered how he knew so much about injuries. Had he been hurt often in his work? I didn't ask, because he seemed eager for me to leave. I moved to the office, started the computer, and looked at the previous day's work on the Port document. It didn't look as good as it had the day before. I fiddled with it, changing a word here and there, without improving it.

As Harold had suggested, I stood and stretched. My mind wandered. Better put the bloody turtleneck on to soak or it will never come clean. And might as well do some laundry. I went into the living room. Harold sat at the dining room table with his eyes closed. I started back to the office, but he asked, in a neutral voice, "Did you want me?"

"I thought I'd do a couple loads of laundry," I whispered. "Have anything you want done?"

"Sure, I'm running low on underwear. Thanks."

I gathered the towels and my clothing while he got his, then went downstairs with the load. Harold's shorts weren't wild, I noticed, just small nondescript patterns. Too bad. I held his undershirt to my face for a moment before dropping it in the washer. The scent of him brought back the feel of his arms around me so strongly that I ached and wanted to cry out.

What's the matter? Does he regret everything he said? The words of a song from Camelot came to mind, something about loving in miserable silence, finally talking about love, and then being more miserable than ever.

Oh, God! I raged at myself. Thinking in song lyrics! Then I got mad about dumping on myself, and then decided song lyrics sometimes said important things. I spent more time in the basement than necessary to get the laundry started, but was composed when I went back up.

"Do you mind if I set the microwave timer to tell me when the wash is done?" I asked Harold.

"No, that's fine. How do you feel about not having lunch until after Walt leaves?"

"Sure." I set the timer and went back to the office. When the timer went off, I had accomplished nothing more at the computer. I put the clothes in the dryer and started the next load of wash, setting the timer to measure dryer time. As I marched up and down the stairs at the timer's command, I made a point of not disturbing Harold, who was on the phone once and reading every other time I went through the living room. I noticed he had moved on to Allan Gurganus' Oldest Living Confederate Widow Tells All.

As I sat at the computer, the words on the screen blurred, and I grew more and more frightened. I'd nearly been killed the night before, and now the Killer might be coming right into my home! The Task Force hadn't protected me well last night. What if they didn't succeed if Walt was the Killer? And what was wrong with Harold? The defeating thoughts rolled around inside me. I'd never thought much about my own death, not even when I had major surgery several years before, but here it was! Not now, I wanted to scream. Life is looking good! Not now!

I remembered discussions with friends when they'd said,

"What's so awful about death? What if we're just moving on to another, better, phase of our existence?" Somehow, that didn't comfort me. I thought about people who willingly sacrificed their lives for others, and about what I had told Harold about not having a choice. None of that comforted me, either. And then I thought, I don't know what's the matter with Harold, but I don't want to be alone with these thoughts.

I went into the living room again. Harold was in the recliner, his eyes closed. I put a hand on his arm. "I'm sorry to wake you," I whispered, "but I need to talk."

He opened his eyes and forced a smile. "I wasn't asleep. What's up?"

"I'm getting afraid," I said, forgetting to keep my whisper breathy enough. It hurt. I adjusted my voice. "After last night I'm feeling very mortal. Walt's going to be here in about an hour, and I'm scared. Has the Task Force found anything on him?"

"Nothing implicating or excluding him yet, but they're still checking. He's still only a possibility."

"Okay. So he's coming and we don't know much about him. I'm supposed to greet him as naturally as I can. I'll be wearing the alarm. You'll be in the office with your gun. The surveillance teams will be ready to jump. And half the Tacoma Police Force will be waiting around the corner, but I'm still scared. Before last night it didn't seem possible anybody was trying to kill me. Now I know somebody is. And that paralyzes me."

"Do you want out? You can go away and we'll pick Walt up when he gets here."

"On what grounds? Bringing fruit to an injured friend? You know better than I that you couldn't hold him if you did arrest him. The Killer still hasn't left anything you didn't have before except one more necktie that could belong to anyone. If you catch him in an attempt on me, you can at least hold him on that until you get more evidence or a confession or something."

I stood, moved behind the barrel chair I had been sitting in, and leaned forward on its back. "I still don't have any choice. I can't go away. I'd never be free of him until he's caught, but also I'd never live peacefully with myself if I flubbed this chance to help stop something evil. If I'm this scared with all the protection around, how do you think those girls felt before he killed them?"

Harold's face worked, but he didn't say anything. I thought for a moment he was going to cry, but then he controlled his face and I couldn't read his expression.

"I'm going through with it, but I'm feeling alone. I heard what you said last night about me being weak now and you being in authority. I'm not sure I agree, but I respect it. I'm not trying to proposition you or change your mind about what you need to do." I grimaced. "But I feel as though you've stepped back about twenty paces and I don't think I can do this well with you that far away. Can we at least try to get back to where we were before last night?"

His face worked again, and he came and stood behind me, resting his big hands on my shoulders. I couldn't see his face as he started talking. "I was wrong last night, Sarah. I'm sorry." He paused, and my heart dropped so hard and fast I could almost hear it hit. "I did say you were vulnerable—not weak—and I was in authority, but in the night I realized I'm just as vulnerable here. Nobody I especially care about has ever been involved in a case I was working on until now."

He kneaded my shoulders as he talked, and I leaned into the kneading. "I was able to do a good, professional job as long as I was detached. Sure, I felt fear whenever I went into something dangerous, but it helped, like a shot of adrenaline. Today I'm feeling a kind of sick fear, not for me, but for you. I thought I was okay before you woke up, but after we talked I started thinking about what Walt might try to do to you."

His hands moved up and massaged the back of my neck and head. "I was trying to hide my fear so you wouldn't feel any worse. If you want, we can get somebody else over here to protect you, someone who isn't emotionally involved."

I guess it should have scared me that Harold was afraid, but instead all I felt was relief. I turned and hugged him hard for a moment. "I don't want someone else. I think I can handle it if I don't feel like I'm out there totally alone. It was just when it felt like you had gone away . . . ."

"I'm sorry I pulled back, Sarah. I'm here, and I'm with you. So let's talk about exactly what might happen when Walt comes. And let's hope he's not late. This waiting is hell!" ≠

Chapter 22

Walt arrived at 2:03, bearing an ostentatious basket of fruit wrapped in cellophane and tied with a bow. It looked like the biggest offering the supermarket had for Christmas, the kind of thing you get when you realize you've forgotten to get anything for Aunt Sadie and you're having dinner at her house in an hour.

I'd used the folding gate to shut the dogs in the kitchen. Harold was just inside the office doorway, ready to come to my aid if needed. I went to the door alone. It was hard to greet Walt, and not just because my throat was sore. I'd tensed up so it was hard to get any words out.

Walt didn't seem to notice. He started talking the moment I opened the door and didn't slow down for the first several minutes. Frank was right about his being on stage all the time.

"Sarah! I'm so sorry about your accident, and Frank is just devastated! He could hardly sleep last night, he felt so responsible. I've never seen him so upset." Walt strode across the room and put the basket down on the dining room table. "Hope you like fruit. I would have brought flowers, but didn't know your color scheme. These are from Frank and me, of course."

He dropped his coat on a chair; he wore a brown medium-weight wool sports jacket and a bowtie. He looked around the room before focusing on Jesse and Golda in the kitchen doorway behind the gate, wagging their tails but not barking. Their manners had improved a lot since Harold's coming.

195

"Oh, these are the dogs Frank told me about," Walt said, barreling straight toward the kitchen. I heard a slight noise from the office as Harold scuttled to where he couldn't be seen. "What was that?" Walt asked.

"Probably the cat," I whispered.

"Your poor voice! But at least you can talk. Frank didn't mention you had a cat."

"He didn't see her. She's shy. She hides whenever someone comes over." It occurred to me I was good at this. I guess I haven't lost my talent for lying, even after all those years in ACOA and other twelve-step groups trying to be honest. Wonder how I can capitalize on it?

"I just love animals, and Frank takes after me that way," Walt said, stroking the dogs' heads. They both seemed to like him; so much for believing dogs and children could always tell what kind of person someone was. "Can't we let them out with us?" he suggested.

"No, I like them to stay in the kitchen when I have company," I said, wanting the dogs out of the way if there was any action. "Would you like some coffee?"

"Sure, Sarah, black."

I poured two mugs and handed them over the gate to Walt. I had to push the dogs back to keep them in as I went through the gate.

"You stay here, babes," Walt said to the dogs as we went back to the living room. They sat, but Jesse thumped his heavy tail solidly on the floor and kept his gaze focused on Walt. Once this was over, I'd need to have a talk with Jesse about character discernment.

Walt seemed less hyper when we sat down. If I hadn't been so frightened, I'd have thought he was just shy. He looked me in the face for the first time. "Are you okay? Frank didn't say much except you got mugged and had to go to the emergency room and he felt responsible. I'm sorry about your voice."

"I'll be okay," I said. "I'm pretty achy, but no permanent harm done. And it wasn't Frank's fault at all. In fact, he came after me right away and scared the mugger away. He was a real hero!"

"I'm glad you don't blame Frank. And I'm glad you weren't hurt worse."

I stifled a bit of a laugh. It was bad enough he made a fuss over the dogs after trying to kill them. Now the day after he tried to kill me he was saying he was glad I wasn't hurt worse! "Thanks, Walt. And thank both of you for the fruit. It's awfully nice of you."

"I wanted to make sure you were okay and to talk with you about Frank. And to apologize. I'm sorry I yelled at you on the phone Monday night. I even listened in when you and Frank were talking. I want you to understand that's not the way I usually act."

What is this? I thought. Walt's confessing to me before he tries to wipe me out? This is crazy, like a bad movie!

He seemed embarrassed, but he continued, "You see, Frank's the most important thing in my life. His mom and I didn't get along real great, and we don't even talk any more. I hardly ever see Frank's sister. I do okay at work, but it's not worth a rat's ass in the long run. And then there's Frank. Most of the time I don't even know how to talk with him, but I'm so proud of him I could bust."

He fumbled in his shirt pocket and I wound up tight again. "You don't smoke, do you?" he asked.

I shook my head.

"Okay, I can wait. Frank doesn't like me to smoke anyway. Did he tell you he's on the honor roll? And he made Eagle Scout? And he has a part-time job? I even like his girlfriend, though I'm a little afraid he might be getting too serious too fast."

"He's a great kid, Walt," I whispered. "You have a right to be proud. He's fun to be with, too."

"Yeah, but you're probably wondering why I'm telling you all this. You see, I don't want Frank to know, but your mugging might be connected to that girl we found up on the Skagit."

I almost choked on my coffee. Is he trying to figure out how much I know? "What do you mean?"

"That couple that got killed in Gig Harbor—you must have read about it—they were on the raft with us. I think maybe the Killer is after everybody who was on the raft. I phoned the police, and they just thanked me and said they knew and please keep it quiet. They didn't send anybody out to question me or anything and they didn't take it seriously when I said Frank and I might be in danger. First the Rimbauds and then you. We might be next, but nobody will listen."

"This is incredible," I murmured.

"I know. I feel like I'm trying to run underwater. I can't get anywhere at all." He put down his coffee cup and looked straight at me, his face pleading. "Sarah, you didn't know you and Frank might be in danger when you went to Zoolights last night, did you?"

"No, Walt. Why should I think either of us would be harmed? Especially in a public place?"

"I didn't think so, but Frank told me Sunday you'd talked with that detective and I thought you might know something we don't. The whole thing sounds so far-fetched, but I just want my son to be safe."

He stood up. I tensed again. Is this it? Was he disarming me so he could attack now?

"I don't mean to sound like I'm not concerned about you, too," he said. "It's just that Frank's my son and I don't know what to do now. You feel real helpless when you can't protect your kid." His shoulders slumped, and he didn't seem the same person who had bounded into the room just a few minutes earlier.

I couldn't help it. I stood up and gave him a light hug. "Walt, Frank's a good kid and you're doing your best to be a good father. And I'll tell Detective Workman what you've told me."

I moved Walt toward the door, picking up his coat as we went.

"It's none of my business," I said, "but why don't you tell Frank how much you love him?"

"I can't say that kind of thing to him!" he said with some of the force he'd had when he came in. "It's hard enough telling you how I feel about him. I don't want Frank getting a swelled head, either."

"Trust me, Walt. Just tell him. I don't think it would make him conceited."

As soon as Walt had pulled his car out of the drive, Harold burst into the living room. "What just happened here? Everything he said sounded like a loving parent. Did he know I was here? Did he do anything I didn't catch?"

"I don't think he suspected anything," I said, "and I don't think he's the Killer."

"He's an actor. Couldn't he have fooled you?"

"I don't think so. I kept trying to think of him as the Killer and waiting for him to make a move, but it just didn't fit. And nothing in his voice reminded me of the Killer. Finally I couldn't think of him like that. Even the dogs liked him. I think he's good-hearted and rather simple, but not dumb. And he does love Frank."

"Was there anything visible that might help?" Harold persisted. We seemed to have reversed positions. Now Harold thought Walt was the Killer and I was convinced he wasn't.

"He wasn't wearing a long necktie, if that's what you mean. And he didn't limp from a dog bite. Didn't drool and rub his hands together, either, while gloating, 'I've got you, my proud beauty.' I just think I was wrong to suspect him."

Harold tried a chuckle, but didn't succeed well. "Okay, Sarah, but don't eat the fruit," he said in a cautionary tone.

That struck me as funny, and I started laughing; even that hurt. After a moment, he joined me. When we quieted down, he said, "I'll tell the Task Force we're back to waiting. But I'm serious about not eating the fruit. We'll get it tested."

I let the dogs out of the kitchen while Harold telephoned from the office. He broke off to call me, "Sarah! Something on Call Waiting."

I picked up the kitchen phone and whispered, "Hello." It was Sharon.

"Oh, Sarah, hi. Did you just love Zoolights? Wasn't it everything I told you?"

"All that and more," I answered. "I see why you keep going back."

"We must have a bad connection; I can hardly hear you. Are you okay?"

"Getting a sore throat," I whispered, "and a little achy, but not too bad. Can't talk loud."

"You poor thing! You're probably getting the flu. That's what Hugh had, but he's lots better now. It lasts only a few days. Why don't I come over with some chicken soup after work? And what else do you need?"

"Thanks, but you don't want to risk getting it."

"Oh, pooh! I'm healthy as a horse, and besides, Hugh's already exposed me. And I've got a tremendous favor to ask, unless you're feeling just too rotten."

"What?"

"Hugh wants to talk with you about our group! While he was sick he did a lot of thinking about it. What I said about your helping me stuck with him and he wants to see you. He asked if we could come over tonight. I think it really is important that he wants to talk about it!"

"I can't talk much, Sharon, with this throat. Can it wait?"

"It can if it has to, but he's eager to get things started and I'm afraid he might back out if he doesn't follow through right away. Once he decides to do something, he likes to move quickly. I know it's an imposition, but it would mean a lot to me if you would see him. And besides," she said, "it'll give you a chance to do some twelfth-step work. Hugh needs somebody besides me to tell him about the program."

The twelfth step is all about spreading the word about twelve-step programs to others. "That's hitting below the belt!" I protested. "You know I can't say no when you put it that way."

She was silent.

"Okay, at least we can get started," I said, caving in. "But we'll have to make it early and keep it short."

"Thanks, Sarah. How about right after work? I'll stop by home and pick up the soup and we can be there by 5:30."

"Could you bring a loaf of Poulsbo bread and a half-gallon of skim milk as well? Oh, and a dozen eggs. I haven't been shopping since before my trip and I'm about out of everything."

"Be happy to. We'll see you at 5:30 or a little later, then. And, Sarah, Hugh's worse than Paul about dogs, so could you close them up?"

I started to ring off, but she stopped me. "I forgot to tell you. Paul called me yesterday and asked if I'd trade partners for this month and let him partner with you. I said he'd have to wait until next month, but he said he was going to contact you anyway and get some book to you. He planned to get it to you last night, but I told him you were going to Zoolights. He's really being hyper about talking with you soon."

I thanked her and went to tell Harold. "This is the legislator I told you about, Sharon's friend. He's not been interested in her twelve-step work, so this is important to her. It might be a milestone in their relationship, too."

"You've got to help out in such a situation. But are you up to it?"

"I guess so. And she'll bring food," I finished up. "I wasn't sure what all we needed, but at least we'll have bread and milk and eggs."

"And the chicken soup. As soon as I call the Task Force about your visitors, I'll fix us some lunch. Then we can have the soup tonight."

"Can you wait to eat until they leave? I need a nap; all of a sudden I'm wiped out. We could have some cheese and fruit to hold us over."

"Not Walt's fruit!" he protested.

I smiled. "There are still some apples in the refrigerator," I said. "Walt's can wait. Oh, and Sharon told me Paul might be stopping by with a book. I hope he'll call first, though. Anyway, you might want to tell the surveillance teams." ≠

Chapter 23

I don't know whether Tylenol was still in my bloodstream or I was just emotionally exhausted, but I slept deeply for two hours, waking only when the clock radio went off at 5:00. I was stiff again, but not as much as I had been in the morning.

"Anything happen while I slept?" I asked, joining Harold in the living room.

"Phone call from Bert. Wanted to know if he could use the computer for an hour or so later this week. All the details are on the machine."

"Didn't even hear it."

"'Course not. You were snoring too loud."

"Harold! I didn't, did I?"

"No, but I thought that'd get a rise out of you like it did this morning!"

"Anybody ever tell you you're rotten?"

"Frequently, but I don't let it go to my head. How are you feeling?"

"Not too bad. A little stiff. How'd you learn so much about working out the soreness, anyway? This kind of thing happen to you often?"

He laughed. "Not too often, but anybody in law enforcement has had a few run-ins. I'll tell you about them sometime. Right now, I'd better start getting ready for when Sharon and her friend come. I'll wait in the bedroom again so you have privacy, but you take all the precautions you took Monday night. Then call me when they leave and I'll make cornbread to go with the soup."

We were back to waiting, but we were also back on an easy footing with each other. Sharing a stakeout was a heck of a way to get to know somebody, but it sure cut through the superficial stuff. I wondered if Harold could be right in suggesting I might want to forget him and everything about this time once it was over. I didn't think so, but maybe that would depend on how much longer it lasted—and how it came out.

Harold headed for the bedroom when we heard the crunch of tires in the gravel drive at 5:50, but didn't close the door until he heard Sharon greeting me at the front door. "Sarah, this is Hugh Treadwell. Hugh, Sarah Tierney. And you've each heard plenty about the other! I'm sorry we're late, but I thought you'd want some oranges and romaine and tomatoes and broccoli and stuff like that, too. I told Hugh we'd have to bring you lots of vitamin C fruits and veggies if we made you meet us when you don't feel good."

Each of them held two Queen Anne Thriftway bags. Sharon marched back to the kitchen with her load. Hugh started to follow, but stopped short when he saw the dogs. Golda barked once, and Jesse stood at the gate, tail still. I took the bags from Hugh and deposited them on the dining room table.

"I thought they were going to be shut up," Hugh said in a raspy voice, retreating to the living room.

"They are," I whispered in surprise. "They won't bother us in there."

"I was mauled by dogs when I was a child," Hugh said. "I have never gotten over it, and they sense my fear and react badly in consequence. Can you put them outside, or shut them behind a door?"

"Jesse would go wild if I tried that. He'd claw at the door and yelp and bark so loudly we couldn't talk. They've *never* knocked the gate down, and I've used it ever since I got them."

"They're wonderful dogs, Hugh," Sharon reassured him, "and they *always* stay behind the gate during our group meetings. They won't bother us."

She looked worried, and no wonder! This wasn't the most auspicious way for her best friend and best guy to meet.

"We could do this another time and meet someplace else, if you'd like," I offered.

Hugh squared his shoulders and forced a smile. "No, I guess I can stand it. You are good to see me like this when you do not feel well. Maybe Sharon told you I did a lot of thinking when I was sick, and decided maybe I should look into this twelve-step program of hers."

I smiled back at him. "Well, in that case, let me take your coats and get you some coffee or tea."

"None for me, please," Hugh said, taking off his coat with stiff movements. "I find caffeine makes me more achy when I am getting over the flu." He wore jeans and a navy-blue pullover over a white polo shirt. He was short, but I could see what Sharon meant when she said he was fit. He helped Sharon off with her coat, then handed both to me. She was still in her lady-lawyer gabardine suit and was shorter than he, even in high heels.

He wasn't especially good looking, but handsomer than he appeared in his campaign literature and in newspaper photos. His compact ruggedness was appealing. Reddish-brown hair grew far back over his forehead. He had a ruddy complexion and pale blue eyes. His prominent jaw muscles—as if he clenched them, I thought—broke the symmetry of his roundish head.

"I'm delighted to meet my State Rep," I said, taking a seat in the yellow barrel chair near the front door. He and Sharon sat side by side on the sofa, where he couldn't see the dogs. "I voted for you, and I haven't been sorry. You're having quite an impact on the House Education Committee."

He and Sharon both beamed at me. "I appreciate that, Sarah," Hugh said, still raspy. "I feel I can make a substantial difference to the young people of our state. And while I believe in separation of church and state," he segued, "I want to learn more about what you and Sharon believe. You do not feel well, so I do not want to keep you overly long, but it seemed important to find out now about this higher power."

"Oh, Hugh, surely Sharon told you my belief has practically nothing to do with church. Also, I'm no expert," I whispered. "I muddle along. But believing in a higher power helps me stay relatively sane in an insane world. Also, it helps me with a sense of right and wrong and gives me strength to act on my beliefs."

"What do you mean, 'act on my beliefs?'" Hugh asked.

"Well, for instance, I have to measure my actions against some sort of standard. I try not to judge what anyone else believes, but trying to follow the twelve steps makes me accountable for my own actions. This legitimizes those actions for me and gives me a sense of solidarity I didn't have when I was just a 'fuzzy-headed sixties liberal.'" I grinned when I said the last phrase, since Hugh had been accused of being that.

He grinned too, a sort of Jack Nicholson grin, and I had a glimpse of why Sharon found him so fascinating. "But as a former 'fuzzy-headed sixties liberal,' you must have doubts about how much sense religion—any religion—makes," he said. "Is it not just a crutch, 'the opiate of the masses,' a way to justify intolerance?"

"A higher power doesn't necessarily have to do with religion. And religion frequently is all of those things," I admitted, "but at its best it promotes joy and peace and love and altruism. I'll grant you little of it makes any *sense* to me. All I know is I'm a happier and better person when I'm working the steps, and—with notable exceptions—I like people in the twelve-step community."

He kept silent and waited for more. "Maybe Sharon told you that belief in some sort of higher power is part of the twelve-step program," I went on. "That was crucial in helping me turn my life around, and if it works, who am I to doubt it?"

Sharon had listened to our exchange. "You two jumped right in there," she said with a sort of maternal pride in both of us. "You don't need me, so I'm going to put away the food."

When we'd started talking, Hugh had glanced at the dogs several times, but now he seemed less worried. We hardly registered Sharon's leaving or rejoining us as he and I kept up a rapid-fire intellectual jousting. I'd missed this kind of discussion since I rarely attended university gatherings after I quit the staff, and I enjoyed the exchange. However, my voice wasn't up to it.

"Hugh, I'm enjoying this, but I can't keep talking. I'll get complete laryngitis."

"I am sorry, Sarah. You have given me a great deal to think

about. Can you spare me another half hour if I do most of the talking?"

I nodded.

He turned to Sharon and put an arm around her shoulders. "Dear, I need to talk with Sarah privately. Could you go away and come back in half an hour?"

"Sure," Sharon said, looking somewhere between dazed and delighted. "I can do some last-minute Christmas shopping at the Pacific Northwest Shop up in the Proctor District and be back here in half an hour."

"Just blow the horn when you come. I will be waiting at the door."

"I'm not sure what's happening, but this is great," Sharon whispered in my ear as she hugged me good-bye. "He needs this. Thanks! I'll talk with you later." I let her out and locked the door.

The atmosphere in the room had changed while I was letting Sharon out. Hugh seemed about to move from our general discussion of belief to his specific needs.

We talked for several minutes, without getting to whatever Hugh wanted to talk about. He had turned more formal, and our easygoing conversation was gone. I wanted to let him move at his own pace, but this was agonizing!

Finally, groping for words, Hugh leaned forward and asked in evident distress, "Sarah, if one wants to change, is it possible to become different?"

I groped, too, with my response. "I think so—and I *believe* so. It worked for Sharon and me with ACOA and our twelve-step group. But maybe you should come to meetings and get a sponsor, someone more knowledgeable than I am. You and I can set up a temporary partnership agreement like Sharon and I have, though. In fact, we can do that now, if you'd like."

If Hugh hadn't fallen silent then, I wouldn't have heard the slight noise at the front door, even sitting as close as I was. I stood and went to the door, just in time to see Walt turn away and start down the stairs. ≠

Chapter 24

Maybe I was wrong about Walt after all, I thought in panic. *What's he doing here?*

"Walt, wait," I called, unlocking the door.

Walt turned toward me and started back up the stairs. "I heard voices," he said, "and I didn't want to bother you. But I dropped something off."

I glanced down to the right of the door. A large bouquet of red-and-white chrysanthemums and holly was propped against the wall. Again, Walt seemed to have bought the biggest and best the supermarket had to offer.

"Thanks, but why?" I asked, leaving the flowers where they sat.

Walt grabbed them up and thrust them at me. Reflexively, I took the strong-smelling armload.

"There's a note to explain," he said, beaming. "I think this is going to be a good Christmas. You'll see." He moved down the stairs and trotted to his car.

I looked at the flowers in my arms. The surveillance teams must be going crazy, and I had an idea of what Harold would think if he knew about this. But I was the one who had to decide what to do.

Too many things were coming at me all at once, but Hugh was waiting and he needed me now. I went with my gut feeling about Walt, took the flowers and put them on the bookcase near the door, and locked the door behind me.

"I'm sorry for the interruption," I said to Hugh, whispering to protect what was left of my voice; calling to Walt had strained it even further. "I think I'd just asked if you wanted to set up an agreement like Sharon and I have."

"No," he said, his face closed off as though a trap door had fallen, "but Sharon has offered something good in my life. I do not want to hurt her."

I wondered how he meant that statement. "You wouldn't want to hurt her, but you can't force something like this, either," I said. "You have to be ready for it yourself. I hope you'll give me a call when you are ready."

The doorbell rang then, and the dogs sat up with ears perked. "It's like Grand Central in here," Hugh said, looking at the dogs in distaste.

I cautioned Jesse and Golda to stay quiet and went to the door. Paul stood there with a book in his hand. "Can you put the dogs away for a minute so I can come in?" he asked. "I brought that book for you so you can read it before we discuss it next month. Sharon wouldn't trade partners with me, and she said you wouldn't be in last night, but I'd like to tell you a little about it now."

"I'm sorry, Paul. Now's not a good time because somebody's here. Why don't I take the book now and you can tell me about it later on the phone?"

"Bummer!" he said, his favorite word, it seemed. He usually looked bland and unconcerned, but I suspected he hadn't yet learned to trust our twelve-step group and kept something hidden from us. Tonight he looked angry.

He handed me the book with ill grace. "This gave me some insights," he said, "and I really want to talk about it with you. I'll call when you're not too busy for me."

"C'mon, Paul. You could have called first if you had to talk with me right away."

He turned away and went down the stairs limping a little, as he had after our twelve-step meeting on Monday. Again I closed and locked the door. I put the book on an end table and went over to Hugh.

He stood to go, and I stood next to him, realizing for the first time he was a little shorter than I.

He reached out and caressed one of the chrysanthemums on the bookcase behind me, then took my hand and said, "Thenk you, Sarah. Thenk you very much."

Like Ed Sullivan! My eyes widened and I hoped my face was under better control.

"You know," he said. "I was afraid of that."

"Know what?" I whispered, fumbling for the alarm at my waist. It wasn't there. I hadn't put it back on after my nap. There was no way I could yell for Harold; my voice was almost gone. If I couldn't get away, Harold might not know until it was all over.

"Know about all the girls," he answered.

It would take too long to unlock the door, even if I could get there. I tried to position myself to run toward the bedroom, but Hugh caught me.

"I am much stronger than I look, Sarah," he said, "even injured. I will have to finish the job I started last night. And unfortunately, I will have to take care of Sharon, too. I am sorry, but I cannot risk everything."

The raspiness had left his voice. Now I recognized the extreme precision of his speech.

I jerked as hard as I could, but he held me fast from behind. I kicked back at his shins, but the soft heel of my loafers didn't seem to hurt him. Then I thrust my hands up through his arms and broke his grip for a moment. I turned and tried to kick him between the legs. He caught my foot and jerked, so I fell on the sofa with a soft thud.

Golda barked once and Jesse whined, but they stayed behind the gate. *Damn all that training!* Hugh moved toward me, a yellow and blue polka-dotted tie stretched between his hands. I tried once more to kick. He sidestepped and hit the top of my thigh with his right fist. Tears blurred my vision as my leg exploded in a blaze of pain.

The tie disappeared from in front of my eyes and Hugh was on the floor fighting with a snarling, vicious Jesse. Golda stood behind the gate, barking continuously.

A tremendous thump sounded from the bedroom. I tried to rise, but the leg Hugh had hit seemed a solid spasm of pain and wouldn't hold me. Hugh and Jesse rolled on the floor, Jesse snarling and snapping rather than holding on.

A strange, high-pitched noise filled the room. It was Hugh, keening through his nose as he fought Jesse. I grabbed a lamp from the table behind the sofa and crashed it down on Hugh's head just as I heard Harold thunder "SIT!"

The ceramic lamp shattered, Jesse sat, Golda stopped barking, and the silence was deafening. Hugh slumped on the floor in front of me. A trickle of blood started from the top of his balding head, and numerous channels of blood ran from bites on his hands and arms.

"Come over here, Sarah, while I cover you," Harold directed me. He held his gun in both hands, aimed at Hugh.

"I can't, not without crawling over him," I whispered, barely loud enough to be heard. "He did something to my leg."

"If I pitch you the handcuffs, can you get them on him?"

"I think so."

Harold tossed me the cuffs. I had a moment of confusion trying to pull them open. "Just push them through," Harold explained.

I slid to the floor with a leg on either side of Hugh and fastened his wrists behind his back. They were slippery with blood, and he still clutched the tie in one hand. I pushed back toward the sofa as Hugh moved his head from side to side and seemed to be coming to. As he opened his eyes, he looked straight at Jesse, who slurped as he cleaned blood from his teeth and lips. Hugh closed his eyes and started keening again.

"It *is* him, isn't it?" Harold asked.

I nodded. "He admitted trying to kill me last night. And he said he'd have to take care of Sharon."

"Did you hit the alarm?"

"It's on the bed," I said, "under a pillow, I think."

"And the bed's on the floor," he said. "I leaped up as soon as I heard the commotion, but I crashed into your bed in the dark and knocked it down. That's what took me so long."

Harold backed up a few steps, reached into the bedroom, and

flicked on the light. Rummaging around in the mess of bedclothes on the floor, he found the alarm and pressed it. Just then I heard Sharon's horn sounding for Hugh. *What am I going to tell her?* I thought, as Harold moved to unlock the door for the Task Force. ≠

Chapter 25

A horde of plainclothes cops poured through the door, pushing Sharon with them. I'd never seen so many drawn guns outside a movie.

"That's the Killer," Harold said, raising his voice so they could all hear him, "and Sarah and Jesse collared him."

Sharon pressed toward Hugh, but someone held on to her arm. "I'm sorry, ma'am. This man is under arrest."

She looked as though she had been hit in the middle with a two-by-four, then crumpled to the floor. Someone carried her to a chair.

Several men gathered around Hugh, who was still making that high-pitched keening noise. His eyes were closed as he rocked backward and forward, hampered by the handcuffs.

"Why's he doing that?" a man asked.

"He's afraid of dogs," I responded, hurting with every word. "He flipped out when Jesse attacked him."

"He looks like Representative Treadwell," another man said.

"He is, but he's still the Killer," I said. "He admitted it."

I still sat on the floor behind Hugh. The pain in my leg was intense, but ebbing. Jesse looked from person to person, delighted at being in the center of things. Harold came to help me up. "Get Jesse out of the way and check him over," I whispered. "I can wait." He touched the back of his hand to my cheek, then stood and called Jesse.

I followed Harold and Jesse with my eyes. The gate was still standing. I'd never say Jesse was dumb again. Knocking the gate down wasn't allowed, so he'd leaped over it while Golda barked an alarm. Harold put Jesse behind the gate, then knelt in the doorway and wiped the blood from the dog with a dampened dish towel, checking for injuries as he went. Golda licked at Harold's face, hampering his efforts.

The tableau of man and dogs was precious to me. Then someone went to the kitchen phone and blocked my view.

People milled all over my small living room until a man who seemed to be in charge ordered most of them to wait outside. As the room started to clear, I looked up and saw the FBI man making an "okay" sign at me.

"Arrest him and read him his rights, in case that's an act," said the man in charge. "The representative's an attorney. He could be setting up for his defense." One of the remaining men pulled out a card and intoned a list of rights to Hugh. The keening noise didn't stop.

Harold came back and lifted me to the sofa. "Jesse's fine, Sarah. No injuries at all; the blood's all from Treadwell." He knelt next to me and asked, "Now, what did he do to you?"

"I tried to kick him in the crotch, and he punched me right here with his fist," I whispered, touching the top of my thigh. "My whole leg cramped, but it's not as bad as it was. He was coming at me with the tie when Jesse attacked."

Harold's fingers probed through the wool slacks. "Feels swollen, but I don't think it's broken. The paramedics will know."

"Harold, what's going to happen to Sharon?"

"We'll explain her connection and they'll probably let her wait 'til tomorrow to give a statement."

"Could you call Rosalie and ask her to come over? She's a member of the group. Tell her whatever you need to. Sharon's going to need more help than I can give her tonight." I gave him Rosalie's number and hoped she'd be home.

A siren rushed closer, before cutting off right outside the house, followed almost immediately by another siren. Several slicker-clad men and women came in and started working on Hugh. The man in charge said something to one of the newcomers, who came over to me. At least it wasn't one of the paramedics who had taken me to the emergency room the night before.

"What's the matter, ma'am?"

I explained what had happened and he helped me ease my slacks down so he could look at the eggplant on my leg. *Marilu would have been proud of me*, I thought, remembering our jokes about wearing good underwear in case we had an accident and everybody saw it. Then I realized it didn't hurt to think about Marilu. Maybe I was ready to let her go.

"Your leg's going to hurt like mad for a while and you'll be sore for several days," the paramedic said. "See your doctor if the pain doesn't get a lot better in the next couple of days. For now, ice packs will help. Did he do these other bruises, too?" he asked, noting several mementos of the night before.

"I already had them; don't worry about them," I whispered.

The paramedic glared at Harold, who came back and looked at the purple bruise. Bending over me, oblivious to the paramedic's frown, Harold murmured, "Looks like hell. No wonder it hurt so much. I like the freckles better. Rosalie's on her way, and she'll try to bring her minister with her."

"Thanks. Will you explain to Sharon?"

"Sure, but I'd like this guy to look at her first, as soon as he's through with you."

"I'm done here," said the paramedic, sighing. "Who's next?"

An officer unlocked one side of Hugh's handcuffs, then secured it to the gurney as soon as the paramedics loaded him on. The paramedics belted him on the gurney and a police officer secured his ankles with a plastic strap. He was still making that keening noise.

The paramedic followed Harold across the room to Sharon as I pulled up my slacks. He bent down and started talking. "I'm okay," I heard Sharon say. "I don't need any help."

The paramedic moved away, and Harold spoke to Sharon. She burst into tears and clung to him. *Harold's getting a lot of practice at this*, I thought. *I'm glad he's so good at it.*

"Good job, Ms. Tierney," the man in charge said. "We're leaving now. Detective Workman will see we get statements later from you and your friend."

I whispered my thanks, and the officers and firefighters cleared out, taking Hugh with them. Harold helped Sharon to a chair next to me and set a box of tissues beside her. I reached out and took her hand. "I'm so sorry, Sharon."

"Oh, Sarah! *I'm* so sorry," she said in a broken voice. "I don't understand anything. What do they think Hugh did?"

"We're pretty sure he's the Skagit River Killer."

She shrank back into the chair, turning paler than before, if possible. "That's what that man told me," she said, pointing to Harold. "But Hugh *helps* people. He doesn't kill them!"

"I'm sorry," I said again. "I don't understand, either. But he tried to kill me. And he admitted killing others." I couldn't bring myself to tell her he had planned to kill her, too.

We both fell silent. I sat in a stupor, holding Sharon's hand and feeling only my pain for her and the pain in my leg. Harold began restoring order around us. He picked up pieces of the broken lamp and moved chairs back into place, then brought rags and a pail of water and cleaned the blood from the rug. After sweeping up the ceramic shards he moved the gate away and let the dogs in. Jesse ran straight to me and sat to have his ears scratched.

Golda went to Sharon, who let go of my hand, grabbed the dog in a tight grip, and cried into her fur. Sharon's wracking sobs tapered off, then she held Golda and let the dog lick her face until Rosalie and her minister arrived. Rosalie greeted me and whispered, "I'll call you tomorrow." Then they gathered Sharon and left without any questions.

At last everyone was gone but Harold, Jesse, and Golda. "Move over," Harold said, making room for himself next to me on the couch and putting an arm around me. "You and the dogs did great, Sarah. I knew you could handle whatever you had to."

"I'm glad *you* knew that; *I* wasn't so sure. Especially when it seemed to go on forever and I couldn't make a noise to alert you. I thought I'd be dead before you knew there was any trouble."

He pulled me close, so hard I felt every bruise yet felt wonderful at the same time. "I couldn't have borne that," he said. "You might have been, if it hadn't been for Golda and Jesse. I didn't hear a thing until they started barking and snarling."

Jesse's tail thumped on the floor when he heard his name. I nestled against Harold and said, "Then you didn't hear Walt, either. He tiptoed up to the door and panicked me. I thought for a minute he was the Killer after all, and he'd come back for another try. He left those flowers and took off without explaining anything. But he did say there was a note with them."

Harold retrieved the note and handed it to me.

"'I told Frank how proud I am of him,'" I read. "'You were right. Thanks, and Merry Christmas.'"

"And after Walt left, Paul showed up to give me a book. He'd never just stopped by before, and he was still limping. Monday night he said he tripped while jogging, but when he got here and was so insistent on seeing me, I wondered if he might be the Killer."

I leaned back against Harold again. "I'm awfully glad it isn't Walt—or Paul—but I can hardly believe it's Hugh. How in the world could he do such good things as a Representative and at the same time be the Skagit River Killer?"

"We'll probably never know, just like we never learned the reasons for Ted Bundy," Harold said, "but half the psychiatrists in the country will try to find out. His legislative work probably gave him a reason to travel around. It'll be interesting to see if any of your other ideas check out."

"Poor Sharon," I said, snuggling a little closer. The phone rang. *Damn phone!*

"Let the machine get it," Harold suggested. "The Task Force will try to keep your name from the media until tomorrow, but they might not succeed."

"It might be something important, and we can't hear it from here," I protested.

Harold picked me up, something no one else had ever done. I felt strong and protected at the same time. He carried me into the office and set me down on the desk. At the beep a voice said, "This is Sheriff Carl Potter. Please have Detective Workman call me at . . ."

Harold hit the speakerphone button. "This is Harold."

"Congratulations! Fine job. We just got the news."

"Thanks, but Sarah deserves all the credit. She and her dogs got him by themselves. The Task Force just helped mop up and cart him away."

Potter chuckled. "Good. Then she's in line for the reward money. It's up to a couple hundred thousand." I gasped and looked at Harold. He nodded.

"Important as all that is, that's not why I'm calling," the Sheriff said. "I'm going to patch a call through to you, and this time you deserve some of the congratulations, at least. Hold on."

Another voice came on the line, "Dad? This is Connie. Dad, the baby's here and we're both fine. She came so fast we didn't have time to call you first. She's seven pounds five ounces, and her name's Lisa. She's beautiful!"

Harold's face registered everything from laughter to tears and back again as the conversation continued. *This man has fine and deep emotions*, I thought, watching him. *But he was wrong in thinking I might want to forget about him.*

"I'll be home tomorrow, Connie, and I'll be in to see you as soon as I can get there," he said. After hanging up he bowed his head for a moment.

Then he looked at me with a questioning expression. "If you think you might be interested in a grandfatherly type, I'd like for you and the dogs to stay with me through the holidays. No strings, no expectations, and no pressure. It'll protect you from the media until you're ready for them. And we can try for an old-fashioned Christmas. I can even get a boat and take you down the river to see the eagles if you want."

I thought of a million reasons why I couldn't go with him and said, "We'd love to." ≠

The End

About the Author

Jean McCord represented the State of Georgia at the National Teen-Age Press Conference in Detroit, Michigan while in high school and wrote several prize-winning articles while in high school and college—one of which was translated and published in French, Spanish, and German. The need to earn a living took precedence for most of her life after college, but she started doing ride-alongs with police and fire and writing articles on "Along for the Ride," which were published in two weekly newspapers in Tacoma, Washington. She took a class for Reserve Deputy Sheriffs as research, but graduated third in the class and was asked to be commissioned; for three years she worked once a week as a Reserve Deputy. Now retired and living as an ex-pat in Cuenca, Ecuador, she has resumed writing, first with "Home Free," and a mystery novel, "The Eagle Murders."

Made in United States
Troutdale, OR
12/05/2024